'I've never taken a kiss from a school-ma'am before.

'It's a novelty. Worth repeating, I think.'

'No…*no*! Don't *dare* to handle me so.'

Letitia's fury was not only for his contemptuous embrace, but for herself, too, for she ought to have seen it coming, or at least made it more difficult than she had.

He watched her brilliant flint-stone eyes spark and glisten with rage, her beautiful mouth tremble with shock, and the flippant words he was about to deliver, the laughing retort, did not emerge as he intended. His eyes grew serious, suddenly contrite. 'A woman of independence and courage,' he said, relaxing his grip.

Despite the sage-green velvet that covered her own breast, Letitia could still feel the imprint of that bulky silver braid, the ache in her arms, and the assault of Lord Rayne's mouth upon her lips. That was bad enough, but worse still was the pain of his contempt, which she believed was less for her indiscretion on the parade ground than for the fact that she was, as he put it, a 'school-ma'am', and therefore less entitled to his respect than her sisters.

Dear Reader

If you take a peep at the first pages of any Mills & Boon book you'll see (perhaps with a smile) that the address in England really *is* Paradise Road in Richmond, Surrey, which is also where a great medieval palace stood beside the River Thames. So I made this romantic address the setting for my Regency trilogy, of which this story is the third part, because I felt such an appropriate name ought to be celebrated for the 100th Anniversary. There is, in fact, a previous story—ONE NIGHT IN PARADISE—concerning the distant ancestors of my Regency characters, set in Elizabethan times when the palace was still in use.

What do my Mills & Boon editors think about my using their address for such a romantic purpose? Well, I know that if I were to set a story around the royal manor of Shene (the original name for Richmond) in Anglo-Saxon times, they'd be as enthusiastic about the eleventh century as they have been about all the other periods. They are, of course, as unashamedly romantic and imaginative as their writers and readers—just one of the reasons why working with them is such a joy.

Happy Anniversary, Mills & Boon!

Juliet

THE RAKE'S UNCONVENTIONAL MISTRESS

Juliet Landon

MILLS & BOON™

Pure reading pleasure™

First published in Great Britain 2008
Harlequin Mills & Boon Limited,
Eton House, 18-24 Paradise Road, Richmond, Surrey TW9 1SR

© Juliet Landon 2008

ISBN: 978 0 263 86272 0

Set in Times Roman 10½ on 13 pt.
04-0808-87415

Printed and bound in Spain
by Litografia Rosés S.A., Barcelona

Juliet Landon's keen interest in art and history, both of which she used to teach, combined with a fertile imagination, make writing historical novels a favourite occupation. She is particularly interested in researching the early medieval and Regency periods and the problems encountered by women in a man's world. Her heart's home is in her native North Yorkshire, but now she lives happily in a Hampshire village close to her family. Her first books, which were on embroidery and design, were published under her own name of Jan Messent.

THE RAKE'S UNCONVENTIONAL MISTRESS is the third in the *Ladies of Paradise Road* trilogy. They feature descendants of characters you will have met in ONE NIGHT IN PARADISE.

Recent novels by the same author:

DISHONOUR AND DESIRE*
A SCANDALOUS MISTRESS*
THE WARLORD'S MISTRESS
HIS DUTY, HER DESTINY
THE BOUGHT BRIDE
THE WIDOW'S BARGAIN
ONE NIGHT IN PARADISE

Ladies of Paradise Road

Chapter One

Richmond, Surrey. 1814

'Well?' said Letitia, closing the door of the parlour behind her, shutting off the gentle hum of voices. 'What do you think? Shall you beg Mama to come and rescue me, or shall you tell her how capable I am?'

Garnet placed an arm through hers and pressed it to her side. 'Mama *knows* how capable you are, dearest. She simply didn't want you to do this all on your own, that's all. It doesn't fit in with her plans for any of us, least of all her eldest daughter.'

'Well—' Letitia smiled, acknowledging the truth '—she always knew I'd go down a different path. She must have expected it. A pity she couldn't find time to come and see for herself, though. She knows how to make her displeasure felt, doesn't she?'

Persephone, Garnet's twin, was like her sister in everything except in the degree of assertiveness. 'Oh, Mama's displeasure is no rare thing these days, Lettie,' she said. 'You know how easy it's been to set up her bristles since we lost Papa. You're well out of it, but not too far for us to visit whenever we like.'

'You approve, then?'

'Of *course* we do,' the twins chorused. '*Very* select. Seven lovely young ladies. Hanging on your every word. So respectful. Yes, Miss Boyce, no, Miss Boyce.'

'Stop!' Letitia begged them, laughing. 'It's only their first term. They'll soon be pitching the gammon like the rest of us.'

The white hallway was bright with spring sunshine that bounced off the jug of creamy lilac blooms and shone in patches upon the pink-toned Axminster rug. Through two open doors could be seen a polished post-chaise with the Boyce crest upon the panel, a liveried postilion sitting erect upon one of the horses while another waited on the pavement beside the folding steps.

A large bay gelding was brought to a standstill behind the coach, its rider showing no sign of impatience as the three, with arms linked, came to stand beneath the elegant white portico, still finding last-minute messages to send, approvals to be repeated, thanks and farewells mixed like potpourri.

'Lord Rayne is to escort us back to London,' Persephone whispered, unable to prevent a deeper shade of pink creeping into her cheeks. 'He's *so* gentlemanly, Lettie.'

'He's taking us to Almack's this evening,' Garnet added, her eyes shining with excitement. 'It will be the most *horrendous* bore, but Mama insists on it.'

This, Letitia knew, was intended to convince her that they would not enjoy it much and that *she* would enjoy it less, even if she too had been invited by the handsomest beau of their acquaintance. She glanced up at him, then wished she had not, for he caught her eye in a look that seemed to reflect, with added amusement, a certain perception that was by no means enthusiastic. Without prejudice, her glance might have agreed with her sisters' description of him as the most perfect tulip, the best-dressed, the most eligible *parti,* a Corinthian out of the very topmost drawer.

But Letitia *was* prejudiced by the other epithets she had heard, not so glowing, that although he was wealthy and titled—and who in their right minds could ignore that?—he was also a rake. And what was her mother doing to allow her younger sisters to be seen exclusively in his company, she would like to have known. Granted, her lovely sisters had reached their twenty-second birthday some months ago, quite a serious matter for any ambitious mother. But Lord Seton Rayne, younger son of the Marquess of Sheen, must by now have had every heiress in London hurled at him, despite his reputation, and still he had not made a permanent choice.

The look Letitia caught, the one that made her turn hastily away, seemed to have read her like a book. His slow blink returned to her, telling her in words as clear as the town crier that she might disapprove all she liked, but *she* had nothing to fear, that unmarried females who ran seminaries were of no interest to him except as objects of amusement, however well connected they might be.

But if Letitia hoped to avoid an introduction, it was not to be. 'Come,' said Garnet, gently urging her forward. 'Will you not allow me to present Lord Rayne to you before we leave? My lord, you said how you longed to meet our elder sister. Well, here she is.'

He bowed from the saddle, touching the brim of his grey beaver with the silver knob of his whip, his dark eyes taking in her tall figure as if—she thought—he was about to make

a bid at Tattersalls for a good general-purpose sort of hack.
'Miss Boyce,' he said, 'I am pleased to meet you at last. I had
begun to suspect that you were a figment of your sisters'
imaginations.'

'I can well believe it, my lord,' she replied, unsmiling. 'I
suppose you must meet so few women of independence, these
days.' Making it clear that this briefest of exchanges was at
an end, she turned away to place a kiss upon her sisters'
cheeks, to shoo them into the carriage and to watch them
move off, waving merrily.

Responding to a signal from his rider, the bay gelding took
his place on the far side of the carriage and pranced away,
swishing his tail as if to cock a snook at the lone figure on the
pavement who could not quite understand why she felt so
buffle-headed and gauche. Had she been unnecessarily defensive? Had she taken his greeting the wrong way? Would he
have noticed? Did it matter if he had?

She walked back into the shadowy hall, studied the nearest
brass doorknob, then turned it and entered the room, relieved
to be back in her natural element. Seven heads lifted, sure that
Miss Boyce would find something complimentary to say
about their drawings of daffodils.

It was not that she begrudged her sisters a single moment
of fun with the pick of London's available bachelors, never
having enjoyed being caught up in the social whirl of balls,
routs and drawing-rooms, house-parties and assemblies. Her
twin sisters did, and popular they were, too. Well mannered,
well dressed and gregarious, they graced every event with
their petite charm and blonde curling hair, not least because
there were two of them. Good value by any hostess's standards. By their demanding mother's standards they were

worth their weight in gold *and* a liability, for she could not conceive how one could be married without the other, and where did one find two equally wealthy titled bachelors, these days? The twins were just as sceptical.

The problem of mates for her eldest daughter had rarely occupied Lady Boyce's sleepless nights as it did with the twins, for Letitia might as well have been a boy for all the interest she showed in finding a husband. For her, the schoolroom had never been a place to escape from, her father's vast library had been a favourite haunt, and a visit to a museum, a lecture on the structure of the ode, or a discussion on Greek vases and their classification was more in her line than an obligation to dine with her mother's gossipy guests in their gracious Mayfair home. She did, of course, do her duty in this respect, but most of her friends were artists, poets, politicians and writers.

Her late father had understood his daughter perfectly—her socialite mother did not. After her father's sudden death in the hunting field, Letitia had made her bid for complete freedom away from her mother's dominance. Her father would have approved, though it was her mother's elder brother, Uncle Aspinall, who had helped her to purchase Number 24 Paradise Road in Richmond, in the county of Surrey. He had also been the only one of her relatives, apart from her sisters, to approve of her plan to open a seminary there.

'A *seminary*?' Lady Boyce had said, as if her daughter had blasphemed. 'How do you ever expect to attract a *husband*, Letitia, if you're stuck in a seminary with young *gels* all day? Really, how *can* you be so vexatious?'

'I shall not be stuck in it all day, Mama,' she had said. 'It's not going to be *that* kind of seminary. And they won't be much younger than seventeen, just on the eve of their coming-out. There's so much they ought to know at that age,' she added, remembering the deficiencies of Mrs Wood's Seminary for the Daughters of Gentlemen. 'If Papa had not talked to me about interesting things, I would have been as tongue-tied as most of the other girls at Mrs Wood's.'

'And tongue-tied is one thing no one could ever accuse *you* of being,' her mother retorted, not intending the compliment. 'But I wish you would consider *my* feelings for once, Letitia. How I'm going to explain this to my friends I really don't know. They may look on eccentricity in the older generation as something to be expected, but no one expects it from a twenty-four-year-old who ought to be turning her mind to raising a family. It's *most* embarrassing.'

'It was never my wish to be an embarrassment, Mama, and I have nothing against men, or marriage, or families, either. But I have never been able to understand why educating one's mind is acceptable in a man, but frowned on in a woman. Papa never thought women's brains were inferior to men's, did he? It was he who taught me to read.'

'Your Papa, God rest his soul, had radical views about most things, Letitia, but when he left you a sizeable legacy to do with as you pleased, I doubt if he ever thought it would please you to run completely wild, buy your own house and make an utter cake of yourself.'

'Uncle Aspinall doesn't think so, Mama. And thank heaven for it. Without his help I don't think I could have managed half so well.'

This comparison did nothing to mollify Lady Boyce. 'Aspinall,' she snapped, 'has no children of his own, which is why he knows so little about what parents want. I hardly expected he would side with me on this matter, and I was right as usual, but if he likes the idea of having a *blue-stocking* for a niece, there's little I can do about it. Indeed I suspected you were inclined that way when you tried to conceal a *Latin dictionary* in your reticule when we went to Lady Aldyth's rout party. Was there *ever* such a trial to a devoted mother?' Lady Boyce's imposing figure described a convincing swoon that would have done justice to Mrs Siddons, landing gracefully on a striped brocade settee with lion's paws feet.

It was from both parents that Letitia had inherited the height that had not afflicted her sisters to the same extent. For a woman, she was taller than average, which had never done much to help when she was obliged to look down upon so many of her dancing partners. Sitting down with men to talk was more comfortable for both parties, Letitia being blessed with a serene loveliness that, combined with an ability to talk interestingly and without affectation on any number of current affairs, captivated the more liberal-minded men of her acquaintance. Whether it helped for her to have fine ash-blonde hair that strayed in wisps over her face and neck resisting all efforts to contain it, or to have large eyes the colour of thunderclouds rimmed by unusually dark lashes, or to have a figure that Juno herself would have been proud to own, were not things that occupied Letitia's mind, for in the wide unchartered territory of men's preferences she was lamentably ignorant.

The priority in most men's minds, her mother had told all three of her daughters, were that they should remain innocent, be adept at all the social graces and, above all, show no inclination to be bookish. If there was anything a man deplored above all else, it was a woman who knew more than he did on any subject except domestic matters. The twins had no wish to argue with that, but Letitia understood that it was far too generalised to be true, for there were men she knew personally who had accepted her exactly as she was, bookish or not. Unfortunately for Lady Boyce, these same men were not interested in marrying her eldest daughter, either, because they were already married or too engrossed in their own special subjects to be leg-shackled to a wife and family.

If Letitia was affected by this lopsided state of affairs, she never let it show except, occasionally, by an inclination to pity both the men and women who lived by such shallow conventions. Nevertheless, the stark truth was that book-learning and marriage rarely mixed and that, as she had now earned a reputation as being 'Lady Boyce's unconventional eldest daughter', she was highly unlikely to find a mate of *haut ton* as her mother would have preferred.

'What will people say?' whined Lady Boyce for the fiftieth time. 'That I threw you out to make shift for yourself? You have no need to earn your own living, Letitia. It's simply not *done* by women of your standing, you know.'

But it *had* been done, and so far Lady Boyce had been too busy to visit Number 24 Paradise Road, relying on the twins' information to fuel the smouldering fires of her disapproval. Naturally, she urged them to tell Letitia about the ball she was planning, the guests she would be entertaining, the visits, the soirees, the titled men they were meeting. They had brought her a copy of the newly published novel by the author of *The Infidel*, which all society had talked about last year. They were sure it would not be available in Richmond for some time, though their mother had deemed it a wasted gesture. 'Lettie will not read *that* kind of thing,' she had told them.

'What kind of thing, Mama?' they had asked, innocently.

'*That* kind of thing. Novels. Racy novels.'

'Is it racy, Mama?'

'Oh, I don't know, dears. It looks racy to me. What's it called? *Waynethorpe Manor*? *Sure* to be.'

'So you haven't read it, Mama?'

'Me? Read such rubbish? Why, no, of course not.'

'Then how can you judge it, Mama?'

'Oh, I flicked through it when I was in Hatchards, and I could tell. I don't see Letitia reading it unless it explains how to tell a Turner from a Reynolds, which I'm sure I don't care about unless there's a difference in the price.'

Meant to tease, the conversation veered predictably into areas about which Lady Boyce had strong views, but no knowledge. The twins smiled and took the book to Richmond, just the same.

Letitia picked up the brown paper package and opened it, finding the three volumes of brown leather tooled with gold lettering. She peeped at the title page of the first one.

Waynethorpe Manor
A Novel in Three Volumes by the Author of *The Infidel*
London
Printed for the Mercury Press, Leadenhall Street
1814

She closed it again, smiling. But seven faces could not conceal their curiosity. 'May we read it, Miss Boyce? Please may I be the first? Is it the new one? *The Infidel* was *so* romantic. My mama told me I should not be reading it, but *she* read it. I *know* she did.'

Letitia chuckled. 'Perhaps I shall look through it first, and, if I think it's suitable, I'll lend you my copy. I would not wish to offend your mamas. Now,' she said, glancing at the clock on the mantelpiece, 'it's almost time for our accounting lesson. Mr Waverley will be arriving at any moment, and we must not keeping him waiting. Leave your paintings as they are, and we'll come back to them after tea. Come, girls, into the parlour.'

Rewrapping the volumes, she carried them away to safety.

The Honourable Bartholomew Waverley was indeed arriving on foot as she spoke, to take the Friday lesson that would, in theory at least, initiate Miss Boyce's pupils into the mysteries of household accounting that every good wife, wealthy or not, needed to know. It was the kind of thing Letitia included in her curriculum, which other seminaries did not, and so far there had been plenty of parents who agreed with her that it was essential learning. Mr Waverley had been a friend of Letitia's since they had met at a lecture to which her father had taken her many years ago in London. By good fortune, he lived in a beautiful house that faced north-west across Richmond Green, and his willingness to become involved as escort, guide and tutor was one of the reasons why Letitia was sure she could take on such a responsibility. Their relationship was warm, but never more than that—more like that of brother and sister. They were both quite content to have it so.

Mr Waverley was not only a reliable friend, but also an excellent companion who saw nothing remarkable in Letitia's exceptional interest in subjects deemed to be a man's territory. They attended meetings and discussion groups together where his keen mind and knowledge of things scientific and mathematical balanced nicely against her preference for the arts subjects. He was, in fact, the perfect friend. He stood with his feet upon the fanlight's semi-circular shadow that fell upon the Axminster. 'I'm standing on your cheese segments.' He grinned.

'So that's what I can smell. And, yes, you *are* invited to dinner. Come inside, Bart. The girls are in the parlour already.'

'With Gaddy?'

'Yes, Gaddy's in there, too.'

Miss Gaddestone was Letitia's cousin who lived with her by dint of a reciprocal arrangement whereby she received board and lodging for her services as chaperon whenever she was required. And since several of the tutors employed by Letitia were gentlemen, Miss Gaddestone was always there in a corner of the room for the sake of propriety and to keep an eye on good manners. She was kindly and well liked, a stickler for correctness who took her duties very seriously, sitting there with her basket of sewing, saying little, but hearing all.

The exchanged smile needed no explanation, for both of them were aware that one or two of the pupils harboured fantasies about Mr Waverley that had very little to do with accounting. He was tall and pleasant-faced, brown-haired and courteous with well-manicured hands, and eyes that smiled easily. He was also the son of a viscount, wealthy and unmarried, quite a catch for any woman, if he had shown the slightest interest. Naturally, the pupils were sure that he and Letitia were more than just good friends.

'I'll go in, then,' he said.

'Yes. The twins have been.'

'Oh? Not Lady Boyce?'

'No. They brought me something, Bart.'

He studied her laughing eyes, almost level with his. 'Not the book? But you've already got your copies. Did you tell them?'

'Heavens, no. Mama's sure it's not suitable reading.'

'She's probably right, dear heart.' He smiled. 'So do I get to read it now? Come on, that's part of the bargain, remember.'

'All right. You can take it home after dinner. Go on in.'

'Promise?'

'I promise.'

It was getting late by the time Mr Waverley left, though Letitia had not minded having the three boarders stay up for an extra hour or two of good conversation, since the morrow would be Saturday and free from lessons. Miss Gaddestone had contributed with hilarious tales of her childhood in rural Wales, and their next-door neighbour at Number 22, Mrs Quayle, with whom the three young ladies had their rooms, had connections with society women that made her a fount of fascinating information, mostly of a cautionary nature.

By the light of a single oil lamp, Letitia unlocked the drawer of her writing-desk and carefully lifted out a scuffed leather-bound book where the pages of the first half had grey well-thumbed edges, the second half still pristine. It seemed to open by itself at the last page of handwriting.

Unscrewing the silver top of her inkwell, she peered in to check the shine of liquid against the light, picked up her quill and studied its sharpened end. 'Stop prevaricating,' she whispered to it. 'Go on, write it. It's what you want to say. Write it, before you forget.' Obediently, the quill dipped and began to describe.

He sat the huge bay gelding like a god, scowling at the sun until he was obliged to acknowledge her, though she did not wish it. His eyes she could not see, though she knew how they looked at her, how they refused to light, but scanned in one

*glance from head to toe, touching a nerve of her anger, making
her fists clench, halting her breath. She said something ungracious that did not, as she had intended, make him smart,
but dismiss her as too clever by half and not worth his time.*

*She felt her heart thudding, her eyes wanting, but not
wanting, to take in more of him, his gloved hands on the reins,
now reaching to pat the glossy neck before him, settling his
mount as she wished he would settle her. She had never felt
so unsettled. So overlooked. There are more interesting things,
she told herself, to occupy your thoughts. Yet for the life of her
she could not will them to return.*

The quill was laid to rest as a shuddering sigh wafted
across the page, and for several moments she stared at the
words as if someone else had written them. But that was what
writers must do to record every scrap of information that
came their way, especially writers to whom such things came
with exceptional rarity, as one had today. Was it worth record-
ing? she asked herself, closing the book and returning it to the
drawer. Yes, it was. Comfortable or not, she could hardly
afford to let it pass, her experience of men being what it was.

The ride to Hampton Court Palace on the following day,
ostensibly to visit Mr Waverley's elderly mother, was aug-
mented by five of Letitia's pupils, two of whom were local
day girls who, if they had wished, could have stayed with their
parents. So while Miss Gaddestone and Mrs Quayle rode in
the barouche, the others rode their own horses, some of which
were stabled with Letitia's. As a good horsewoman, she had
been keen to introduce riding lessons into her list of subjects,
there being too few young ladies of seventeen, she said, who
knew how to look easy in the saddle. She had no say, however,

regarding the quality of the mounts their fathers had provided for them, which was something she would have to work on, once things became more established.

The cavalcade of one carriage and seven riders ambled along the river path to the village of Hampton with not quite the striking image Letitia had had in mind at the outset, though she did not believe they would be much on show at a place like Hampton Court. The last time she had visited, the gardens had been overgrown and the elderly inhabitants too intent on their feet to notice any passing horseflesh.

While Mr Waverley rode round to the south side of the palace where his mother had a grace-and-favour residence, Letitia led the way round to The Green, and from there in through the West Gate, which, she had been informed, would lead them directly to the place where they could leave the horses and go on foot into the courtyards.

What Mr Waverley had failed to mention was that the large area from gate to palace, known as the Outer Green Court, was the province of the cavalry academy where recruits underwent intensive training before joining Marquess Wellington's army in Spain. Along the left-hand side ranged the red-brick barrack block, the yard in front of which was packed with mounted men in blue tunics with silver frogging across their chests, white pantaloons tucked into shining boots, tall fur helmets, with braids, tassels, belts and buckles, sashes and saddle-cloths, curved scabbards and yards of silver cord. As the barouche and six riders began to cross the parade ground, large glossy horses with stamping hooves and jingling harness moved off in synchronised groups, with civilians around the perimeter to watch the exercise.

But Letitia's elderly coachman, slightly deaf and revelling

in his audience, could not hear her call to him to stop, the blast of a trumpet coinciding with her warning and, at the same time, spooking several of the horses. Almost unseating two of the pupils, the mounts half-reared and pranced out of control while others scattered and wheeled, preventing Letitia from reaching the coachman who, still oblivious to the danger, thought it unlikely that a group of cavalry would take precedence over his carriage and pair. In this, however, he was mistaken, for the cavalry recruits threatening to mow him down were the 10th Light Dragoons, who believed by divine right that they took precedence over everything at all times.

Torn between stopping the carriage and rounding up her struggling pupils, Letitia yelled at Miss Gaddestone who was half-standing, waving her arms like a windmill at the advancing line of dark blue tunics in the hope that they would wait. Using a more immediate approach, Mrs Quayle took up her parasol like a golf club and swiped wildly at the coachman, sending his top hat bouncing like a football under the feet of the cavalry horses. She said afterwards, by way of apology, that she had been aiming for his shoulder. Nevertheless, it brought him at last to an abrupt halt.

The six attractive female riders having trouble with their mounts and the coachman having trouble with his dignity were immediately surrounded by the elite cavalry corps, aged from eighteen to twenty-two, who were not so disciplined that they could conceal their grins in view of the farce before them. Nor could they totally ignore the plunging, whirling, side-stepping and reversing mêlée that blocked their way. Unable to resist the temptation, a few of the young men caught the reins of the worst-behaved horses just as their commanding officer, on a very large bay gelding, rode through the ranks as if the Red Sea was parting for him, and came to a halt beside the coachman's box.

Beneath the black fur of his helmet, the officer's expression was thunderous as he barked at the furious coachman. 'I take it you were never a part of His Majesty's Services, man?'

'No, sir. I was not!'

'Then you may not be aware that a blast on a trumpet is some sort of *signal*, and that not even a dimwit with half a brain would take a carriage forward across a line of cavalry unless he had a *death wish*. Who is in charge of this *nursery*?'

'I am responsible for the safety of these young ladies,' Letitia called out to him. 'And if the commanding officer had *his* wits about him, he would have seen that all was not clear *before* he issued his command. I hope this will be the worst that can happen to your men when they go into battle, for they will be—'

Although the two antagonists had recognised each other instantly, Captain Lord Rayne had decided not to listen, turning his mount away before her insults were finished, snapping and barking at his men and Letitia's coachman, bringing order to the chaos so quickly and efficiently that even the horses obeyed him. Letitia was the last one to pass him, but neither of them cared to acknowledge the other by so much as a glance, and she was left to bring up the rear, seething with anger and humiliation under the barely controlled grins of the men and the wide-eyed stares of the spectators. There was a scattering of applause as she left.

The drumming of hoofbeats on the gravel behind her made her turn to see a young cavalryman with a boyish face drawing alongside, holding out a battered top hat that had once been black. 'Captain's compliments, ma'am,' he said.

The discomfiting episode of the parade ground was bound to have repercussions that would follow Letitia's party, quite altering the purpose for which she had brought them, which was to see the palace architecture and for the riding experience. Now, the excited pupils were far more interested in the young men who had dashed to their aid—which was how they preferred to see it—than in the beauty of the patterned brick chimneys, and they begged to be allowed to watch, if only for a few minutes, the men performing their battle drill. Letitia could hardly refuse. So, leaving the girls with their two chaperons, she went off in search of the grace-and-favour apartments where Mr Waverley's mother lived.

The maze of stone-flagged passages in the Tudor part of the palace soon gave way to the more recent but equally convoluted muddle of courtyards and poky chambers of the William and Mary additions, which had once been the royal apartments, but were now shabbily redundant. After wandering without success from one long passageway to another, she sat down upon a dusty windowseat in a small bare room that might in earlier days have been a butler's pantry. Looking out on to yet another cobbled courtyard, she tried to remember by which side she had entered it, and which might conceivably be the south side.

Before she could draw back, a tall uniformed figure strode through the colonnade opposite her and stopped to look about him. Almost identical in dress to dozens of others, there was no mistaking the set of the powerful shoulders, the length of muscular leg, the officer's arrogant bearing that singled him out from all the rest. She did not watch to see where he went, but held herself flat against the cold wall, hoping that the sage-green velvet habit would not be seen against the mossy brickwork. He was the last, the *very* last person she wished to bump into here, of all places.

Listening for the smallest sound, she held her breath while

trying to distinguish the rattle of roosting pigeons and the thudding of her heart from the hard echo of a footfall upon stone floors. It grew louder, then stopped at the doorway and took a step inside.

Lord Rayne ducked his head beneath the lintel. 'What's this?' he said, softly. 'Abandoning your chickens, Mother Hen?'

Letitia glared at him, then looked away, fixing her eyes on the flaking distemper of the opposite wall, disdaining to answer such a nonsensical question. She felt very vulnerable, for though he had not bothered to close the door, the passage-way behind him was completely deserted.

'Mute?' he said, coming forward to rest a hand high on the wall near her head. 'Interesting. You had plenty to say a few moments ago out there, Miss Boyce. Would you not like to continue, now I have your undivided attention?'

One lightning-quick glance told her that his eyes were as brown as chestnuts, hard and mocking, and that it would not be the first time he had ever had a woman so completely at a disadvantage. Still, she refused to give him any more ammu-nition, it being clear that her ungracious retort yesterday was remembered and that he was angered by today's unladylike response in front of his men. It *had* been unladylike. There was no getting away from that.

'An apology, then? Would that be too much to ask?'

'Yes, my lord. It *would*. Please leave me alone,' she said with as much dignity as she could summon, though he must have heard her voice waver. He was uncomfortably close on purpose, she thought, to intimidate her.

'Leave you alone…here? Ah, no, that would be ungentle-manly, Miss Boyce. You are either hiding, or you are lost. Which is it?'

Taking refuge in silence, she turned her head to one side, her cheeks burning under his intense scrutiny, her mind working furiously towards a way to resolve this dreadful hindrance. Not for the world would she give him the satisfaction of an apology, nor even an explanation. But he was between her and the door and, although hoydenish behaviour was not her style, whatever he chose to believe, a quick dash for freedom seemed to be the only way to extricate herself.

Riding habits, however, were not designed for the quick dash. No sooner had she gathered up her skirts with one hand than his long leg moved to prevent her, his body pressing her back against the wall with a determination she could not break. She felt the shameful pressure of his thigh against hers, and the warmth of his face, so closely restricting. 'Let me go!' she whispered. 'You insult me, Lord Rayne. This surely cannot be the gentlemanly conduct you offer my sisters.' She pushed against his shoulder with her riding crop, but even her well-built frame was no match for him, and there was little she could do to prevent his mouth slanting across hers, taking the apology she had refused to offer.

It was no mere peck, and when she tried to end it by breaking away, he caught her chin to bring her back to him, stopping her protests with another angry kiss more searching than the first. Even through the thickness of uniform, braids and buttons, she could feel the surge of authority that he felt obliged to impose, left over from the earlier incident and now aggravated by her refusal to yield. His arms were controlling her, determined to humble, demanding submission. It had nothing to do with desire, she was sure, but with obedience, the same obedience she had refused him earlier before crowds of onlookers.

'No,' he growled, 'this is not what I offer your sisters, Miss Boyce. I am not offering anything, but *taking* your apology. No one is allowed to walk off my parade ground yelling insults at me, not even a woman. Besides, I've never taken a kiss from a schoolma'am before. It's a novelty. Worth repeating, I think.'

'No...*no*!' Letitia snarled. 'Don't *dare* to handle me so. Get off me! I owe you nothing, and that was *not* an apology. I never apologise to *hooligans.*' Her voice, hoarse with rage, spat out the last word as she found a space to bring up her riding crop with a backhander that would have left a mark had he not caught it in time.

Her fury was not only for his contemptuous embrace, but for herself, too, for she ought to have seen it coming, or at least made it more difficult than she had. There was also the painful truth that her first kiss from a man had been taken from her with such ill will rather than for reasons of tenderness and affection that she had always believed were the prerequisites for lovemaking. His intention had quite obviously been to chasten her, making it doubly humiliating.

He held her wrist and riding crop in mid-air, clearly taken aback by the vehement eruption of her fury, his other hand ready to catch her next move. He watched her brilliant flintstone eyes spark and glisten with rage, her beautiful mouth tremble with shock, and the flippant words he was about to deliver, the laughing retort, did not emerge as he had intended. His eyes grew serious, suddenly contrite. 'A woman of independence *and* courage,' he said, relaxing his grip. 'Steady now.... I've had my say, and I would not wish you to believe your sisters have a hooligan as an escort. Can we not call a truce now?' He held out a hand. 'Friends?'

But Letitia whisked away out of his reach as if he'd offered her a viper. 'After that *disgraceful* behaviour towards a lady, my lord? If you can believe I need *that* kind of friendship, you must indeed be more queer in your attic than the rest of your kind,' she snarled. Lifting her arms, she replaced her hat over her brow, wishing she had worn a veil. 'Stand aside and allow me to find my way out of this *damned* place.'

He might have smiled at the strong language, but his mouth formed a soft whistle instead while his eyes took in the neat waist and voluptuous curves, the arch of her back and the proud tilt of her head on the long neck, which yesterday she had kept hidden. He cleared his throat. 'I know this place like the back of my hand. I will be glad to—'

'I'm sure you *do*, my lord. Every little nook and cranny. I can find my own way, I thank you.'

'What were you trying to find?' he said, ignoring the innuendo.

She had to give in, or run into yet more problems. 'The Gold Staff Gallery. Lady Waverley's apartments.'

'Number 17. So you know Lady Waverley, do you?'

'No,' she said, enigmatically. She swept past him through the door, but a distant shout put further bickering at an end.

'Lettie! Lettie, where are you?'

Relief swept over her, flooding into her voice. 'Here!' she yelled. 'I'm here…*Bart*!' The voice cracked on the last note, giving her away.

Mr Waverley strode round the corner, quickening his stride at the sight of her, reaching out. 'Lettie, where've you been? You here, Rayne?'

'How d'ye do, Bart. Miss Boyce was lost,' said Rayne. 'We were on our way to find your lady mother. Number 17, isn't it?'

Smiles, indulgent and comforting, warmed Mr Waverley's face. 'Little goose,' he said, tucking her arm through his. 'You'd get lost in your own backyard, wouldn't you? Thank'ee, my lord. That was kindly done.'

'You…you *know* each other?' Letitia whispered.

'As lads,' said Mr Waverley. 'Both at Winchester together. Live in the same town, too. I never went in for all *this* stuff, though.' He grinned, flipping a hand towards the silver frogging across Rayne's broad chest.

But despite the sage-green velvet that covered her own breast, Letitia could still feel the imprint of that bulky silver braid, the ache in her arms, and the assault of Lord Rayne's mouth upon her lips. That was bad enough, but worse still was the pain of his contempt, which she believed was less for her indiscretion on the parade ground than for the fact that she was, as he put it, a 'schoolma'am' and therefore less entitled to his respect than her sisters.

Chapter Two

❦

Far from being disturbed by the parade-ground incident, Letitia's five pupils rode back to Richmond brimming over with excited chatter about the way they had been saved from bolting horses or, at least, being thrown and trampled to death. Their exaggeration served two purposes—first, in masking Letitia's quietness and, second, in providing Mr Waverley with all the details that she did not particularly want to repeat.

He had not attached any importance to finding Lord Rayne there at the palace, or to the fact that he had been helping Letitia to find her way about. It was, he agreed, a devilish place in which to lose one's bearings. And it was not Letitia who asked him about Lord Rayne's exact function as a captain of the 10th Light Dragoons, but Mrs Quayle and Miss Gaddestone, who were still chuckling like girls about the poor coachman's top hat.

'He trains cavalry for Marquess Wellington,' Mr Waverley told them. 'Not just the 10th Light Dragoons, the Regent's Own, but other regiments, too. He's done his share of fighting, but he sold out once and was re-commissioned. There's no one better than Rayne for preparing young lads for battle. He lives with his brother and sister-in-law up at Sheen Court for some of the time.'

Mrs Quayle of Number 22 knew his brother. 'That's Lord Elyot,' she said to Miss Gaddestone, holding her broken parasol across her knees. 'Lady Elyot's a lovely lady. She's on the Richmond Vestry Committee, in charge of the strays that wander into the town.'

'Stray dogs?'

'*Women*, dear,' said Mrs Quayle, pursing her lips, implying a certain condition. 'Lord Elyot is Assistant Master of Horse, you know. The Royal Stud is there at Hampton Court, so he and his brother work hand in glove with the King's horses. Breeding,' she whispered, raising an eyebrow and leaning towards her friend. 'Horse mad, that family.' She might as well have said 'breeding mad'.

Letitia made no contribution to the conversation, nagged by the thought that it was her own untypical defensiveness that had brought about that outrageous scene in the little room, not in defence of her charges, which would have been understandable, but in defence of her own position as their guardian. Had it been anyone else but Lord Rayne who had appeared, she would probably have said very little except to admit their mistake. But at first sight of him, it was as if all the hostility in her being had rushed to the fore, to pay him back for the perceived slight she herself had provoked yesterday. It was all so farcical, when she cared not a whit what the dreadful man thought of her.

Yet she cared very much that she had been shown such shocking disrespect, kissed by one of the most notorious rake-hells in town, not because she was what he wanted, but because he suspected that was what would upset her most, a blue-stocking, worth in his eyes only the novelty value. So much for leaving the protection of her family. So much for independence.

After dinner she pleaded tiredness, leaving her two companions, Mrs Quayle and Miss Gaddestone, to their own company. This was the time she usually reserved for writing her thoughts while she was unlikely to be disturbed.

Tonight, the pen refused to speak for her.

For the best part of an hour she struggled for a way to translate her confusion into words, to describe the physical sensations and to explain her emotions, but this time not even anger would untangle itself sufficiently to make the slightest sense, and eventually she closed the book in weary surrender. Perhaps tomorrow she would be able to see it better from a distance.

That, she told herself, was half the problem, for while she could see perfectly to read and write, to sew and draw, she needed her spectacles to be able to see *anything* clearly at a distance, and only amongst friends would she have been seen wearing them. If only she'd had the courage to wear them that afternoon, she might have been able to anticipate the trouble before it happened. Locking away her notebook, she reached for her reticule and took out the leather- and silver-banded case that held her plain steel-rimmed eyeglasses.

Coldly, they clamped each side of her face, but instantly each dark recess of the room came to life with detail, the faint rose pattern on the bed-curtains, the reflections on glass and metal, the sharp moulding around the ceiling. The lamp flame was a little miracle.

Her maid, Orla, entered with a tray, smiling at the bespectacled figure that stared about her in wonderment. 'The day will come, ma'am,' she said, 'when every other lady will be wearing those.'

'In public? Never.'

'In public, ma'am. You mark my words.'

Letitia was silent. Her father had refused to wear his except in private. Letitia had been with him when he approached the fence and ditch all wrong, and she had never hunted since, knowing that it could have been her. He had died in her arms.

Her inability to put down in words what she had gained by the experience of that disturbing day kept sleep at a distance. Her success as a writer of novels depended to a large extent on her sincere and often vivid accounts of passionate relationships, which, for the most part, were the result of an active imagination combined with brief and surreptitious observations. It was not a satisfactory method for any writer of integrity, even though her first novel to be published, *The Infidel,* had been a runaway success. The second, recently published, seemed just as likely to please, if her pupils' eagerness was anything to go by.

Her notebook was her lifeline, a personal record, added to daily, where not only her own thoughts and experiences were logged, but other people's, too, including those of her pupils, relatives and friends: their mannerisms, figures of speech, and the tales they recounted. Descriptions of places were important, too, which had been one of her reasons for wanting to visit Hampton Court Palace that day. She needed the details, the colours and scale, the sounds and patterns. She had returned with an indigestible muddle of emotions, too contradictory to string together in words.

But therein lay another problem—that of writing about relationships when she had only her own to draw on. If she wished to continue giving her readers the kind of detail they craved, it surely made some sense for her to gain a deeper understanding, a more informed perception of the human heart in all its seasons. Some had dubbed her novel 'racy', even 'scandalous', because she had followed her characters into places where other writers had not, but as long as she remained anonymous, she was perfectly safe from the disapprobation of those who felt shamed by such personal matters. How could any young woman enter matrimony, she wondered, without knowing the first thing about the state of mind, and body, of the man she would be tied to for the rest of her life? If her own pupils read her books, then so much the better for them. No one would ever suspect her, Lady Boyce's eccentric daughter, of writing about people in love.

Later that night, however, long after Orla had plaited her tresses into a silver pigtail as thick as a wrist, the notebook was brought out for a second airing to receive a scattering of adjectives, which, while they added colour to a new kind of scene, had little to do with the emotion that simmered behind it. Nevertheless, as she climbed back into bed, she could not resist taking a look at two faint bluish marks on her upper arm. 'Lout!' she whispered. 'Ill-mannered *boor*!' He would have laughed about her with his comrades, for certain, marking up a score for the superior male sex.

At that moment, the thirty-three-year-old lout in question lay sprawled across his bed staring up at the dim pool of light made by a single oil lamp on the canopy. He had scarcely moved for the last hour, but now he rolled off to the edge and sat there with his dressing gown gaping, his hands dangling in repose between lean thighs.

Feeling unsociable and critical of his behaviour that afternoon, he had left the company of his brother and sister-in-law, unable to convince himself that Miss Lettie Boyce deserved all she got. Nonplussed by his uncharacteristic discourtesy, he wondered what devilry had made him follow her, insisting on playing out an incident that would have been better put behind them. A bevy of silly females and a deaf coachman were not, after all, the worst thing that could have happened to disrupt his exercise. To make matters worse, the woman he had shamed was the elder sister of the twins he was currently escorting, the sister they had fondly told him about.

He had formed a picture of a dowd, a frumpish bookworm securely on the shelf. He had caught a glimpse of her yesterday when she had clearly formed *her* own picture of *him* and decided he was not worth her civility. So he had not suffered any guilt at dismissing her as a sharp-tongued hen-of-the-game, even without a closer look. But today he'd seen her on horseback, superb, stylish and proud, the only one of the women to keep control of her mount. Later, he had come across her in that grubby little room where her dignity had been no less impressive, defying him, refusing to be intimidated, spitting fire from her remarkable eyes and rousing in him the kind of aggression he kept only for male opponents with whom he fenced and boxed. Never before had he vented it on a woman.

She was a beauty, too, once he'd got close enough to see: tall and athletic, and undeserving of the 'schoolma'am' he'd taunted her with. Now he would have to find a way to put things right, if only for the sisters' sakes, his first try having been justifiably rejected. He sighed and stood up, dropping his gown to the floor. The thought of seeing the bubbly twins again did not, for once, give him any particular pleasure.

His chance came quite unexpectedly at church next morning when the two Misses Binney asked him if he could find the time, just once, to attend their supper party in the company of his brother and sister-in-law. 'It's several months since you've been,' Miss Phoebe Binney complained, touching his arm with the tip of one gloved finger. 'You brought Mr Brummell with you last time, remember. Such an interesting man, and such good company.'

'Dear Miss Phoebe,' said Rayne, taking her hand between his own, 'I remember it well, and so does he. But I usually return to barracks on Sunday evening ready for work in the morning.' From the corner of his eye he could see the tall plume of dark blue feathers on a velvet hat moving towards the west door, and he knew that, if he stayed talking to Miss Phoebe, his chance would be lost.

'Oh, dear. Then you won't be able to get to know our latest addition to Richmond's talent, will you?' Miss Phoebe's eyes searched, pausing at the vicar's latest captive. 'Miss Boyce, you know. Bart Waverley has promised to bring her with him again. Such a bright star. Her father was Sir Leo Boyce, the architect of those magnificent… Well, of *course*. Your parents are neighbours, are they not?'

But Rayne's refusal had already begun to veer like a weathervane towards acceptance. 'I can return to barracks early tomorrow, Miss Phoebe. Thank you, I look forward to this evening.' Surrounded by several other females, the plume was fast disappearing down the path towards the lychgate, leaving Rayne in little doubt about the reason for the haste.

The terraced three-storey building on Maids of Honour Row facing the Green was well known to the Richmond set as one of the most popular literary salons outside London, not only for its attraction to 'blues and wits', but as a place of political neutrality where complete freedom of speech was actively encouraged. The home of the two elderly Misses Binney, both of them highly intelligent and well educated, its guest lists were noted for assembling people of all ages and experiences, the only requirement being that their manners must be impeccable and that they must contribute to the evening with at least a modicum of cleverness. Needless to say, an invitation to one of their 'supper parties' was an honour few ever declined and, as the best society hostesses were celebrated for their brilliant repartee, the contribution of women to the discussions, whatever the subject, was treated with due seriousness.

When Rayne arrived with Lord and Lady Elyot, the drawing room already buzzed with conversation, and the first notes of a song on the piano, followed by a voice, then laughter, made them smile even before the door closed behind them. Heads turned with greetings, absorbing them into the pool of black and grey, ivory and amber, the blue-white flash of diamonds and the wink of a quizzing-glass.

'Ah, Rayne, old chap. Come over here and tell us about…'

Courteously, he nodded, but preferred to wait a while. This was not the kind of place to which he would normally have come to pursue a woman, nor was he quite sure why he'd accepted the invitation so optimistically when Miss Boyce was unlikely to give him the time of day, let alone engage him in conversation. She was not his type anyway; he preferred his women friends to be affable and accessible, not needing too much effort on his part and certainly not as enraged as she had been by his kiss, even if the reason behind it was controversial. Unsurprisingly, she was a complete innocent and more than likely to stay that way if she was as determined as she appeared to be to redirect her social life. A *seminary*, of all things. Why, with the blunt Sir Leo had left her in his will, she must be one of the best catches of the decade, but for her non-conformity.

'Eccentricity is all the rage these days,' murmured a sweet voice in his ear. 'There are plenty of them about, if you think on it.'

Rayne smiled. 'Amelie, my dear, what are you talking about?'

Slipping an arm through his, Lady Elyot squeezed gently. 'You know well enough what I'm talking about, brother-in-law dearest. I'm talking about the one your eyes could not keep away from in church this morning. The one who sits over there in the corner talking to Miss Austen. It's not like you to be so hesitant. Nor, come to think of it, was it like her to dash off without coming to speak to us. I don't suppose she was the reason you changed your mind about delaying your return to Hampton Court, was she?'

He looked down at her, catching the teasing in the lustrous dark eyes, remembering the time, nine years ago, when he and his brother had first seen her in Rundell and Bridges choosing silverware, both of them wanting her, as most men did. Even after bearing three children, she was still a stunningly lovely woman, gentle and compassionate, whose love had tamed his brother's wild heart as no other woman could have done. Rayne trusted her opinion as much as his brother's.

'Nonsense,' he said with a sideways grin. 'Whatever gave you *that* idea? You've met her then, have you?'

'Well, of course I have, love. I was one of the first people she contacted about opening a seminary in Richmond when there are already six others, not to mention all the boys' academies. As a member of the Vestry, I was probably in the best position to discuss the idea with her, and had she not proposed to make hers different from the others in many ways, I'd not have been so encouraging. Besides, I know her mother, as you do.'

'What ways?'

'Subjects about which young women of a marriageable age seem to know so little these days. The art of conversation, for one. That's sadly neglected by so many mamas. She takes them on visits to places of interest, to art galleries and studios of the leading painters, visits to the House of Commons to hear debates, to the theatre and the royal palaces. She wants them to learn better riding and driving skills, too. You'd be surprised how many young women are unable to ride really well,' she added, waving to a friend across the room.

'No, I wouldn't,' he said.

'I believe she has a lot to offer that others don't. We have Kew just across the park and I'll lay any odds that half her pupils' parents have never been to see the gardens, let alone the succession houses. She intends to teach them how to keep household accounts, and to plant a herb garden, and to cook with them.'

'To cook? What on earth for?'

'Seton dear, you're so old-fashioned. What do you expect a wife to do these days? Stand around like a gateau and simper?'

'Gateaux don't simper, dear Amelie. And I think it sounds like an expensive exercise, since you ask.'

'Ah, but Miss Boyce is no fool. She knows one cannot start such a venture on a shoestring, but don't be supposing her fees are anything like the usual. Nothing but the best for Miss Boyce's pupils. She had the house extended and refurbished before she moved in, and her pupils are from Richmond's best families. Colonel and Mrs Lindell's daughter is one, the vicar's eldest daughter is another, and Sir Mortimer Derwent's girl, too. Oh, and Sapphire Melborough from up on the Hill.'

'Mm…' said Rayne. 'Interesting. Quite a handful.'

Whether he meant the entire package or Sapphire Melborough alone, Lady Elyot did not ask, though she might have been able to guess. 'With her connections,' she said, 'she's had no problem attracting the right kind of client. How do *you* find Lady Boyce these days? Has she tried to interfere with your friendship with the her twin daughters yet?'

'Not yet.'

'She will.'

'She'll only try it once, Amelie.'

'Oh, so you're not *so* keen, then?'

'There are plenty of other fish in the sea. Lady B. is a shark.'

'Yes,' she whispered, 'but some will be harder to catch, I believe. Like the elder Miss Boyce.'

'Hah!' said Rayne, laughing off the suggestion. 'I wouldn't even know which bait to use to catch *that* one. I leave her to the *literati*, m'dear.'

Lady Elyot withdrew her arm, responding to her friend's repeated beckoning. 'Well, you *do* surprise me, Seton dear. I would not have thought you were too old for a challenge as lovely as that. Stay with the safe twins, then. You can hardly miss there, can you?' She drifted away before he'd realised he'd forgotten to ask her who the Miss Austen was, talking so earnestly to Miss Lettie Boyce. But her taunt rang in his ears rather like a warning bell, overlapping the cheery male greeting behind his shoulder.

'Seton, good to see you here. Having an evening off?'

He was aroused from his reverie just in time to catch the remains of a smile on Bart Waverley's attractive face that had been directed, not at him, but at Miss Boyce, who had clearly been heading in his direction until she saw who he was about to address. Then she had smoothly stopped by the side of Baron Brougham, the Member of Parliament who was talking to Sir Joseph and Lady Banks, greeting all three with a kiss to both cheeks, turning her back upon the two who watched.

'Oh, that looks rather like a cut to me,' said Mr Waverley with a laugh. 'I wonder what we've done to deserve that.'

'I cannot imagine,' said Rayne. 'Who is the lady in the corner, Bart? Did I hear the name Austen correctly?'

'Miss Jane Austen. She's staying here with the two Misses Binney. Lives over at Chawton. Shall I introduce you?'

'Yes, if you will. She looks like a homely sort, and I feel a bout of charity coming on.'

'Then a word in your ear, old friend. A little less of the condescending manner. Miss Austen and most of the ladies here could give you an intellectual run for your money any day of the week, so if you start off in patronising mode, you'll find yourself tied up like a bull in a pen. Just be warned.'

'Thank you, Bart. What is Miss Austen's forte?'

'Writing,' said Mr Waverley. 'Even Prinny is one of her admirers.'

'Good grief. Then I'd better tread carefully.'

'The trouble with you, Seton, is that you've never fished in deep waters, have you? Come on, I'll introduce you.'

With the metaphors becoming increasingly visual, Rayne and Mr Waverley waded through the company to reach Miss Austen, only to find that they had been beaten to it by both Lady Elyot and Mr Lawrence the court painter, both of whom had been waiting in line for the chance to speak with her.

Nor was it quite as easy as he had thought to capture a few moments of Miss Boyce's time when she was surrounded by artists and poets, publishers and politicians, writers, actors and musicians and, in one case, a painted scent-drenched play-wright who seemed desperate to hold centre stage until Miss Phoebe and Miss Esme, her sister, drew him kindly towards the supper table, still declaiming *King Lear.* Rayne eventually discovered her standing with her back to him, listening intently to Mr William Turner talking about his latest tour of the northern counties, a small untidy man whose strong Cockney accent was at odds with those who asked questions of him.

Among others, Miss Boyce wanted to know what his plans were for the Royal Academy Exhibition. 'You only presented one painting last year, Mr Turner. Will there be more than one this year?'

He obviously knew her, fixing her with an impish glare down his beaked nose, rather like an outraged gnome. 'Virgil,' he said. 'Begins with a D.'

'Dido?' said Miss Boyce, promptly. 'Dido and Aeneas?'

The amusement and applause was as much for the master's pretend-anger as for Miss Boyce's sharpness, but he scowled and shook her hand, telling her she had no business to be guessing in one. Then, because there was some turning and teasing, she saw who stood behind her and allowed the rav-ishing smile to drain away, edging past her friends with a quick look of annoyance over her shoulder, which, Rayne suspected, may have been partly to do with the fact that a pair of steel-rimmed spectacles rested halfway down her nose.

Striding away towards the supper room, she attempted to outpace him, but was prevented by a group of chattering guests who hesitated, then parted to let her through, allowing Rayne to meet her on the other side of them. 'Miss Boyce,' he said, 'may I help you to some supper?'

Rather than move her spectacles up, she tilted back her head to look down her nose, just as Mr Turner had done a moment earlier. 'Help, Lord Rayne?' she said, scanning his figure like the proverbial schoolma'am with a tardy child. 'Help? Why, no, I thank you. Your assistance, I seem to remember, comes at the kind of price I'm not prepared to pay. Go back to your gaming tables and whatever Sunday-evening company you usually keep. You seem to be out of your depth here.'

'You look even better with spectacles than you do without them,' he replied, refusing to flinch under the lash of her tongue.

'And you, my lord,' she said, removing them with a haughty flourish, 'look much better *without* them.'

'You flatter me, ma'am.'

'No, do I? I beg your pardon. I didn't mean to.'

'Still way up in the boughs, I see. Isn't it time you came down?'

'To your level? Heaven forbid. I fear I should be trampled on.' Tucking her folded glasses into her reticule, she turned away, heading once again for the supper room.

Rayne's own brand of cynicism would, at times, have been hard to beat, but this woman's meteoric put-downs would have silenced most hardened cynics. He followed on, more slowly, watching the swing of her hips under the charcoal-grey beaded half-dress over pale grey satin, the low-cut back and peach-skin shoulders, the long wisps of moonlight-blonde hair escaping from her chignon to curve into her graceful neck. Needled, curious, perplexed, he followed her to the array of food, not sumptuous, but plentiful. But it was not easy to identify the tiny pieces of something, the squares of something else, rolls and balls garnished with greenery, jellies and glasses, and a confusion of cakes.

Without a word, he took the plate from her hand, placed a selection of bite-sized delicacies upon it and gave it back to her, poured two glasses of lemonade and bade her follow him. 'This way,' he said, as if he could sense her relief. He found a vacant sofa beside a table and waited for her to be seated before he asked, 'May I?'

She glanced at the space beside her as if to estimate how much of it he would need, then she nodded, refusing to meet his eyes, taking the lemonade from him with a mechanical 'thank you', and placing it on the table. 'Is this all for me?' she said, looking at the plate. 'Where's yours?'

'I wondered if we might share it,' he said, watching for her reaction.

She made a small involuntary move backwards as if trying to steel herself for something very unpleasant. 'I have suddenly lost my appetite,' she said. 'And anyway, such a gesture would be taken to mean that I have accepted you as a close friend, which is very far from the truth, my lord. If it were not for the fact that you are known to be on good terms with my sisters, I would not be sitting here with you like this. Certainly not sharing a supper plate. Mr Waverley usually does this for me.'

'I accept what you say entirely, Miss Boyce. So may I suggest that, for the time being, you pretend that I am Mr Waverley?'

Dipping her head with a genteel snort of laughter, she turned her dark grey eyes to him at last. 'Lord Rayne, my imagination is in perfect working order, I assure you, but there are some things it would find quite impossible to tackle. That is one of them.' As she spoke, her eyes found the black frockcoat and white breeches of her friend, resting there affectionately. 'Mr Waverley's manners are faultless,' she said. Picking up one of the tiny squares of pastry, she placed it absently in her mouth, still watching until, catching her companion's amused expression, she realised what she had done. Instantly, she stopped chewing and blinked.

'There, now. That wasn't difficult, was it? Having vented some of your spleen, you've found your appetite.'

Swinging her head away, she finished the mouthful. 'Fudge!' she snapped. 'I have not *vented my spleen,* as you put it, in years. In fact, I'm not sure where it is, so long has it been unvented. Here, have one of those. They're quite good. But don't take it as a peace offering. You may be the bees' knees with my sisters, my lord, but if they knew what I know, they'd not be so convinced that you're as gentlemanly as all that.'

'Yet you have agreed to sit and share supper with me,' he said, taking two of the tasty pieces.

'Don't be bamboozled by *that,*' she said.

'Why not? Is it not true?'

'Because,' she said, taking another piece and studying it, 'there is a limit to the length of time I can stay blue-devilled, that's why. I have rarely had reason to hold a grudge against anyone, so I lack the practice. I suppose it's a form of laziness, but I find the effort not worth the reward. I might have been able to keep up a high dudgeon for a few more weeks if there were not so many people known to both of us who would wonder why I insisted on being so uncivil to you. Which I *could*.' The piece disappeared into her mouth at last.

'Oh, I have absolutely no doubt of that, Miss Boyce.'

'But,' she munched, 'I should find it so *tedious* to explain. Naturally, I can accept that men of your…*experience*…may become confused from time to time about who to bestow good manners on, and who not to. That's not the problem. The problem is that when one is on the receiving end of shabby behaviour, one tends to take it personally. If I'd known you had such an aversion to women like me, my lord, I would never have ventured near the parade ground yesterday. Not in a million years. And had I known that your tolerance extends only to women of my sisters' sort, pretty, gregarious women, you may be sure I would have taken my pupils round to the back entrance. So, you see, it's not so much that I've decided to forgive and forget how insulting you can be towards *some* women and mannerly towards others, depending on who is watching, but that I really cannot be bothered with people of your sort. The world is so full of really *interesting* people to spend time with, don't you agree?'

Taking the glass of lemonade, she downed half the contents in one go, replaced the glass on the table and, withdrawing her spectacles from her reticule, replaced them on her nose. Then, treating him to an innocent wide-eyed stare, she rose. 'Thank you for sharing your supper with me,' she said sweetly, and walked away to join a group, linking her arm through one of them like a favourite niece.

Leaning back, Rayne let out a silent whistle like a head of steam being released. 'Whew!' he murmured. 'The lady is certainly not stuck for words, is she? I think there may be more work to be done here, old chap, before this episode can be closed.'

Chapter Three

Creamy white pages danced with shadows. Hovering like a merlin, the loaded quill point swooped, squeaking on the line, eager to tell what it knew.

Even George Brummell himself would have approved of the cravat, spotless white, perfectly creased against the bronzed outdoor skin around the jaw, touching the dark curl of hair before the ears. One could not tell whether the hair had been combed or not, but the way it rumpled on to the forehead might have taken others some time to achieve. A broad forehead, straight brows, deep watchful eyes, still mocking, a nose neither hooked nor bulbous, a wide mouth without fullness, but showing perfect teeth. Taller than me, for a change, and, I suspect, no padding upon the shoulders. My sisters say he boxes, shoots, fences and hunts, and this I can believe for he has the athlete's grace and assuredness, thighs like a wrestler's under skintight white breeches, well-shaped calves. The tables were turned, this time. I was amongst people I knew and liked, at ease and not inclined to sham a confusion I did not feel. I see no need to like him for their

*sakes, but I will say that, as far as looks go, he must be called
a Nonpareil. Would that his manners matched his appearance.
My sisters must see quite another side to him, which makes
one wonder which side is the right side and which the reverse.
Outwardly, some semblance of politeness must be maintained,
I suppose. In Miss Austen, for example, I detected no other
side than that which I saw her present to everyone, whether
they knew of her books or not. Such a delightful lady, well into
her thirties, she has asked me to call on her tomorrow before
her return to Chawton. To be granted a private meeting—what
could be more excessively civil?*

As usual, the cathartic labour of love released her pent-up
thoughts and tumbled them on to the page, ready for use in
another form in the story she had only recently begun. It was
work that had to take second place nowadays to the needs of
the seminary, still occupying several hours of each day. Apart
from the emotional satisfaction of daily creating her own
characters and scenes, the financial reward was a bonus she
had never anticipated. *The Infidel* she had sold for £80 to the
publisher who had seen in her writing an extraordinary talent,
and the first edition had sold out in less than a year, bringing
in a reward of £200. That had been more than enough to spur
her into the next one, *Waynethorpe Manor*, just published
with a subscription list that took up the first three mottled
pages and glowing reviews from *The Lady's Magazine*, and
even *The Lady's Monthly Museum*, usually cautious about
what it recommended.

For a woman possessed of such an independent spirit, the
delight of being well paid to do what she most enjoyed was a
welcome boost to her confidence that had given her the courage
to set out along her own path. Her father's legacy and her

uncle's active encouragement had made it possible. Now she was truly a woman of means, and if that brought with it a certain non-conformity that made her family uncomfortable, then it would have to be so. She could devise her own romances and walk away from them without the slightest loss of sleep.

Her enthusiastic publisher, Mr William Lake, had never met his most popular novelist face to face, however. Not even Letitia could bring herself to talk to him about her work, so Mr Waverley was the one who took her manuscripts to Leadenhall Street, to convey Mr Lake's comments and to negotiate on her behalf. This had been, so far, a very satisfactory arrangement which meant that, for his services, Bart was usually given his own copies to read before anyone else, and a vicarious share in her wild success. Knowing the author only as Miss Lydia Barlowe, the publisher had agreed that the creator of *The Infidel* should be known only as 'A Lady of Quality', since it was abundantly clear to him that, with a friend of such superior breeding as the Honourable Bartholomew Waverley, that was what she was sure to be. It was not his business, he assured the go-between, to probe any further.

Leaving her young charges to the Monday-morning care of the two elocution, play-reading and singing tutors, Letitia set out alone to the Misses Binney's house, wearing a favourite but rather worn velvet pelisse of faded lilac, keeping the nippy April breeze out with a swansdown tippet inside the neckline. She had noticed last night that Miss Austen had worn a long-sleeved brown gown trimmed with black lace, an acknowledgement of the death of the Queen's brother last month.

This morning, the mood had lightened to a white gauze gown under a sleeveless spencer of pale green quilted silk complemented by a soft Paisley shawl and satin slippers made to match. Partly covered by a pretty lace cap, her dark curls framed her sweet face, though, in the daylight, Letitia could see shadows beneath her brilliant eyes and the delicate, almost transparent skin that she understood had once been flawless. Life, she saw, had not passed Miss Austen by without leaving its mark upon her, though she moved with the grace of a much younger woman, her welcoming smile as open as ever.

Their meeting last evening had been too brief for either of them, with so many others awaiting their moment of glory, and now Letitia could not hold back a pang of guilt for the strain that more talking might impose.

'My dear Miss Boyce,' said Miss Austen, 'it's no strain to talk to those who share a love of good literature. Especially—' she twinkled '—without the background noise. That's what I find most difficult. The politicians do tend to *boom*, don't you find?'

Letitia loved her puckish sense of humour. They sat opposite each other by the long window that looked out across The Green where people strolled like coloured beads caught in the sun. 'I think the playwright did his share, too...' she smiled '...but I must not be too harsh. He is to escort us all to Mr Garrick's Temple after lunch. He knows Mrs Garrick well, so we shall be introduced.'

'Then we shall not say another critical word about loud voices. I take it you have tutors to come in daily. Are they there now?'

'Indeed. Elocution and music on Monday mornings. The "voice day" we call it.'

'Music...ah! It *is* important,' she agreed, 'for every woman, young or not, to be able to entertain her guests and to sing for her supper, too, when asked. Not to contribute in some way would be exceedingly poor form. But I have always thought it to be a little…well…insincere, even dishonest, to pretend to an enthusiasm one does not possess, as if other people's likes and dislikes carried more weight than one's own. Without sounding pompous, Miss Boyce, this is why I think you and I could become good friends, for you do not appear to me to be afraid of showing what you do. For a young woman of your background, the pressures to conform must have been very great indeed. But here you are in a fashionable place like Richmond, running an exclusive seminary, which I own I would rather have attended than The Abbey at Reading. It's nothing short of courageous. I suspect there is very little you would hesitate to try, despite what society thinks of it.'

Beneath such a misplaced tribute, Letitia was faced with an instant dilemma of whether to accept it with thanks and to say nothing about Miss Austen's suspicion, or whether to confide in her about the writing, which no one but Mr Waverley knew of. It was a decision that could not be delayed, for upon her response would depend the true nature of any future friendship. On the one hand, Miss Austen would see nothing especially difficult in admitting to a profession at which she herself was a success but, on the other, the kind of writing for which 'A Lady of Quality' was known would most certainly not come within Miss Austen's approval. The friendship would end before it had begun. Letitia could not bring herself to shock so excellent a writer whose books she truly admired, for it had been made quite clear during their previous discourse that Miss Austen's opinion of writers who 'stepped over the bounds of propriety with too colourful imaginations', as she had delicately phrased it, were definitely not to be recommended.

Nor was there any chance that Letitia might admit to being a writer *without* saying what she had written, or how very successful she was, the very idea of pretending to be unpublished being too full of pitfalls to contemplate. So, in the time it took her to smile, she decided upon an even greater deception as the price of Miss Austen's much-needed regard and the approval of a like-minded spirit.

'You honour me with your friendship, Miss Austen,' she said. 'I don't know that I would call it courage, exactly, but I believe my bid for independence of mind may have begun as soon as I gave my first yelp. Or so my mama always maintains. May I ask about your next book? Is it soon to be published?'

'About May, I think. It seems so long since I began writing it I can sometimes scarce remember what it's about. It isn't quite the seamless progress it appears to those not in the business,' she explained. '*Mansfield Park* was begun in the year 1811, almost three years ago, but there are usually some overlaps when parts have to be revised or even rewritten, and then I may find I have two books in hand, the one I *thought* was finished and the one I'm in the middle of.'

'I see. So when one is published, you re-read it after quite an interval? That must be quite refreshing.'

'In a way. But I'm always struck by what *could* have been written, rather than what I actually wrote. Several years later, one's experience of life is slightly changed. Small changes, but enough to make a difference.' Her tone became wistful, reflective. This was exactly what Letitia needed to know.

'Experience is vital, then? Does not the imagination and observation make up for what one can never hope to experience in life?'

Miss Austen sighed, speaking with less assurance.

'Marriage is what you mean, I suppose. Yes, on that subject you may be right, for I shall never enter that estate now and you yourself have taken a brave risk in placing yourself outside your family's protection. And although I can observe some of the tenderness of married love from my relatives, that's probably as far as I need to go in my stories.'

'But before that? In the wooing? The relationship of lovers?'

There was a pause, and the hands that lay in Miss Austen's lap began to move and caress. 'That, too,' she said. 'There were two occasions: one of them I had hopes of, the other could never have progressed. I withdrew my consent immediately. It was a mistake. Without love, you see.' She smiled sadly as the moment of pain lifted. 'One needs to *feel* the love. It's the same with writing. One *can* write about the anguish and uncertainty; one can write about the wonderful sensitivities of the mind, men's minds, too. But as I get older, I realise that it's the true experiences that have informed my writing as no mere imagination could possibly do, even though it was quite some time ago now. There's no substitute for sincerity, is there? I think my readers would demand it from me now, Miss Boyce.'

'I'm sure they won't be disappointed in *Mansfield Park*. I look forward to reading it. Have you another one planned?'

'I have another,' she smiled. 'I shall call it *Emma*. And this heroine will have faults, for a change. They cannot all be so perfect, can they?'

They continued to talk for another half-hour, which was much longer than Letitia had intended. By the time of her departure, they were on first-name terms, had exchanged addresses and had given promises to write and to visit. They embraced at their farewell, Letitia both elated and cast down by her most significant artifice. Deception on such a scale weighed heavily upon her.

There was one thing, however, that afforded her some relief, for in denying her writing, she had been spared the obligation that would inevitably follow of having to talk about her stories. Miss Austen had seemed happy enough to explain her published heroines' attributes and foibles, but Letitia could never have done the same with anything like her skilled understanding. Perhaps, she thought, that was because she did not understand them as well as Miss Austen understood hers.

Another aspect of her meeting with the famed Miss Austen was the conviction that, whatever the authoress had meant to say, there was no substitute for experience. This was something that no page in her notebook was ever likely to supply. She was going to have to take the bull by the horns, one day very soon. The question to be answered was—how?

Her return to Number 24 Paradise Road, taken at a very brisk walk, coincided perfectly with the mid-morning break when the pupils gathered in the garden room to take a cup of chocolate and a biscuit while conversing, as a good hostess should, with the tutors and chaperons. Their lessons that morning had been more in the nature of rehearsals for, in five days' time, all seven pupils were to entertain an invited audience of local guests, including tutors and parents, at the Richmond home of Sir Francis and Lady Melborough whose daughter Sapphire was a pupil at Letitia's seminary.

Understandably, they were nervous, but nerves, they were told, were no excuse for trying to opt out of it, or for unnecessary displays of modesty. The second half of the morning was a run-through of the singing, leaving the piano solos and duets, the harp-playing and poetry recitals, for the days ahead.

The afternoon sun and sharp breeze were perfect for their outing to Hampton House, the home of the late Mr David Garrick. That same morning, Letitia's pupils had been studying one of the actor's most acclaimed roles as Shylock in Shakespeare's *The Merchant of Venice*, and the invitation to visit Garrick's Temple to the Bard had come at a most opportune moment, even if the exuberant playwright Mr Titus Chatterton was hardly the one she would have chosen to escort them. But Mr Chatterton and the old Mrs Garrick were personally acquainted, and this was the kind of connection one needed if six adults and seven young ladies were to descend upon a frail ninety-year-old widow all on the same afternoon.

To buffer her against Mr Chatterton's incessant theatricals, Letitia had requested the company of their elocution tutor, Mr Thomas, whose popularity was almost on a par with Mr Waverley's. The latter was also one of the party, riding horseback like everyone except Mrs Quayle and Miss Gaddestone, who sat behind the coachman, his dignity having been restored by the presentation of a replacement hat from the late Mr Quayle's wardrobe. This time, Letitia warned the girls, they were unlikely to interfere with any cavalry drills.

It was when they rode through Bushy Park's avenue of chestnut trees towards the Diana Fountain that Letitia realised how close they were to Hampton Court Green where the cavalry offices and stables were situated and that, as they turned right on to the avenue of limes, they had been recognised. A group of helmetless recruits sat on the white-painted fence waiting for orders, swinging round to ogle the riders who passed behind them.

Coming under the multiple stare of male eyes, the seven young ladies adjusted their posture and became alert as if, Letitia wrote in her notebook that night, someone had pulled their strings and brought them quietly to life. At the same time, several of the horses reacted, too, exchanging whinnys and pricking ears, rolling eyes and prancing under tight reins, responding to unintentional messages.

Letitia reined in her pretty grey Arab mare. 'Keep going!' she called, resolving to have their riding tuition increased now that the good weather was here to stay. Waiting until they had passed her, she brought up the rear alone since Mr Chatterton, with his captive audience of two ladies, rode beside the barouche. The other two men were some way ahead, oblivious to the cavalcade behind them. From the corner of her eye, she could see the uniformed young men donning helmets, mounting horses and heading for the gate that would release them on to the avenue. Soon, the drumming of hooves followed her, keeping a respectful distance but ready to overtake her pupils as soon as she relinquished her rearguard position.

One young man, more reckless than the rest, cantered on to the grass beside her, laughing at his comrades for their prudence. A sharp command brought the young man's mount wheeling round on its haunches and, before Letitia could turn to look, the captain's bay gelding was beside her, towering over her dainty mare, garnished with tassels and braids and padded with several inches of white sheepskin under the ornate saddle. Shining black boots and silver spurs caught her eye, but she would not look at him. In front of her, the swish of a tail away, Jane Doveley's horse had taken a fancy to walking crab-wise, highlighting yet again the sad fact that all was not as it should be with the young riders and their mounts.

'I see you could not stay away, Miss Boyce,' said Lord Rayne in a voice that held more than a hint of amusement.

'This is the way to Hampton House, Lord Rayne. We are obliged to avoid the public highways, but the last thing we need is a cavalry escort. We have our own chaperons, I thank you.'

'Not very effective, are they? They don't even know we're here.'

He spoke too soon. Responding to the calls, Mr Waverley and Mr Thomas had turned and were cantering back, astonished to find that their duties had been taken over by at least a dozen mounted men. The first help Mr Thomas offered was to take Miss Doveley's horse by the bridle.

Mr Waverley greeted his old school friend and asked—foolishly, Letitia thought—if he intended to go to the Garrick house with them.

'No, he certainly does not!' she replied with more emphasis than she had intended. 'Poor Mrs Garrick would suffer a fit of the vapours to see such a crowd on her property. Please return, my lord. We shall go on nicely as we are.'

'What you need, Miss Boyce, is a good riding instructor for some of your young ladies. Do you not agree, Bart?'

'Well, I, er…'

'The good riding instructor to be yourself, of course,' said Letitia. 'So, having got that detail out into the open, perhaps you should know, my lord, that it doesn't matter what Mr Waverley thinks about it, their lessons are in *my* hands, and I shall arrange any extra ones myself, I thank you.'

'No need to take a pet about it, Lettie,' said Mr Waverley,

reasonably. 'Rayne's only making a suggestion, and there's no one more experienced than he.'

'Yes,' said Letitia. 'That's exactly what I am afraid of.'

'And if he was offering me his help, I'd take it. He might even reduce his fee for seven of them.'

'You mean I'd be expected to *pay* him for an hour in the company of my pupils? I think not. And anyway, Lord Rayne is fully occupied with his own business all week, and our weekends at Paradise Road are not for lessons. It's quite out of the question.'

'I could make an exception,' said Rayne. 'I'm sure the parents would notice the difference.'

'I'm sure the parents would also notice the difference if some of the mounts they've provided were not the ones they've had since the girls were ten, or the ones they use to pull the family dog-cart. But that's not for me to tell them, unfortunately.'

'But *I* could,' Rayne persisted. 'Coming from me, and knowing that it was myself who'd given them some schooling, they'd allow me to find them something more suitable for their daughters. These nags hardly add much to *your* image, either, do they? Unless your intention is to entertain, of course.'

'My image is my own affair, my lord,' she snapped.

His low reply was meant for her ears alone. 'Yes, my beauty, and I could make it mine, too, if you could curb your sharp tongue. The nags are not the only creatures around here that need some schooling.'

She pretended not to have heard, but she had, and the words bit deep into her shell, angering and exciting her at the same time. Why did he think, she wondered, that it was not obvious why he wanted access to seven attractive young ladies on a regular basis, with her personal approval? Did he think she was a dimwit not to see what he was about?

'Your persistence must be an asset when you're teaching battle tactics, Lord Rayne, but I find it irritating. Thank you for your offer, but I prefer to do these things in my own way and in my own time.'

She had not, however, made any allowance for the timely interference of Miss Sapphire Melborough, whose parents were important members of the Richmond set and who, at almost eighteen years old, saw in Lord Rayne a close resemblance to Sir Galahad of Arthurian fame. What she knew of his reputation made him all the more dangerously attractive to her. By falling behind her companions and by making her dapple-grey dance about naughtily, she allowed herself to be caught by Lord Rayne's hand on her bridle and brought back to the wide path, blushing in confusion. It was doubtful whether the performance had fooled anyone, Miss Melborough being one of the better riders, her mount usually well mannered, but it served to reinforce Lord Rayne's argument tolerably well.

'Oh, thank you, my lord,' she said, slightly breathless. 'I cannot *think* why Mungo should choose to be so wilful when I was trying so *hard* to do everything Miss Boyce has told us about looking where we're going.'

'Perhaps,' said Rayne, with a glance at Letitia, 'Miss Boyce also finds it difficult to see where she's going.'

'But Miss Boyce is the most *elegant* of horsewomen, my lord. You must have seen that for yourself. And her beautiful grey mare is…'

At the merest signal from Letitia, the beautiful grey mare bounded forward on delicate hooves towards the barouche, which was approaching the village of Hampton, and although her instructions to the coachman were hardly needed, neither would she stay to hear the silly exchanges between those two, or to his impertinent observations about not being able to see. It was not hard for her to believe that this deficiency was partly behind his offer, knowing as she did that, in order to correct anyone's riding, one must be able to see perfectly. Yet she did not think his offer was entirely for her sake, either. The man was nothing if not an opportunist.

Entering the riverside grounds of Hampton House, she left Mr Waverley and Mr Thomas to dismiss the cavalry in whatever way they chose, going with the playwright Mr Chatterton to meet their hostess in the sadly neglected mansion that David Garrick had lovingly referred to as 'his pretty place by the Thames-side.' Bound to the upkeep of two grand houses under her husband's will, old Mrs Garrick was now reduced to doing almost everything for herself and understandably did not wish anyone to see the dilapidations of the house. She was happy for them to go down to Mr Garrick's 'Temple to Shakespeare' by the river, which is what they had most hoped to see.

It was a domed, octagonal, brick-built place with steps up to a portico of Ionic columns and a room beyond where, they were told, the actor used to entertain his friends or learn his lines in full view of the river. A statue of the bard was here, too, with objects said to have belonged to him, though the glass cases were dusty and a mouldy smell hung in the air. Between them, Mr Chatterton and Mr Thomas, a young Welshman with the most perfect diction, took it upon themselves to be the guides.

Miss Gaddestone, Mrs Quayle and Mr Waverley hovered on the edge of the group while Letitia, hoping for a few moments to herself, wandered down the sloping lawn to the water's edge. A weeping willow swept the grass with new fronds like pale green hair and, as she passed through its curtain, a figure moved away from the trunk and into her view. Against the mottled shadows, she had not noticed him.

The fur helmet was cradled under one arm, his dark hair caught by patches of light, thickly waved and long enough at the back to be tied into a pigtail, which she knew was a badge of this regiment. She wished he had stayed with them.

He followed as she turned away, though she felt rather than heard his presence. But there was nowhere for her to hide and her impulse to run was held in check, and she was gently steered away from the direction of the Temple, feeling rather like a hind evading a dominant stag.

'Out of the frying pan into the fire,' she snapped. 'I came here to avoid the commentary, but perhaps I should have braved it, after all. Don't captains have duties to perform on Monday afternoons?'

'Surely, Miss Boyce, you would not begrudge me a few moments of your time?'

'Oh, be assured that I would, my lord. I thought I'd made that plain last night at the Misses Binney's. However, if you are also hoping to claim a few moments of Miss Melborough's time on the way home, I would rather you respect my wishes and do your flirting when she is under her parents' protection, not mine. I cannot be held responsible for what *you* get up to. Is that too much to ask?'

'Not at all. I am happy to oblige. So, having dismissed the young lady from our thoughts once and for all, I wonder if you would care to reconsider your objections to allowing some help with the riding problem. You admit that you do have one?'

'I neither admit nor deny it, Lord Rayne. It is my concern and nothing to do with you. Thank you for your offer. The answer is still no.'

They had been walking quickly, and now Mr Chatterton's distantly garbled ranting came to them on the breeze combined with the honking of geese on the water. The winding path had taken them downhill out of sight of the Temple and into a dell where they came to a standstill, their antagonism almost tangible as they faced each other like a pair of duellists waiting for the next move.

'Do you answer no to everything, Miss Boyce, as a matter of course?' he said, softly.

She hesitated, suspecting that he had re-routed the subject towards something more personal. She could not be sure. 'No,' she said, 'but I find it a useful tool to use when an alternative won't do.'

His head bent towards her. 'Surely you don't think there is only one alternative, do you? There are many tones between black and white, you know. There is *maybe,* and *perhaps*, or *let's discuss it*, or *what exactly do you have in mind?* And dozens more.'

'I know exactly what you have in mind, Lord Rayne.'

'Tch! Miss Boyce!' he exclaimed in a dramatic whisper. 'That is the most unintelligent thing I've heard from you so far. Would you believe me if I said the same to you?'

'No, of course I would not.'

'I should hope not indeed. Still, if you're quite determined not to accept the best offer you'll have for some time, then so be it. We shall consider the matter closed because Miss Boyce has a bee in her bonnet about my precise intentions. Which, by the way, are not at all what she thinks.'

'Lord Rayne,' said Letitia, looking towards the silver ribbon of water and the blobs of white floating upon it, 'I think we ought to return. I have nothing to gain and much to lose by taking a walk alone with you. Perhaps you should allow me to walk back on my own.'

'I do not think you should be allowed to go anywhere on your own, Miss Boyce. Will you take my arm up this bank? We'll go up towards the house.'

'I'm not exactly *blind*, my lord.'

'So defensive,' he said, crooking his arm for her. 'Come on. Mind that branch.'

She hesitated, unaware of any obstruction on the path. It was shadowed and dappled with greenery, and it would be unnecessarily foolish to ignore his offer of help, and she *was* defensive, and insecure, and a whole lot of other devices acquired during years of having to battle against convention, her mother, her desires, her poor eyesight and its disadvantages. Her hesitation was interpreted as obstinacy.

'Can you not bring yourself to accept help of *any* kind?'

'I can't see any branch!' she yelped.

Unable to stifle a chuckle of exasperation, he went behind her, bending to unlatch the skirt of her sage-green habit from a mossy twig projecting from a branch. 'Now,' he said, offering his arm again, 'shall we go, or shall you fight the elements single-handed?'

Subdued, she took his arm and used his steely strength to negotiate the overgrown path up to the house, unsure how she had come to this point in a relationship that could not have begun in a worse manner. She understood that everyone had at least two sides to their characters, but so far she had allowed him to see only one of hers. It was her own bizarre two-sidedness that concerned her most, for she was not sure which of the two was the real Lettie Boyce, nor did she approve of the deception she was being forced to present, especially to those close to her. For some reason she could not explain, it mattered to her that this man's opinion should be placed on a firmer footing.

'Lord Rayne,' she ventured, not quite knowing what to say.

'Miss Boyce?'

'You may have…well, you see…I am not quite what you think.'

'And you are about to tell me what I think, are you? I thought we had agreed on the absurdity of that, just now.'

'I *meant* to say, if you will allow me, that I may have given you the impression that…well, you spoke earlier about my sharp tongue, and—'

'And the fact that you might personally benefit from a little schooling? Yes, I remember, Miss Boyce. Are you taking up my offer, then?'

'Lord Rayne, you are the most *odious* man of my acquaintance.'

'Abominable,' he agreed, smiling broadly.

Chapter Four

As a result of her meeting with Miss Austen Letitia came away with a feeling of relief that she had not revealed anything of her own writing. Yet with every sentence she wrote, she was reminded that, apart from one derisory kiss from the odious Lord Rayne, her heroine and her heroine's creator were both still innocents with fervent imaginations. Although the kiss was very clear in her memory, it had not been given in the right circumstances and was therefore untypical.

Mr Waverley had told her that afternoon how much he was enjoying *Waynethorpe Manor* as much as, if not more than, the first novel. His mother, he told her, had begged to be the next to read it.

'Is that wise?' Letitia asked him before he left that evening.

'She's one of your most avid readers. Of course it's wise.'

'I hope she doesn't suspect…'

He took her by the shoulders in brotherly fashion, laughing at her touchiness. 'She doesn't suspect anything, Lettie. She and Lake are well acquainted, and he's told her that the author is a certain Lydia Barlowe, but no more than that.'

'Perhaps I should have used different initials.'

'Nonsense. No one is ever going to make the connection.'

Her friend's approval of *Waynethorpe Manor*, however, satisfied her that the author's lack of emotional experience had not in any way affected his enjoyment, though whether she could convince her readers for a third time remained to be seen.

'What's the new one about?' he asked.

'About a young lady called Em…er…Perdita, rather like one of my pupils, in some ways.'

'Which pupil?'

'Any one of them. Inexperienced. Looking for excitement.'

'Looking for love, you mean.'

'Yes, that, too,' she said, giving herself away at each reply. Surely Bart would recognise the heroine?

'You have only to look at the material right under your roof.'

'What d'ye mean?' she asked, rather too sharply.

'I mean your seven young ladies, who else?' They had reached the pavement where Mr Waverley's horse was being held by the young groom. Taking the reins with a nod of thanks, he spoke to Letitia in a confidential whisper. 'As a matter of fact, there is a young lady who might fit your Perdita's description, up to a point. The lass from Scotland. One of the boarders.'

'Edina Strachan? In what way?'

'Nothing I can quite put my finger on, but you must have noticed how inattentive she's become this new term. Her mind certainly isn't on her household-management accounts, and I'd swear she'd been weeping before she came to the dinner table yesterday. She moons about like a lovesick calf.'

'You don't think she might be in love with you, do you, Bart?'

'Good grief, no, I do not. She's either still homesick or lovesick, I tell you. Perhaps something happened while she was at home at Easter. You might keep an eye on the situation.'

'Yes, thank you for the warning. I will. I'll ask Mrs Quayle what she knows about it.'

But Mrs Quayle, the widow in whose house next door the three boarders had rooms, had nothing to add to Mr Waverley's observations. 'Homesickness, my dear,' she said that evening. 'It's only her second term away from home. We may have to work harder on her Scottish lilt, for if she cannot be understood, she's not going to make much headway in the marriage mart, is she? Perhaps we could get Mr Thomas to give her an extra half-hour each week?'

'So you don't think she's in love?'

'Who knows? With all those young Hussars swarming about, it wouldn't surprise me if all seven of them were. Don't worry, I'll keep a look out.'

'Yes. Thank you.'

That same evening, Letitia sat with the attractive seventeen-year-old Edina, whose guardian grandparents lived at Guildford. After talking at length about her family, it seemed that Edina was relieved to be away from their strait-laced Presbyterian influence and more involved with the kind of social life she had previously been denied. The symptoms that Mr Waverley had identified could not be homesickness, Letitia decided, therefore it must be love.

That evening, Edina's early signs were written into the notebook with some elaboration to make up for what Letitia had not personally observed.

* * *

The remainder of the week passed uneventfully except for the visit on Thursday of Miss Garnet and Miss Persephone Boyce in the company of Uncle Aspinall and Aunt Minnie, the latter requiring a tour of the house and redesigned gardens. Sir Penfold Aspinall, a bluff, good-natured giant who had done so much to help his sister's eldest daughter to set up house, approved of everything he saw, partly because he trusted her good taste and partly because he liked the idea of being surrogate father to his remarkable niece. His wife, shrewish and disapproving, had come chiefly to take note and then to convey to Lady Boyce every detail to which they could mutually object.

The twins' main purpose in visiting their sister seemed to be to catch sight of Lord Rayne, whose absence had been the cause of some concern. They asked if it was true that he was visiting her.

'Visiting me? You must be bamming!'

'Has he?'

'Of course not. Why would he visit *me*?'

'We heard he was riding with you on Monday.'

'Me and about twenty others on the way to Garrick's Temple.'

'Oh, well, if that's all.'

'That *is* all. I suppose he'll be escorting you on Saturday?'

'No,' said Persephone, pouting.

'Too busy with preparations for the foreign visitors. Apparently they'll all need mounts,' said Garnet. 'We shall go to Almack's, anyway.'

'It won't be the same. He's such a tease.'

'Is he?' said Letitia, relieved to hear that his commitments would keep him away from Richmond that weekend.

'Come to the garden and see my new summer-house. I think you'll like it.'

Aunt Minnie had found it first. She was taking tea there, dunking an almond biscuit in her cup before she heard them coming. 'Ridiculous waste of money, Letitia,' she said, brushing away dribbles of tea from her lace tippets. 'What are your fees for this place?'

'With extras, usually twenty pounds a term. More for the boarders.'

'Hmm! I don't know what your mama will say to that.'

Uncle Aspinall chuckled. 'It has nothing to do with Euphemia,' he said. 'Cheap at the price, I'd say. What are your young ladies doing now, Letitia?'

'French, with Madame du Plessis, Uncle.'

'Tch! French indeed,' said Aunt Minnie, sourly. 'That monster Bonaparte has a lot to answer for.'

But Uncle Aspinall had nothing but compliments to offer about the way his niece had furnished the rooms, the feminine colour schemes, the new garden layout and the adjoining conservatory. The hanging baskets, potted palms, window-boxes and newly planted vines had brought the garden well into the white painted room. 'Like a jungle!' Aunt Minnie carped. 'Ridiculous!'

It was not until Saturday evening when Letitia gathered her pupils into the downstairs parlour for a last check that she discovered an unwanted addition to the guest list that she could do nothing about when the invitation had been issued by Miss Sapphire Melborough, the daughter of their hosts.

Letitia kept her annoyance to herself, though she would like to have boxed the pert young woman's ears. 'I don't mind you inviting Lord Rayne, Sapphire dear,' she said, fastening the pearl pendant behind her neck, 'but it might have been more polite if you'd asked me first. And your parents. We have to be very careful about the audience, you know.'

'But they *like* Lord Rayne,' said Sapphire, understating the case by a mile, 'so I know they won't mind him coming with Lord and Lady Elyot. And I didn't think you'd disapprove, now that you and he have made up your differences. I told him about our concert and he said he'd like to hear me sing.'

'Next time, dear,' said Letitia, turning Sapphire to face her, 'ask me first, will you? He may be one of Richmond's *haut ton*, but the 10th Light Dragoons, or Hussars, whichever you prefer, have quite a reputation.'

Sapphire's bright cornflower eyes lit up like those of a mischievous elf. 'The Elegant Extracts is what I prefer, Miss Boyce. It's so fitting, isn't it?'

'It's also one of the more repeatable tags. There now, let me look at you. Yes, I think your family will be proud of you. Nervous?'

A hand went up to tweak at a fair curl, and the eyes twinkled again. 'With Lord Rayne watching me, yes.' Provocatively, she lifted one almost bare shoulder in a way that some women do by instinct. It would only be a matter of time, Letitia thought, before this one and her parents managed to snare the Elegant Extract, unless one of her own sisters did first.

'Stay close to Edina, Sapphire. I think she feels the absence of her parents and guardians at a time like this.'

'Yes, Miss Boyce. Of course I will.'

There was more to Letitia's annoyance than having to show friendship to a man she would rather have avoided. He had told her sisters that he would be too busy on Saturday to escort them when he must already have accepted Sapphire's invitation to hear her sing. Persephone and Garnet would be sadly out of countenance to learn that he was not as committed to them as they thought. Their mother even more so. All that was needed now to set the cat among the pigeons was for them to believe that *she* had invited him to the Melboroughs'. She could only pray that they would not come to that conclusion as easily as they'd learned of his precise whereabouts on Monday.

As it transpired, this particular problem faded into insignificance beside the others of that evening. Though she had made every effort to present her pupils to perfection in appearance, manners and performance, the one who outshone them all without the slightest effort was herself. Gowned modestly in palest oyster silk and ivory lace, her aristocratic breeding and her refined silvery loveliness drew the eyes of the appreciative audience before, during and after each individual contribution. Making good use of her gold enamelled scissors-spectacles that hung from a ribbon looped about her wrist, she was able to see most of what was happening while combining an image of seriousness with a charming eccentricity, for the folding spectacle was not an easy accessory to use.

When she was not using it, it seemed hardly to matter that she could see only the indistinct shapes of the guests for, with Mr Waverley to help her through introductions and to murmur reminders in her ear, she felt the disadvantage less than she might otherwise have done. It also quite escaped her notice that the admiring eyes of so many men turned her way, or that the women's eyes busied themselves with every perfect detail of her ensemble.

Miss Gaddestone, petite in a flurry of frills, mauve muslin

and bugle beads, and Mrs Quayle, like a plump beady-eyed brown bird, were the other two who knew the seriousness of Letitia's handicap, but who were too interested in their own roles to play chaperon to her as well as the pupils. They knew Mr Waverley would do that.

Sir Francis and Lady Melborough had taken a fancy to Letitia from the start, looking upon her at times as one of the family, though it had always been one of her policies to maintain a respectful distance between herself and the pupils' parents to avoid any appearance of favouritism. Lady Melborough was a perfect forecast of how Sapphire would look in another twenty years, kindly and flighty and of a more blue-blooded ancestry than Sir Francis. She had prepared well for this event, her house being the most perfect setting, high-ceilinged and spacious, gold-and-white walled, moulded and mirrored.

As a newly knighted city banker, Sir Francis was self-important and ambitious, handsome and middle-aged with an eye for the feminine form, and for his own form, too. He stood facing a very large gilded mirror to speak to Letitia where, with lingering looks, he could see over her shoulder both his own front and her back, the curve of which he thought was enchanting. Letitia found his closeness uncomfortable, his affability fulsome, his attentions too personal for politeness. She edged away, trying to identify Mr Waverley's brown hair amongst so many others, and when she noticed the unmistakable frame and dark head of Lord Rayne approaching from across the room, the sudden relief she felt was quite impossible to hide.

'Why, Miss Boyce,' he said, 'am I dreaming, or did I see a fleeting welcome in your smile? Do tell me I'm not mistaken.'

'It would be impolite of me, to say the least, Lord Rayne,

to admit any feeling of relief. Sir Francis is our host and I'm sure he's doing all he can to make the evening a success.'

'Then I take it you would not appreciate a word of warning?'

This was the first time she had seen Lord Rayne in evening dress, and she found it difficult to reconcile the former soldier in regimentals with the quietly dressed beau in charcoal-grey tail-coat, left open to show a waistcoat of grey silk brocade. Whatever else she disliked about him, she could not fault his style. 'Warning?' she said. 'Are you the right person to be warning me of *that*?'

'Of what, Miss Boyce?'

'Lord Rayne, you take a delight in putting me to the blush. But I shall not rise to your bait. You of all people must know what I refer to.'

'Will I never be forgiven for that, Miss Boyce? Am I not to be allowed to warn you of similar dangers from old married men who ought to know better?' Despite the teasing words, his eyes were seriously intent.

'It is not necessary. I am not a green girl, my lord, and I have Mr Waverley to protect me.'

'Ah, Mr Waverley. So you do.'

Their eyes roamed together, identifying the elegant figure in dark blue and white only a few paces away. Side by side, he was talking and smiling with Mr Jeffery Melborough, Sapphire's older brother, shoulders almost touching, their backs reflected in the long mirror above a semi-lune table. Before Letitia could withdraw her glance, a slight movement in the mirror caused her to squint, trying to understand why young Mr Melborough's hand was slipping between the long tails of Mr Waverley's coat, its white cuff almost disappearing.

'What's he doing?' she frowned. 'I think he's picking Bart's pocket. I must go and warn him.'

'No, come away…over here.' Lord Rayne's voice was suddenly commanding, his arm across her waist urging her forward. 'Look, here are Mrs Quayle and your cousin. It must almost be time for the second half. Ladies,' he bowed. 'May I procure—'

'But what if he *was* trying to reach Mr Waverley's pocket? Is there not one in the lining of the tails?'

'—a glass of punch for you?'

Face to face with the two chaperons, Letitia had little option but to abandon Mr Waverley to his predicament, whatever it was, in favour of the excited chatter covering every aspect of the evening, including Lord Rayne himself, as soon as his back was turned.

'Did you *know*,' said Mrs Quayle, 'that he actually *offered* for your house when it first came on the market? I had no idea, but that's what Lady Adorna Elwick has just told me. She's his sister, you know. Lives at Mortlake. Over there, with the tall gentleman. Her *beau*,' she whispered. 'Isn't she a *vision*?'

'Yes, I met her earlier,' said Letitia, recalling the stunning beauty in gossamer gold-threaded muslin that seemed to reveal more than it covered. The Merry Widow, they called her, with good reason. 'Strange that no one mentioned it before. Lord Rayne has said not a word.'

'Well, perhaps he doesn't want you to know,' said Mrs Gaddestone.

'That he wished to purchase my house? Why not?'

Miss Gaddestone opened her mouth to answer, but was checked by her friend's elbow connecting firmly with hers. 'Oh! Am I not meant to say?'

'Say what? Gaddy, what *are* you talking about?' said Letitia.

Helplessly, Miss Gaddestone blinked at Mrs Quayle, who rose to the occasion as if this was what she'd intended. 'Lord Rayne,' she breathed from half behind her fan, 'is still recovering from a thwarted love affair, his sister says. Number 18, you see, belongs to the Bostons, and Lady Boston is Lady Elyot's niece, and when the two of them lived there before they were married, Lady Boston and Lord Rayne formed an *attachment* to each other.'

'Before she was Lady Boston, you mean?'

'Yes, she was plain Caterina Chester then, but she—'

'Mrs Quayle,' said Letitia, 'what are you implying? That Lord Rayne wanted Number 24 so he could live near the lady he once had a *tendre* for? If that were typical, he'd have to offer for dozens of properties a year, wouldn't he? Anyway, Number 18 is empty for most of the year. I was told that the Bostons live up in Northumberland. Or is it Cumberland?'

Fluffing up her feather boa and settling it again upon her shoulders, Mrs Quayle tried again. 'It is,' she said. 'The Bostons keep a skeleton staff there. They come down from the north about twice a year. Still, it sounds to me as if he's not quite got over the lady, doesn't it? I wonder if she feels the same way.'

'I think you're probably jumping to conclusions,' said Letitia. 'Perhaps he had his sights on Number 24 because Richmond houses don't come on the market too often. Well, not the kind he'd want to buy.'

But the information, so carelessly given, found a corner of her mind into which it did not fit as snugly as it ought. The notion of Lord Rayne being capable of a lasting affection for a woman seemed uncharacteristic of such a man. More than that she would not allow herself to dwell on, though it became quite a struggle to prevent certain images from developing in her mind that had no business there in the first place. Especially when she did not even like the man.

As if she could not resist the chance to needle him for something as indefinable as that, she joined him towards the end of the interval as he and Mr Waverley were chatting together. Instead of greeting her with his usual smile, Mr Waverley was studying his shoes as if they had been the subject of some discussion while Lord Rayne's expression held traces of sympathy.

'Ye…es,' Mr Waverley was saying. 'Right. Ah, Lettie. It's all going rather well, don't you think?'

'It is indeed,' she replied. 'And just think, if Lord Rayne had been with my sisters as they expected him to be, he would have missed such high-class entertainment. But one must choose, I suppose, between hearing Miss Melborough sing and thereby pleasing two prospective parents-in-law on the one hand, or escorting two Miss Boyces and pleasing only *one* parent. It must have been a very difficult decision to make, my lord. I hope the concert is worth the sacrifice. Shall I let my sisters know who took their place, or shall you be the one to explain the problem?'

Rayne's eyes, heavy-lidded and patently bored with the subject, looked beyond her. 'There was no problem, Miss Boyce, although if you wish to make a drama of it, please don't let a detail like that prevent you. I realise how dull life must be for you without some kind of diversion, however small.'

'Yes, my lord. You can have no idea how tedious it is to put on concerts of this kind and to be making visits almost every day. Compared to the excitement of routine cavalry drill and the polishing of tack, we live very sedate lives. What is it to be on Monday? Ah, yes, our theatre evening. Oh, what a bore.'

'Lettie, I think Lord Rayne means that—'

'Bart dear, I know what he means.'

'If I may interrupt,' said Rayne, tonelessly, 'I believe we may have covered this ground only recently. We're getting to the "I know what you're thinking" part, if I'm not mistaken. Bart, would you be a good fellow and…?' He touched Mr Waverley's lace cuff with the tip of his fingers.

'Yes, of course. Will you excuse me, Lettie? I'll catch up later.'

Letitia stared at the prompt departure. 'What was that about?' she snapped. 'Why did you—?'

'Because, my sharp-tongued beauty, I have some advice for you.'

'Then I don't think I want to hear it, thank you.'

'Yes, you do. It's about what you saw earlier. With Mr Jeffery.'

'Oh. Were you giving him a set-down?'

'Not at all. It was a fudge between them, and Bart was embarrassed. Nothing was taken from his pocket. It was just a bit of nonsense. It would please Bart if you were not to mention it.'

'Oh, boy's pranks, you mean.'

'Exactly. There are certain things a woman is innocent of when she has no brothers.'

Letitia blinked, not knowing how to reply to that. Without knowing it, he had pinpointed a basic truth that lay behind her writing problem, not simply by being brotherless, but being without the kind of understanding that comes from years of observing what young males do, how they behave together, what they look like under the formal attire and what they say to each other. It was a private jest between friends. She ought to have guessed.

Caught unawares, she foolishly pursued the other matter instead of granting him the last word. 'So what am I to tell my sisters, my lord? I would not want them to think it was I who invited you here this evening.'

'Miss Boyce,' he said, visibly stifling a sigh, 'you appear to be rather obsessed by what other people think, despite your efforts to make it seem otherwise. If I were you, I'd leave me to deal with my own affairs as I think best and try minding my own business.'

'It will be very much my business, Lord Rayne, if my sisters were to suspect *me* of keeping you here at Richmond. In fact, they have already asked me if you have visited me. How foolish is that, I ask you?'

'Extremely foolish, Miss Boyce. I cannot think of a single reason why I should want to call on you at Paradise Road. Can you?'

'Not unless it was to take a look at the alterations I've made since *you* looked it over. Enjoy the music, my lord.'

The tiff gave her nothing like the satisfaction she had hoped for and, if it had not been for her pupils' efforts to please, and her own part in that, she would have felt even more irritated than she did. As it was, the parents were well satisfied that they had made the right choice of school for their daughters and that their money was being well spent on all the right accomplishments. In that respect, the exercise had been well worth the effort.

Sir Francis and Lady Melborough went even further by letting it be known that Lord Rayne had agreed to give their daughter some riding tuition and to find her a better mount

than the one that had been Mr Jeffery Melborough's hack.
Then, it was only a matter of minutes before first one father
and then another approached Lord Rayne with similar
requests, effectively appointing him as personal tutor to their
daughters and charging him with the purchase of suitable
horses to replace the present ones, to Letitia's quietly seething
anger. The only saving grace in her eyes was that the extra
lessons would be outside school hours and it would be the
parents rather than she who paid him. The only one to miss
out on this new arrangement was Miss Edina Strachan, whose
relatives had not attended.

'You did that on purpose, didn't you?' Letitia said to him.

'I didn't actually have to *do* anything, Miss Boyce. It was
Miss Melborough herself who broached the subject to her
father and he who asked me what I thought. What I thought
is what I'd already said to you. Simple as that.'

'You have a knack of getting your own way, that's all I can
say.'

'I wish it was all you could say, ma'am. Unfortunately, I
do not hold out any hopes on that score until you're taken in
hand and held on a tight rein.'

'Which will not be *your* business, my lord.'

'Not yet. You'll have to be caught first. Goodnight, Miss
Boyce.'

This was not, however, the last she heard from him that
night, for as she stood listening to the quietly spoken vicar's
wife, mother of Verity Nolan, the deeper voices of Lord Rayne
and Lord Elyot came to her ears from the other side of a wide
marble column, weaving around Mrs Nolan's opinions of the
piano duets.

'Attracted?' said one, in answer to some question. 'Intrigued, certainly. I can't say I've ever come across such a combination of looks, intelligence and prickliness.'

'So well balanced,' Mrs Nolan was saying, eagerly. 'Of course…'

'You've had it too much your own way, Sete. That's the problem.'

'…there were times when the bass line was a little strong, but…'

'Yes, I know I have. She seems to think so, too.'

'What about the sisters? Not so much fun?'

'….but that's only to be expected. A little more practice, and…'

'Getting tedious, Nick. Too predictable. The elder one is a cracker, and I fancy the challenge. You can see why she and the mother don't see eye to eye.'

'So, you fancy taking on a *blue-stocking*.' There was low laughter and some words about no stockings at all that made Letitia blush. 'Well, give it a try and see how it goes. She may prove to be worth the trouble, if looks are anything to go by. D'ye think she's interested?'

'She's very green, for all her ways. And I think she may be interested, but she'd not admit it. I may need some help, Nick. Are you willing?'

'Of course. You helped me with Amelie. Just let me know.'

'Thanks, I will.'

'Miss Boyce?' said Mrs Nolan. 'Are you all right? You're very flushed, my dear. I was saying—'

'Yes, quite right, Mrs Nolan. More practice, I'm sure. Now, I must go and say farewell to Lady Melborough and gather my brood together.' Slipping away into the crowd, Letitia made her way in a daze between the chattering bodies, her mind reeling from the kind of talk she should not have listened to. As her first taste of the way brothers spoke to each other in private, it would have been more enjoyable if the subject of their speculation had not been herself.

It now became imperative for Letitia and her pupils to take their leave of their hosts, pack themselves into carriages and escape to the safety of Paradise Road away from the controversies surrounding Lord Rayne's unwanted presence. If he had not been invited, Letitia was sure she would not be feeling so annoyed, even if she ought to have anticipated some trouble, in view of her previous experiences.

Her farewell to her host and hostess, however, could not be rushed through in a few brief words, and when Sir Francis took her to one side, impolitely monopolising her attention, it was more than she could do to snub him by refusing point-blank to cross the threshold of his large library where he promised to show her a rare volume of John Donne's poetry before she left. Just to one side of the columned hall, the white double doors were wide open and, since anyone could see inside, Letitia saw no danger in following him.

John Donne was one of her favourite poets, but the library was not well lit and, when Sir Francis opened the book upon his desk and moved it across to show her the handwritten script, she found it impossible to see much except the first decorated letter. Deciding there and then that this was to be the extent of her obligation to him, she bent to look more closely as his hand smoothed over the pattern of words on the page. His body moved too close as only a father would have done, innocent but invasive, nevertheless. His breath smelled of brandy. She was tired, emotional and, she thought later, too keyed up to think sensibly, and what happened next was as much the result of her over-reaction as Sir Francis's uncomfortable closeness.

She moved away and took a hasty step backwards, hitting her heel against some unseen object, and crashing down over the top of it on to the carpeted floor, forcing a yelp from her lips.

Lights tipped and jerked crazily.

Hands reached out.

Shapes bent over her.

A man's face loomed through a haze of shock.

'No…no, don't *touch* me!' she whispered. 'I can manage alone.'

'Miss Boyce, take my hand. It's me, Rayne. Let me help you to get this footstool out of the way. You fell over it, I believe. Are you much hurt?'

Somewhere behind her, she heard the deeply cutting voice of his brother asking Melborough what in hell's name he thought he was doing to invite a young lady to be alone with him, telling him with unarguable finality that it didn't matter whether the doors were open or not, he should have known better. The thud of Sir Francis's footsteps on the carpet was swallowed into the soft hum from the hall.

Letitia struggled to sit upright against the desk. 'My eyeglasses,' she said. 'I heard a crack just now. They're hanging from my wrist. Please, if you would move your foot, my lord.'

There was a tinkle of glass as he obliged. *'Damn!'* he said. 'Oh…oh, *no!*'

Crouching down beside her, he removed the ribbon from her gloved wrist from which dangled the golden scissors-spectacles, one half now empty of glass, its pieces on the floor. 'I'm so sorry,' he whispered. 'I didn't see them there.

Why in pity's name doesn't he get some lights in here?' Carefully, he picked up the pieces. 'Truly, I'm sorry. I'll have them mended immediately. Leave it with me. Come, Miss Boyce, you should go straight home. Can you stand now?' Tucking the broken parts into his pocket, he held out his arms to her as Lord Elyot watched.

Although she had heard, only a few moments ago, how indelicate their talk about women could be, she made no protest as his arms enclosed her shoulders and gently pulled her upright, nor did she object when his cheek almost touched hers. She clung to his arm. 'Yes, I can stand, thank you. Ouch…oh, *ouch*! I'm all right, really. It was nothing.'

'No, you're not!' said Lord Elyot, sternly. 'You've had a nasty fall.'

'Not as bad as I've had on the hunting field, my lord.'

'That was years ago. Rayne and I will support you. See,' he said, offering her his arm, 'this is entirely proper. It will cause not the slightest comment for you to take both our arms, Miss Boyce. Will it?'

Obediently linking her arms through theirs, she winced visibly as the dull pain came pulsing into her knee and elbow. 'Thank you, my lord. You are very kind.' From the corner of her eye, she caught a look from Lord Elyot sent across her head to his brother.

'A little kindness goes a long way, eh, brother?' he said, softly.

Bustling towards them, Miss Gaddestone was all concern. Mr Waverley was not far behind, then came the others, flocking to her with smiles of sympathy and tender enquiries. Her arms were relinquished to others on a wave of affection that bore her out towards a waiting carriage, lifting her into it, settling her with rugs and cushions.

'Bart, will you…?' she began.

'Leave it all to me,' he said. 'Came a cropper, did you, Lettie?'

'In a manner of speaking,' she replied, catching Lord Rayne's eye.

Chapter Five

With so much to be said about the success of the evening, it was very late when the three boarders and Mrs Quayle left Number 24 for their beds next door. Everyone they had spoken to agreed that Miss Boyce's very select seminary excelled in the quality of the teaching and in the astonishing progress of the pupils. The only sad note was the absence of Edina's parents and grandparents, though Letitia did her best to sweeten the disappointment by drawing attention to the absence of her own family, too. It could not be helped, she said, if one's family could not always be where one wanted them to be.

Later, sitting up against a bank of pillows in her own bed, Letitia felt the sadness as keenly as her Scottish pupil, knowing that her sisters would gladly have come if their mother had chaperoned them. What would it take to get her here? she wondered. What would it take to win her approval?

Other incidents had left a sour taste in Letitia's mouth, the last one being by far the most serious and the one her friends had kindly glossed over as being no more than an accident, though they must have realised there was something more to it than that. She had been warned, and had assured Lord Rayne that she was capable of looking after herself, and now he would think she had brought it upon her own head.

It had also served her right for trying to manage without wearing her spectacles on such an important occasion, and now they were broken. Amongst her literary friends it mattered less, for most of them wore them openly. But tonight she had wanted to look her best, to be a credit to her pupils and to set an example of womanly perfection, as far as she was able.

But her efforts to hold herself above the reach of rakes had been less than successful, for the one whose attentions set up her hackles more than any other had discussed her with his brother as if she were a filly ready to be taken in hand. It was what he had rudely told her more than once. Perhaps that was the way they discussed her sisters also—her 'tedious, predictable sisters'. Unlike them, she had always been too threateningly bookish for any man to think of in romantic terms, and even Rayne found her—apparently—intriguing rather than attractive, a challenge, a diversion, nothing too serious. Nor had Bart ever shown her any romantic intentions.

Between bouts of reflection, her pencil on the page described the atmosphere, mannerisms, expressions and ensembles, the music and voices, the colours, the blurred flutter of fans and feathers, the perfumes and the faint, warm, male scent of the man who had lifted her from the floor, effortlessly. The pencil stopped, her head fell back upon the pillow, eyes closed, remembering. Was that how it would feel to be lifted, carried, laid upon a bed?

Busily, the pencil continued its word pictures. Her elbow and knee throbbed. She took another sip of warm chocolate while constructing an image of Lady Boston who would, naturally, be ravishingly beautiful, not at all sharp-tongued or intellectual, and probably pining up in Northumberland for the brother of her uncle-in-law. Was he within the permitted degree of consanguinity? Did it matter these days? She fell asleep, wondering about it, convinced that Lord Rayne did not intend anything more than a light flirtation, being still half in love with Lady Elyot's beautiful talented niece. Yes, she was sure to be talented and experienced. A society high-flyer she would be.

Several times she woke when her knee and elbow pressed upon something, sending her thoughts rushing back into the angry pocket of her mind where Sir Francis's unfortunate lack of manners hovered like a giant question mark over the messages she was unconsciously sending out about her accessibility. Was her learning attracting the wrong kind of man? Was it perhaps to do with her care of younger women? For Lord Rayne to overstep the mark was one thing, but for the father of one of her own pupils to forget the respect due to her was nothing short of shameful. By dawn, she felt as if she had hardly slept at all.

Monday morning, usually kept for music, was taken at a leisurely pace over jugs of barley water and coffee, cook's best biscuits and a continuous flow of laughter and discussion about future events. Sitting outside in the garden, Letitia used the opportunity to show them the new shoots of herbs, dill, parsley, rosemary and thyme, and to make a game of recognising them by smell alone. Then there were formal thank-you letters to be written to their hosts, leaving Letitia to put her feet up in the roomy summerhouse where the footman came to find her with the news that she had two morning callers.

'Lady Elwick and Lady Elyot,' he called to her.

She swung her legs down, but her guests would not allow her to stand for longer than it took to exchange kisses to both cheeks.

'We came to see how you are this morning…'

'…taking a ride through the park…'

'…and to thank you and the girls…'

'…for the concert. We must do it next at Sheen Court.'

Letitia was used to the twins' interwoven sentences, but she had not encountered these two sisters-in-law together until now. Lady Elyot was a dark classic beauty; Lady Adorna Elwick was fair and quite unlike her two brothers. However, she shared with them their noble parentage, so was entitled to be known as Lady Adorna from birth, whereas the title of Lady Elwick came via her late husband. To confuse matters more, she had been known from childhood as Dorna, and the name still held.

Lady Dorna laughed readily, caring nothing for the crinkles around her merry blue eyes, the same shade exactly as the flimsy morning gown and low-cut velvet spencer. Ribbons flowed from her ruched poke-bonnet, and a lacy parasol was furled into a spear as she took the chair next to Letitia. 'Isn't this *cosy*?' she laughed, looking about her at the cushioned benches, basket chairs and rattan tables. 'One could have a secret *rendezvous* in a place like this, Amelie. Couldn't one? Oh, what fun! I think mine is too small for anything as romantic as that. Perhaps I ought to enlarge it.'

Lady Elyot shook her head, smiling at her sister-in-law's artlessness. 'Dorna, you are shocking Miss Boyce, dear. This darling place is used only for taking tea and writing one's journal, isn't it, Miss Boyce? Tell Dorna I'm correct. Mind you, if I had it, I'd use it to do my painting in.'

'That is what I use it for, my lady. Writing *and* painting.'

'Of course you do. As soon as we met I could see you were artistic. Writing and art: two sides of the same voice. You keep a journal, do you? Most women seem to, nowadays.'

'It's one of the subjects we teach. That, and the art of letter-writing. Speech-writing, too. There are sure to be occasions when they'll be expected to say something intelligent in public.'

'You are *so* progressive in your thinking, Miss Boyce.' Sliding gracefully into the other basket chair, Lady Elyot lifted a ladybird off the arm and placed it gently on to the vase of tulips. 'There will also be times when they'll be expected to attend a local Vestry meeting. Our new Vestry Hall is only a few doors away from here. Why not bring them along one day, just to listen?'

'Thank you. That would certainly open their eyes. We shall all be going to the theatre this evening. The girls are studying *The Merchant of Venice* and, by chance, that's the play being performed.'

'A coincidence indeed!' said Lady Dorna, delightedly. 'We have arranged to go, too. We're to have dinner first at the Castle, then straight to the Theatre Royale. Now why don't you join us for dinner, Miss Boyce? You and your boarders. And your two chaperons?'

'Lady Dorna, it is more than kind of you to invite us, but we couldn't possibly all come. That would be far too many because our party includes Mr Waverley and Mr Thomas, the elocution teacher. He wants to come, too. Why do you not come to us instead? It would be much more convenient, I think. We shall be dining early at six o'clock in time for the performance at eight. Just a simple repast. We'd be honoured if you would share it with us.'

Lady Elyot was concerned about the short notice to Letitia's cook, but Lady Dorna had no hesitation in accepting. 'Why not?' she said. 'Seton hopes to be with us, too. What a party we shall be.'

'Is not Lord Rayne at Hampton Court today?' said Letitia.

'Yes, but he's returning in time for our theatre dinner.'

'That's not like him,' said Lady Elyot. 'Seton has never been too keen on Shakespeare.'

'Well, dear, that's what I put to him, but he tells me he's reforming.'

And perhaps, Letitia thought, Lord Rayne has received another invitation from Miss Sapphire Melborough who, like the other day pupils, would be attending with their parents. With this certainty in her mind, she found it hard to accept that she was being used by the scheming young woman as a way of including Lord Rayne in her social life, whether she approved or not. If that were the case, there was little she could do about it, but she would have preferred the Melboroughs rather than herself to have the pleasure of feeding him.

To her relief, Mrs Mappleton, the cook, seemed quite un-perturbed by an extra five guests to cater for. Mrs Brewster, the housekeeper, after indulging in the obligatory astonishment, soon began to warm to the idea of entertaining an extra two lords, two ladies and a captain. It was still before noon, enough time to send for more meat and fish, to prepare more side-dishes and desserts, and enough time for Letitia's pupils to decorate an enlarged dinner table. It was good experience, she told them, opening the double doors between dining and drawing rooms, thinking how right she had been to buy the extending table and matching chairs from Gillow of Lancaster. Lady Boyce had insisted it would be too large for

Letitia's purposes. Rather than set thirteen places, however, she sent an invitation to Mr Titus Chatterton, who lived near Mr Waverley on The Green, asking him to dine with them. He was an entertaining guest, for all his face paint and flamboyance, and one could not help but like him.

For the remainder of the day, she showed her pupils how a good hostess must prepare for last-minute diners without the slightest sign of improvisation or muddling through, and without upsetting one's cook or housekeeper.

By the time the first carriages rolled up at the door, the day pupils had returned home and the duty of receiving the guests was shared by the boarders as part of their education.

Acting as assistant host, Mr Waverley took the head of the table with Lady Dorna to his right while Letitia and Lord Elyot took the opposite end, and although there were more ladies than gentlemen, the arrangement could not have been more comfortable for the three youngest ladies for whom this was a kind of lesson. The guests appeared to understand it well, this being the first visit for four of them, and even though good manners forbade any show of amazement at Letitia's exquisitely tasteful surroundings, it was impossible for them not to appreciate the ivory-handled cutlery and fine engraved glassware, the blue-and-white Wedgwood dinner service matching the posies of bluebells and white lilac filling every space between silver dishes.

It was too early in the year for fresh green vegetables, but root varieties had been made into a pie, with a fricassee of turnips, and roasted potatoes, still a talking point. Nor was there any shortage of lamb, gammon or game, salmon and sole, pies and rissoles, sauces and garnishes and, as the guests were so appreciative and unpretentious, the meal flowed easily along with good wines and home-made orange wine for the younger ones. Tarts and cheesecakes, blancmanges, fruit jellies and creams were toyed with as the talk, inevitably, veered towards the contrast between the pupils' study of Shakespeare and their greater penchant for the novels such as *The Infidel* and, more recently, *Waynethorpe Manor.* The general opinion seemed to be that they could not have been written by a woman, in spite of what the title page told them.

Letitia had no opinion to offer on that, but laughed as she offered her poor excuse. 'Variety? My pupils are encouraged to discuss whatever they read, whether it's classical or popular fiction. If it's well written, it's readable.'

Captain Ben Rankin, Lady Dorna's good-looking friend, was intrigued by this view. 'So you've read them, too?' he said.

'Indeed I have, Captain. I would not otherwise allow my young ladies to.'

'And you approve, I see. Does Mr Thomas approve, too?'

The articulate young Welshman came readily to her rescue. 'If Miss Boyce approves, then so do I, sir. We don't necessarily read these stories *out loud*, as we do with Shakespeare, but—'

But the company had already dissolved into laughter at the idea of anyone reading *The Infidel* out loud, and Letitia's pink cheeks went unnoticed except by Mr Waverley and Lord Rayne who, sitting five places away from her, was finding it difficult to give his undivided attention to Mrs Quayle on one side and Miss Strachan on the other.

As they left the table, he caught up with Letitia. 'Allow me to thank you, Miss Boyce, for including me in your party. That was a memorable meal.'

She had had little choice in the matter of his inclusion, but saw no advantage in saying so. 'Thank you, Lord Rayne. It's given you the opportunity to see how I've changed things since you last saw the inside of the house.'

'I never saw the interior until now.'

'Oh? You would have bought it unseen?'

'My agent saw it. He recommended it to me, that's all.'

'I see. I had heard…' She must not tell him what she'd heard.

'Otherwise?' Deliberately, he looked across the room to the group where Lady Dorna stood talking. 'My sister means well,' he said, in a low voice, 'but she inhabits a delightful world where realities and fancies mix rather freely. None of us would have her any different, but it sometimes leaves us with some explaining to do. Would you like me to explain anything to you, Miss Boyce?'

'No, I thank you. There is room for all of us. But whatever I heard about you wanting my house has completely escaped me. It's of no consequence.'

'None at all. I could never have made it look as handsome as it does now.' His eyes did not follow his compliment, but took a route over her piled-up silvery braids, her graceful neck adorned with a single rope of pearls, her beautiful shoulders and bosom framed by pale grey silk piped and latticed with silver satin.

'No, a house generally does better with one mistress, my lord, rather than a succession of them. Take my *tedious*, *predictable* twin sisters, for instance. Even they might be at odds about some details. By the way,' she whispered, as if about to disclose a confidence, 'the blue-stocking *elder* sister is *not* interested, despite what you believe. I cannot *think* how you came by that notion, my lord, unless you share the same kind of problem with reality as Lady Dorna. Could it be that, I wonder?'

Lazily scanning, his eyes came to rest on hers, slowly revealing an understanding of where her phrases originated. They widened, then smiled, then grew serious again as she reached the end of her disclosure. 'So,' he said, quietly, 'the ears make up for the eyes, do they? No use for me to apologise, I suppose?'

'No use at all, my lord. It merely confirms what I knew already.'

'That's the pity of it, Miss Boyce. It only confirms what you *thought* you knew already. But we've had this conversation before, haven't we? Both of us have preconceived ideas about the other. You believe I am shallow. You *think* I believe you to be—'

'A *challenge* is what you said. You fancy a challenge. Forget it, my lord. You could never hold my interest. My sisters, however...'

'Whom we shall leave out of it, if you please.'

'They'd not be pleased to hear you say that.'

'Then they'd better not hear it, had they? As I was saying, you appear to believe I cannot be serious about a woman, and that what you overheard confirms it, and that I could only be interested in you for the novelty value.'

'I didn't *imagine* that, my lord. I *heard* it.'

'I was being uncivil, on purpose. It was not meant—'

'Oh, *spare* me!' she snapped. 'I'm so looking forward to hearing some *good* acting, aren't you? See,' she said, turning, 'the coats and capes are being brought in. Mr Waverley... Bart...where are you? If you will take three of the ladies in with you, and perhaps Lord and Lady Elyot will take...' She bustled away, managing and marshalling four people into each of the three coaches until, quite by accident, she was the only woman left with one male guest. 'Lord…er…*Rayne*?' she whispered. 'Oh!'

Leaning against the hall table with feet wide apart, he was quietly laughing. 'Managed yourself into a corner, Mother Hen?' he said. 'Come on, then. You and I are going to walk it. It's not far.'

'I know how far it is,' she growled. 'It's not that.'

He did not move. 'You want me to carry you there?'

'Tch!' She sighed, wondering how she could possibly have done something as foolish as this. She would rather have walked with Mr Chatterton in his high-heeled shoes than with Rayne, whose arrogance both excited and annoyed her.

The footman bowed and withdrew, leaving them alone in the hall with a mountain of misunderstandings to keep them apart.

He waited, then reached her in two strides, backing her into the hard edge of the opposite table. She gripped it, leaning away from him, seeing for the first time the crisp detail of his neckcloth, the white waistcoat and its silver buttons, undone at the top. Again, she breathed the faint aroma given off by his warm skin, but now there was to be no making of mental notes for her writing when he was so frighteningly close, no time to express how she was affected, or the sensation of her heart thudding into her throat.

He placed a large knuckle beneath her chin, lifting it. 'Yes, my beauty, I know. This is not what you planned, is it?'

'Don't call me that! I'm not your beauty, nor am I—'

'And you can glare at me all you want, but this evening you will do as I say without argument and without biting my hand off. Do you hear me?'

'I shall—'

'Do you *hear* me? Without argument. Just for once, if you please.'

She nodded, looking at his mouth, then at the faint bluish shadow around his jaw, then back to his eyes that had noted every detour. His thighs pressed against hers, and she understood that, suddenly, he was struggling to suppress an urge to do what he had done once before. She must prevent it. 'Let me go,' she whispered.

He did not move. 'Where are your spectacles? Have you another pair? Do you have them with you?'

'In my reticule. Let me go, please.'

'You will take my arm,' he commanded, 'and you will be civil.'

'Yes, I will be civil.'

'I have your word on it?'

'Yes…now *please*…let me go.' She took hold of his wrist, expecting it to move but, when she looked again at his eyes to find the cause of his delay, she saw how his gaze rested upon the staircase as if to measure its length. Panic stole upwards, fluttering inside her bodice. Her fingers tightened over the soft fabric of his coat-cuff. 'No,' she whispered. 'Don't…please don't.' She saw the reflection of the two wall-lamps in his eyes, heavy-lidded with desire.

'I could,' he said, 'but I suppose they will not delay the performance of Shakespeare for us, so we'd better go. Come, my beauty, adjust your shawl. There, now take my arm, and try to remember what you have agreed.'

Speechless and shaken, she did as she was told. Arm in arm they went out into the cool evening, pulling the heavy door closed behind them.

* * *

Earlier that afternoon she had formed a clear plan of where everyone would sit, herself being nowhere near Lord Rayne. However, arriving at the theatre only a few minutes later, Letitia found her plans already displaced by the earlier arrival of the day girls, their parents and friends. Although Miss Sapphire Melborough clearly hoped that Lord Rayne would join her parents in their box, he merely bowed politely, held a few words of conversation with her mother, then rejoined Letitia, taking the two seats left over after the others had taken theirs. It was not at all what Letitia had intended, and Rayne knew it as he quelled her budding protest with a stern glance, positioning her chair next to his at the back of the box and almost herding her into it with one uncompromising word. 'There,' he said.

She delayed for as long as she dared but, in the end, there was nothing for it but to accept the situation when the musicians in the pit ceased playing and the curtain glided upwards. The scene of merchants and their clients against a background of Venetian waterways would normally have riveted her attention. But this time she was sitting close to Lord Rayne against the high back of the box with a partition on one side of her, and her usually obedient concentration was distracted by the sensation that, for all her determination to deny him any sign of encouragement, he had won that round with ease.

He had another way of putting it, in a whisper, when she turned slightly to glance at him. Catching her angry expression, his unsmiling eyes made his advice all the more telling. 'Stop fighting me, my beauty. I intend to win.'

Turning her attention to her reticule, she drew out a pair of pocket spectacles that swung inside a mother-of-pearl cover, holding them to her eyes as if his words meant nothing. But the spectacles trembled, and she knew he had seen before she transferred them to her other hand.

That evening at Richmond's Theatre Royal was to be remembered for many reasons, the chief of which was the way in which Lord Rayne attended to her needs as they had not been since her father died, not even by Mr Waverley. Independent to a fault, she had intended to take charge of the event, putting herself last, as usual, in spite of there being enough adults to watch over the three boarders. But if she had thought they would prefer her to the others, she was wrong. They did not need her, and she had no other role to play except to stay by Rayne's side, where he wanted her.

'Miss Melborough is hoping you will visit her,' she said.

'Then she will be disappointed. This evening, Miss Boyce, I am with no one but you, and you will not get rid of me.'

'Hasn't this gone on long enough, my lord?' she said, demurely, opening and closing her spectacle-cover. 'You've made your point, I think. You've had your fun and enjoyed the stares. But these girls are my pupils, and you place me in a very awkward position by paying me this attention one evening and then, as you are sure to do, paying the same kind of attention to someone else next time they see you. They all know you and my sisters are seen in each other's company. They know that Sapphire's parents are keen on an alliance. I am not unused to being talked about in one way or another, but this evening will not be easy for me to live down, my lord. Perhaps you think you're doing me some kind of favour, but I assure you, you're not. Surely you can see that?'

Handing her a glass of negus, he took the spectacles from her and popped them into the opening of the reticule that hung on her arm. 'It's a great pity, in a way,' he said, 'that you overheard what you did, for now it will be harder than ever for me to convince you that I am not simply flirting with you.'

'You are mistaken in the matter, Lord Rayne. I was convinced you were doing exactly that at our first meeting. I'm afraid I cannot be unconvinced, nor would any woman be, in the same circumstances.'

'That would not have happened to *any* woman, Miss Boyce.'

'No, of course not. How often does one encounter a short-sighted, lost schoolmistress? Not one of your greatest challenges, I would have thought.'

He sighed. 'Miss Boyce, will you try to dredge from the depths of your *deep* intellect something we agreed on before we set out? Something you gave me your word on, if you need a clue?'

'Yes, my lord, but—'

'Good. Then keep it, will you?'

'But you haven't answered my question.'

'Oh? I thought I had. I wish you would listen as well as you talk.'

'Odious man!' she muttered.

Mr Waverley was amused by the new partnership. 'What's happened, Lettie? The fellow's sticking to you like glue. I think he's smitten.'

'Fudge!' she said. 'Bart, rescue me. Walk home with me. Don't leave me alone with him. He's only trying to show Miss Melborough that she has some competition, that's all. I know the kind of tactics such men use.'

'Maybe, but Sir Francis doesn't look too pleased about it, either, does he? He's been sending you the oddest looks. What's *that* all about?'

She did not explain. She had noticed the crowded Melborough box during the interval but, without peering through her lenses, had not been able to see who the visitors were. Nevertheless, she was receiving the distinct impression that Sir Francis, who would normally have been amongst the first to ingratiate himself with her, was keeping well out of her way.

Undeterred by her watchful escort, she managed to speak to many of her friends, her pupils' parents and their friends, too, and had thought that, as they began to seat themselves for the second half, she might be invited to join their ranks. But Lord Rayne was having none of it and, disregarding the interest and envy of her pupils, he steered her back to the same chair with the utmost propriety, giving them little to gossip about except that their guardian was once again being claimed by him.

And indeed there was nothing to which she could object except his closeness; no touching, no arm across the back of her chair, no flirtatious remarks, no compliments except in his eyes. It was, she thought, as if his aim was to familiarise her with his nearness as he would with an unbroken young horse. Which, after all, would have been the way of any suitor except this one, for whom conventional methods were usually too slow.

Years of watching her vivacious sisters take centre stage, however, had caused her to develop an unhealthy cynicism, enabling her to see through and partly to despise the ploys men used, the foolish games they played. And in view of her previous encounters with this particular buck, she was unlikely to let go of her conviction that she was being used as some kind of instrument in one of his games in full view of the pert and eager Miss Melborough, not to mention her ambitious parents. While she could not help but absorb the exciting vibrations from the man at her side as she had never done before with anyone, it was her steely common sense that pulled her emotions back from taking precedence over her writing, which needed information of this kind more than her starving sensitive heart did. If it was common sense, then it must be right, for what else did a woman like her have to rely on?

Agog with curiosity to see whether Lord Rayne would walk back to Paradise Road with Miss Boyce, her pupils were almost as excited to hear him call farewell to his relatives and to see him take one of the carriages with Letitia and Mr Waverley, which seemed to them a little odd when Mr Waverley lived almost next door to the theatre. Mr Chatterton and Mr Thomas had only yards to go. What the pupils did not discover is that, by tacit consent, Mr Waverley, Lord Rayne, Miss Gaddestone and Miss Boyce stayed up until past midnight in the drawing room, drinking red wine from sparkling cut glasses through which the candlelight danced and winked. Talking like old friends, not one waspish word was heard between them. Then the two men left, Lord Rayne having accepted a lift back to Sheen Court in Mr Waverley's phaeton.

It was usual, at the end of each day, however late, for Letitia to enter notes into her book before they suffered from distortion or, worse, amnesia. This night, the notebook stayed locked in her drawer while she lay against the pillows to watch the shadows move over the bed-curtains, not because she was too tired to write, but because her thoughts were torn by conflict, her heart entering a period of slow ache in anticipation of the pain that was sure to come unless she armoured herself against it. Of *course* he was teasing her. Her sisters said he was a tease. This was nothing but a game to him. Nothing but a game.

* * *

For the next two weeks it began to look as if Letitia's reading of events was accurate, the only communication from Lord Rayne being a formal note of thanks for an enjoyable evening, then a brief visit in person to return her mended spectacles. But since she was out with her pupils at the time, they did not meet. In a way, she was relieved to have missed him, for she had nothing to say except to offer him her thanks.

She was even more certain of her ground when, only two days later, she took her pupils to London to the Royal Academy Annual Exhibition at Somerset House where she found her sisters and mother in Lord Rayne's company. By chance, Miss Melborough was not one of the party, having twisted her ankle the day before and, in some discomfort, had been left to work on her watercolour until their return.

Letitia's sisters, as always, were glad to see her and to unload on her their latest experiences, shopping trips and parties, their mama's dinner party and the men who had caught their attention most. Lady Boyce greeted her eldest daughter more formally with a stand-off embrace and a showy kiss past each cheek that could hardly have been called motherly. After relating to Letitia what she had missed by not being at home, her remarks centred around the attention being shown to Garnet, especially by Lord Rayne. 'There'll be an announcement soon, Letitia,' she said, waving her fan to friends Letitia could not quite identify. 'Mark my words. I'm never wrong about these matters. I can always tell when a man is about to declare himself. Well, heaven knows, it happened to me often enough before your dear papa snared me. Lord Rayne is *very* keen, you know.'

'Yes, Mama.'

'So these are your *gels*, are they?' she said, glancing round. 'They look respectable enough. Isn't that Sir Mortimer Derwent's daughter?'

'Maura. Yes. They live in Farnham. She boards with us.'

'Your papa used to hunt with them. And there's your Mr Waverley. Still faithful, is he? Who are the other two?'

'That's Mr Dimmock, our watercolour teacher, and Mr Ainsley, our drawing master. Rosie has stayed at home with one of the girls, but the lady over there in brown is Mrs Quayle, our next-door neighbour. Would you allow me to introduce her to you? She'd be so thrilled.'

'Another time, dear. Nice to see you. Keeping well, are you?'

It was pointless for Letitia to reply when the orange turban had already turned towards other faces and, since that exchange appeared to be the sum total of her mother's interest, she adjusted her spectacles and moved away to the walls lined with pictures.

Softly, Lord Rayne's voice spoke into her ear. 'You're using them I see, Miss Boyce?'

She turned to face the dark serious eyes and immaculate form of the one man she had hoped not to see. 'Yes, my lord. Thank you for returning them to me. They're quite perfect. I cannot tell where the mend is.'

'Ayscough on Ludgate Street,' he said, gravely. 'My mother gets hers there. He recognised them.'

'He should. That is where they were bought. But please don't let me keep you from your obligation to my sisters. I had not expected to see them here, nor my mother. They don't usually show much interest in this kind of event.'

'I did not come with them, Miss Boyce. I came with Lord

Alvanley and George Brummell. Over there…see? They're helping me to find something suitable for my study.'

'Oh…I thought…'

'Yes, I can see you did. I believe that's what you were meant to think.' His quick glance in Lady Boyce's direction qualified his remark. 'If I may offer you a word of advice, it would be not to—'

'No, please don't offer me any advice, my lord,' she said, quickly cutting him off. 'It's no concern of mine what my sisters do or don't do. All I wish for is their happiness, not to interfere in it. Have you seen a painting you like?'

He paused, obviously not content to be diverted. 'I've seen one prime article in particular I like the look of, Miss Boyce,' he said. 'I wish it was as easy to purchase as a painting.'

'For your study wall?'

'For my study, certainly. For my wall, no.'

'Good day, my lord,' she whispered, trying to hide her flushed cheeks behind the panel of her bonnet. 'I shall leave you to make your choice.'

'And you don't wish to give me the benefit of *your* advice?'

'I don't wish to incur any more of my mother's disapproval than I have already, my lord.'

'By talking to *me*? Surely not.'

'She would misunderstand, and so would my sisters. Need I say more than that?'

'Usually you say too much, Miss Boyce, but on this occasion you have said too little. I thought you had become independent of Lady Boyce's management.'

'I have taken a very big step, my lord, but I have hopes that she will visit me, one day, not cut me out altogether. I am already well outside her plans.'

'But not her influence, apparently. Time you were, then. So, if I am not allowed to advise you, I shall tell you this. Lady Boyce may be allowed to keep a finger in your pie, for the time being, but, by God, she won't put a finger near mine unless she wants it snapped off. When I want a woman, I shall not be asking her permission.'

'Not even when the woman is her daughter, my lord?'

'Not the eldest one, no. Good day to you, Miss Boyce.'

Her cheeks were still very pink when Mr Dimmock joined her to discuss some of the paintings with her and found, to his dismay, that she had so far seen very few of them.

Chapter Six

Leaving William Lake's lending-library in Leadenhall Street, London, Lord Seton Rayne tossed a pile of books on to the seat of his curricle and climbed up beside them, having accomplished what he had promised to do for his mother, the Marchioness of Sheen, who had been unable to find extra copies for her friends anywhere. He was about to call to his tiger to loose the horses' heads when he noticed the tall hurrying figure of the Honourable Bart Waverley leap down the steps of the library and dash across to the other side of the street carrying a leather briefcase under his arm. This was singular, Rayne thought, because there had been no sign of Bart inside the library.

Watching the striding figure disappear round the corner, he then looked up at the windows above the library where the gold-printed words read, Mercury Press, Est. 1790. Publisher W. Lake, Esq. Did Bart know William Lake personally? Was there some business between them? Not being one to poke his nose into other people's affairs, Rayne let the matter rest beside a strange feeling that a connection was escaping him.

* * *

Later that afternoon, he made a detour through the winding corridors of Hampton Court Palace on his way from the barrack block and stables to his own apartments bordering the Outer Green Court, his home during weekdays. Pausing for a moment outside the dingy little room where he and Miss Letitia Boyce had exchanged kisses—oh, yes, she had *exchanged* kisses, he was convinced of that—he smiled and closed the door, continuing his walk round to the gardens on the sunny south side of the palace's grace-and-favour apartments.

Residents and their elderly guests strolled along the overgrown pathways and sat on benches in the shade, snoozing, reading, or watching the boats on the distant river. One erect resident, lace-draped, white-haired and bespectacled, held a book up high as if she were singing from it. She looked up as Rayne approached, lowering the book with a smile. 'Lord Rayne,' she said. 'Finished for the day?'

'I have indeed, Lady Waverley,' he said with a bow. 'And you?'

Her smile softened as she removed her eyeglasses. She was still a lovely woman, arched brows, cheekbones firmly covered. 'No, not me,' she said. 'I have some way to go yet.' She indicated the book and the pages yet to be read. 'It's the newest one Bart lent me. I've been so looking forward to it, you know. Of course, he must be allowed to read it first, dear boy. Come and sit with me a while.' She drew in a heap of soft shawl and lace, moving up to make room for him.

Rayne sat, removed his helmet, and ran a hand through his hair.

'Are you not supposed to powder your hair?' she said,

watching the gesture. 'I thought the Prince's Own had to wear powder and a pigtail.'

'We do on parade, my lady. Makes too much mess for everyday wear.' He looked at the book on her lap. 'Did you say Bart lent it to you? My lady mother is on Hatchett's subscription list, but she wants extra copies to give to her friends. They're very scarce. Where does Bart get his from?'

'From Lake the publisher. He's almost sold out of the first edition, apparently, but we've known him for years.'

'Ah! That explains it.'

'Explains what?'

'Why I saw Bart leaving the Mercury Press this morning.'

'Oh, did you? Well, he brought me this yesterday.' She tapped the book. 'It's his own copy, given him by the author. Perhaps he was there on some business for her.'

'He knows the *author*? So it *is* a woman, then?'

'Oh, yes, he knows her well. He meets Lake on her behalf. A young lady cannot go there on her own, can she? Bart's done all her business transactions with Lake from the very first book. He gets to read it, then he passes it on to me. Am I not fortunate? I doubt I could wait any longer.'

'Is that so?'

'Oh, I've pestered him for ages to hurry up and—'

'No, I meant about the author being a young lady. Does she live in Richmond, near Bart?'

'It may be that she does, but I'm not too familiar with who lives there, so I don't really know, and he refuses to tell me any more except that she's earning quite an income from these.' Again, she tapped Volume One, leather-bound and gold-tooled. 'Mind you,' she continued, 'I have no doubt that Lake is doing very nicely out of it. He's unlikely to be offering her the kind of deal he'd offer a man, even if she is more popular.'

'But isn't that why the author has Bart to act for her?'

She smiled her indulgent, motherly smile. 'Of course. But you know what dear Bart's like, don't you? He was never the forceful kind, was he?'

'No, my lady.'

The sounds of the late afternoon passed them by with a shower of dandelion clocks, as they thought about Mr Waverley's many fine qualities, of which forcefulness was not one. 'Will he ever marry, do you think?' said Rayne, gently.

The shake of Lady Waverley's head would easily have been missed, had Rayne not been watching for it. 'No,' she whispered. 'Shouldn't think so, Seton. Marriage is not for Bart's kind, is it?'

'It's not unknown, my lady.'

'But it rarely works. Best to stay single. He's happy enough.'

'He'd make a wonderful father.'

Lady Waverley took that as the compliment it was meant to be, and said no more on the delicate subject. Rayne, however, returned to the young lady author. 'A Lady of Quality, I believe she calls herself,' he said, smoothing a hand over his helmet's glossy fur. 'So I suppose I must not ask if you know the identity of this mysterious wealthy young woman.'

'Only Bart himself knows that, and he'd not *dream* of breaking a confidence, not even to his mother. Mr Lake knows her only as a certain Miss Lydia Barlowe, but that *must* be a nom de plume. No lady of quality ever had such a common name.'

Rayne bellowed with laughter. 'Lady Waverley, I do believe you're a snob,' he teased.

She agreed, smiling at the notion. 'Yes, dear, I believe I am.

It's one of the few allowances left to a woman of my age. That, and being able to sit and talk to a man like you, alone, without being suspected of flirting.'

'And if I were not so afraid of being called out by your son, I would indulge in some serious flirting with you, my lady.'

The smiling face tipped towards him. 'Does Bart go in for…for calling men out?'

'Duelling? Not by choice, I don't suppose. But if you're asking if he's well enough equipped to protect himself, then, yes, he certainly is. He could do some damage with pistol, rapier *and* gloves, too. And the young lady writer, whoever she is, has chosen an excellent business partner, with Bart's head for accounts.'

'It's pity he won't be offering for her. Even if she is a commoner.'

Rayne smiled, which Lady Waverley took for sympathy, but which was, in fact, nothing of the sort. Lydia Barlowe. *L.B.* How careless of her, he thought. How endearingly, wonderfully careless.

Letitia's proposal to visit Strawberry Hill House at Twickenham, just across the river from Richmond, had an ulterior motive that no one but Mr Waverley could be expected to guess, for it was where Mr Horace Walpole had written, in 1764, his famous Gothic novel, *The Castle of Otranto*. Others, including Letitia, were to follow this trend, literally, while readers made pilgrimages to the amazing house-cum-castle he had built to satisfy his every Gothic whim. No serious romantic novelist could afford to miss such a place with its towers and turrets, chapel, cloisters and chambers littered with historic curios.

The great man himself, son of a Prime Minister, had died seventeen years ago and now it was possible for visitors to look round by arrangement with the housekeeper, a favour that Letitia had gone to some trouble to secure for her party of pupils, tutors and chaperons. She was not inclined to hurry through the rooms, having made it so far with notebook and pencil, sketching and scribbling as they were shown into the long gallery, the library, past carved screens, mock-tombs and suits of medieval armour, gloomy portraits and up winding spooky staircases.

Miss Sapphire Melborough, however, having other things on her mind, had soon seen enough of Strawberry Hill and was incautious enough to enquire of Mrs Quayle, in an undertone bordering on despair, how much longer they might be stuck here. She had asked the wrong person, for Mrs Quayle was thoroughly enjoying herself despite the appropriate melancholic expression. She passed on the plaintive query to Letitia, which Sapphire had neither wanted nor expected her to do.

'Why? Who wants to know?' said Letitia.

'Miss Sapphire. She's had enough.'

'If it's her ankle, she can rest on the bench over there and wait.'

'I don't think it's her ankle, Letitia.'

Beckoning to her pupil, Letitia noted the pouting rosebud mouth. 'What is it, Sapphire? We're only halfway round. There's much more to see.'

'But I…well, you see…' Pulling in her bottom lip, she nibbled at it.

'See what? Are you unwell? Do you wish Mrs Quayle to…?'

'No, Miss Boyce, only that I expected to be home by now because Lord Rayne is to bring my new horse and give me my first lesson on it. I'm afraid I shall miss it if I stay here much longer.'

'Sapphire, I made it clear three days ago that on Friday we'd be having an extended visit. If you forgot to tell your parents, that is your responsibility. My claim on your time takes priority, I'm afraid, and when we've concluded our visit here, we shall be taking tea at the tea gardens in Twickenham. I told you that, too, if you recall. You'll have to have your riding lesson tomorrow instead, won't you?'

Sapphire could not stifle the sigh. 'Yes, Miss Boyce. But Lord Rayne will not be pleased to be kept waiting.'

'Lord Rayne's displeasure is not my concern, Sapphire. You'll be writing an account in your journal of this visit next week, so I suggest you pay attention to what you're seeing.' *Or not seeing. As if I care a fig about Lord Rayne's arrangements.*

The cream tea at Church Street's sunny tea garden could not be hurried any more than the tour of the house, so it was past time for dinner when the carriages arrived back at Paradise Road after taking the day girls home. Letitia did not go up to Richmond Hill House with Sapphire, having no wish to hear about the missed riding lesson.

There was much to be written about by candlelight that evening.

The following day, Saturday, was bright but blustery, a stiff breeze rattling the window frames and rolling the last of the blossom across the walled kitchen garden like drifts of snow. Wandering alone, Letitia peered into the glass frames while the covers were up, at the strawberry beds white with flowers, at the budding cucumbers, the tiny spears of chicory and lamb's lettuce. In the furthest corner, the gardener's son was shovelling gravel on to the path and raking it over. Like coarse oatmeal, Letitia thought, adjusting her spectacles more firmly on to her nose. Fine wisps of hair whirled around her face as gusts of wind moulded her cotton day dress into the contours of her body and, to find a place of shelter, she opened the door of the stone-built potting shed built against the high wall, and entered.

She was instantly enclosed by the earthy aroma of potted plants and trays of seedlings covered by layers of damp newsprint. Racks of tools hung along one side, with buckets and pots, hoses and string, raffia and bell jars. A long low bench was covered with sacking as if the old gardener had used it to indulge in an occasional nap, and a pile of sacks at one end suggested a pillow. Intrigued, she bent to look more closely, to confirm her theory.

A long curling hair lay upon the pillow, clearly not the gardener's. Lifting it carefully away, she held it up to the high dusty window where a beam of light caught its shining gold. A sound behind her made her turn sharply and to frown in annoyance at the hefty figure of the gardener's son filling the doorway. One hand was hooked over the top edge of the door. 'Can I 'elp you, ma'am?' he asked.

His question, and the quiet way he asked it, made her feel as if she'd naughtily strayed out of bounds. Nor did she like being trapped in so small a place. 'No, thank you…er…Tom, is it?'

'Ted,' he replied, not moving or looking politely away, as if he knew of her discomfort and was enjoying it. No more than twenty years old, he had already filled out with brawn, his shirt sleeves rolled up to show well-muscled sunburnt forearms, his front buttons opened too far down for any lady's eyes to dwell there for more than a second. 'Can I do anything for ye?' he asked.

Damsels being pursued and seduced by young males glowing with rude health was the stuff of her novels, and this the kind of situation not too far removed from some of the scenes in them, though so far no major part had been taken by the gardener or his son. Then, she had imagined a kind of helpless excitement rather than the raw anger she now felt at the threat of trespass by an uncouth lad. The girls and Mrs Quayle were in Richmond, shopping. Gaddy was still in her room. The gardener, Ted's old father, was nowhere to be seen. This present danger was very far removed from the harmless entertainment of fiction where one could turn a page and return to safety.

Still frowning, she asked, 'Have you finished the path?'

'Yes, ma'am. All done.' His glance at the sack-covered bench lingered and returned to her, but not to her face, and she knew how he must have seen the clinging cotton of her dress revealing her figure as she bent to the glass frames.

'Then I'll find you another task to do,' she said, suspecting that he would twist whatever she said to mean something different. 'Where's your father?'

'Oh, we don't need to bother about him, ma'am. He'll not be in for a while yet. Got a task for me, 'ave you? Is that what you want, eh?' He spoke slowly, insolently, his words taking on an intimacy far beyond their worth, his pleasant features as relaxed as his body, his blue eyes alight with anticipation.

'Ted, will you move away from the door, please? I want to go out.'

But he took his hand from the top edge, stepped further inside and began to close it, darkening the confined space. 'No, you don't,' he said. 'I know what you want. It's what all you young lasses want.'

Letitia's hand groped behind her, closing over the rim of a terracotta pot. In the very moment she brought it up to hurl at Ted's approaching head, the door re-opened with a crashing force, slamming it into the lad's rear end as he ducked to avoid the missile.

Like an angry bullock, he roared and turned to rush upon the intruder, but his progress was interrupted by a shining Hessian boot across his shins that sent him flying headlong into a stack of logs outside the door. The pot that Letitia had thrown shattered upon the door frame, and as she picked her way through the shards to find out who her rescuer was—supposing it to be Mr Waverley—she was in time to see the stocky Ted about to launch himself upon Lord Rayne.

Assuming that his lordship would certainly go down like a skittle, she let out an involuntary yelp of fright for, though she had once written of a brawl between two rivals, she had never seen a blow landed. She did now, but only just, delivered with such lightning speed that Ted did not see it coming at all. She heard a sickening crack as Rayne's fist connected with the cheek, and the grunt that followed, the thud as Ted fell back hard into the log pile where he slithered and stayed, swaying to one side.

'Get up!' Rayne snapped, standing over him.

Ted struggled and clawed his way up, holding an arm out against the possibility of a second punisher. 'Don't,' he mumbled.

'Get off home!'

'Yessir…I wasn't…I didn't….honest.'

'Out!'

Slouching, clutching at his face, Ted staggered away with a sullen glance at Letitia. 'She wanted it,' he muttered, 'as much as t'other one.'

This insult was not allowed to pass any more than his first had been and, before he had taken another step, he was yanked backwards by a strong hand beneath his arm, only to be knocked sideways by a fearsome blow beneath his jaw, laying him out into a patch of feathery fennel. This time, he did not move.

'Oh, you've killed him,' Letitia whispered behind her hand.

'If he opens his mouth once more, I will,' Rayne said, looking round for a water-butt. Taking up the full bucket of water from beneath the tap, he swung it back and discharged the contents over the prone body. Then, placing the empty bucket upon Ted's chest, he stepped back, removed Letitia's hand from her mouth and drew her like a parent with a child along the path to the door in the wall that led to the house garden.

Closing the door upon the last ugly scene, he released her. 'I'm sorry you had to see that,' he said, 'but unfortunately there was no choice. Are you all right?'

She nodded. 'Yes. Thank you for being there. I'm very much obliged to you. If I'd known he…oh, dear…it must begin to look as if I'm forever getting myself into…well, the truth is that…'

'The truth is, Miss Boyce, that you *do* seem to attract a rather immediate kind of response; while I can understand *why* it happens, I find it more difficult to understand why you *allow* it to happen. One could, I suppose, attribute it to not being able to see clearly, but surely that cannot always be the case.'

'Lord Rayne,' she snapped, coming to an abrupt standstill on the path, 'I do not *allow* any of these…these *incidents* to happen to me. Do you really believe that…oh…this is *too* much! Why should I care a fiddler's thumb what you believe? I have thanked you for dealing with this latest incident but, if you recall, you yourself behaved just as badly, if not worse, because Mr Waverley did not arrive in time to stop you.'

'Miss Boyce, Bart would not have arrived to find what I might have found just now if I'd been five minutes later. It's fortunate that I saw him following you as I entered the garden, but my point is that you need some protection before something truly serious happens to you. Bart is all very well, but he's not here when he's needed, is he? Nor does he have any obligation to be.'

'Why should a woman need protecting in her own garden, my lord?'

'Why? Because you appear to employ untrustworthy servants. That's why.'

'I don't employ him. He's the gardener's *son*, helping out.'

'Helping himself, more like. How many others has he helped out?'

Immediately, she remembered the long curling blonde hair that could have belonged to at least three of her seven pupils, or one of the maids. Surely that young lout had not forced himself upon one of them there, in the potting shed? There was a path that connected her garden with Mrs Quayle's next door along which the three boarders came to lessons each day. But could they also have used it at night to meet that dreadful man? It was unthinkable. They were all highly respectable young women. Like herself. Like the young heroines in her novels. Highly respectable, but eager for adventure, and very vulnerable. Were these young creatures simply more audacious than her, or more foolhardy?

'I don't know,' she said, 'but I intend to find out. If this incident has served no other purpose, my lord, it's certainly alerted me to the danger of—'

'Of not being protected sufficiently and of not being able to see what you're doing half the time. There's an easy remedy for both those problems, Miss Boyce.'

'That's *not* what I was about to say. You are determined to put me in the wrong. Very well, allow me to turn the tables, for once. In future, kindly refrain from organising my pupils' riding lessons while they're still in my care. I have first call on their time and I shall not be releasing any of them before the hour of five, unless there's a very exceptional reason.'

'So you think I'm free before the hour of five, do you?'

'You were yesterday, according to Miss Melborough.'

'Then she was mistaken. I told her father I would bring the new horse over after dinner, which is exactly what I did. I spent an hour or so with them in the paddock while it was still light. Are you jealous, Miss Boyce?'

'Of what, exactly?'

'Of me spending time with the Melborough wench?'

'Oh *do* rid yourself of that addle-pated notion, Lord Rayne. Spend whatever time you wish with whomever you wish, my sisters included, but don't expect me to tailor my time to fit yours.'

'Why not? You're prepared to accept all the advantages and compliments of having your pupils well mounted and taught by the best riding master while refusing to co-operate in any way. In fact, Miss Boyce, you appear to be hellbent on making it difficult for everyone concerned.'

Letitia was silent. He spoke no more than the truth, placing her yet again at a disadvantage. Fortunately, he did not pursue the matter while there were more side-saddle-trained horses to be acquired for the others. Enough time for her to revise her timetable, if she could swallow her pride.

They stopped just in front of the summerhouse as if by mutual consent, in view of what had happened earlier. So far, her anger had overcome other emotions, but now she felt again the sickly fear as the little shed had darkened and the man's swaggering presumption told her that she would not be able to hold him off. Was it mere coincidence that she had been made a target three times since placing herself beyond the protection of her family and friends? Had she been less than careful? In London, Uncle Aspinall had taken the place of her father, but now he, too, was miles away, and the only man to offer her his protection, as opposed to being recruited like Mr Waverley, was one of those who had treated her discourteously. And yet, just a moment ago, he had knocked a man down for less.

Rayne was waiting for a sign from her but, having no particular direction in mind, she took his left hand in hers and turned it to look at the knuckles that she was sure would hurt. A grey-blue bruise was already forming.

'I usually wear gloves,' he said. 'It's nothing.'

Removing her spectacles, she looked more closely. Tears prickled behind her eyelids as she was reminded of her narrow escape and, although she would not submit to pathetic weeping, she was unable to hide the delayed reaction that trembled her hands. Ted had not touched her except with his menace, which had been far worse than the thorough kisses Lord Rayne had given her.

Her shaky breathing was noticed as she struggled to control herself. His hand took possession of hers, with her spectacles, drawing her over the threshold into the shady summerhouse. 'Shh!' he said. 'It's all right. No harm done. You must tell your gardener that his son is not welcome. There's no shortage of labour. My brother's man will find someone for you, if you wish.'

'I'b dot crying, really I'b dot,' she sniffed.

'No, of course not.'

Even so, when he drew her very gently into his arms and held her like a bird against his chest, she stood quietly to absorb the safety and strength of his embrace. 'Why did you cub?' she whispered.

'To take you for a drive in my curricle.'

'But that would give the impression that we're good freds, by lord. And we're dot, are we?'

'By no stretch of the imagination are we good friends, Miss Boyce.'

'It would dot look good.'

'On the contrary, it would send out quite the wrong kind of message. Unless…'

'Unless what?'

'Unless I were to be seen taking you to my sister's house at Mortlake. A social call. That might just disguise any enjoyment we might be tempted to feel.'

She drew herself out of his arms. 'I should not be allowing this,' she said, wiping her nose in an unladylike gesture on the back of her hand.

'Because you may find that you're enjoying it?'

'Because I must set an example to my pupils. If they were to see…well, anyway…it won't do, will it? Young ladies of good birth—'

'Like yourself.'

'—like me, do not allow Corinthians to—'

'Thank you.'

'—to embrace them—'

'As they do in novels.'

'Lord Rayne, would you stop interrupting me for one moment while I try to finish what I'm saying? Please?'

'Certainly, Miss Boyce. What were you saying?'

'I don't know. I can't remember. You've put me off.'

'Then go and get changed, and we'll drive up to Mortlake.'

Predictably, she balked at his tone. 'Do all your female acquaintances promptly do your bidding, my lord?'

'Yes. All except one. Five minutes?'

'Multiplied by three. Shall you wait in the parlour?'

'I shall wait beside my curricle, if it's still there.'

'Well, then, try not to look like the cat that's swallowed the canary, if you please. We cannot have anyone getting ideas.'

'Put these back on,' he said, holding out her spectacles, 'and you'll see that I'm wearing my deepest scowl of discontent.'

'Thank you,' she snapped, putting them on as they entered the house. 'I don't quite understand why I'm agreeing to this. We have nothing pleasant to say to each other.'

Not in the least put out by her cynicism, he held the door open for her. 'Then we shall have to resort to our usual mode of bickering like terriers. See you outside in ten minutes.'

'Fifteen. Not a moment sooner.'

Ten minutes later she tripped down the front steps wearing a cream-muslin day dress under a spencer of apricot kersey-mere and a floppy straw hat tied round the crown and under the chin with a long apricot scarf. Peeping from beneath the banded hem of her dress, a pair of apricot kid half-boots completed the captivating picture.

'Where are your spectacles, woman?' he said, curtly.

'In my reticule.'

'Well, you're not going to see much without them. Put them on.'

'I cannot. They ruin the effect.'

'Miss Boyce, you may take my word for it that the wearing of spectacles out of doors will become all the rage, once you are seen wearing them while being driven in my curricle. Now, put them on, if you please.'

Reluctantly, she fished them out of her cream silk reticule but, because she was wearing kid gloves, they swung upside-down before she could catch them. Taking them from her, he held them open at eye-level. 'Hold your head up…there… that's better. Now I can see you,' he said with a smile, adjusting a wisp of hair beside her cheek.

'You've obviously had some experience as a lady's maid,' she said, blushing at this very public intimacy.

'It would be useless to deny it. One must be versatile, these days.'

Climbing up into the confined space of the curricle, she bit back yet another rejoinder, realising that she would not always be allowed to have the last word with this man, as she did with her pupils, and that to allow him to have it, once in a while, was by no means as unpleasant as she had thought. Quite the opposite. Absorbed in Rayne's dexterity with whip and reins, with the classy paintwork and upholstery of the curricle and the prancing matched bays, she said very little, experiencing for the second time that morning the strange sensation that things were happening outside her carefully laid plans.

But the last thing she wanted was for her name to be romantically linked to his when it could cause nothing but problems and eventual heartache. Could she depend on his discretion when, only the other day, he had made his intentions plain? Would his daring sister jump to her own conclusions about their unsettled relationship? Would she encourage her to?

* * *

As it turned out, Lady Dorna's reaction to her brother's
newest interest was to be the least of her concerns, for they were
seen during that brief journey by at least five acquaintances of
Letitia's sisters and mother, who would be eager to take the
news back to London that same day. Known to be extremely
fastidious in his choice of companions, Lord Rayne had never
before been seen taking up a bespectacled female in his curricle.

Letitia was more disturbed by this unforeseen complica-
tion than Rayne, who brushed it off airily as being no one's
concern but theirs. Forbearing to labour the point that she
could ill afford to upset her mother more than she had done
already, she said no more about it while imagining the indignation at Chesterfield House later that day.

Both the drive and the visit to River Court went well, Letitia
making more effort than usual to respond to Rayne's charming
company if only to show her appreciation of his earlier gal-
lantry. It was unfortunate, she thought, that the problem of her
mother's forthcoming exasperation could not be dealt with as
promptly as Ted's.

As ever, Lady Dorna was delighted to see them together,
and their return to Richmond began with some amusement at
her assumption of a close friendship. 'Nonsense!' said Letitia
as the curricle swung at full tilt out of the gates. 'One single
drive doesn't mean anything at all.'

'Of course not. Quite meaningless.'

'I hope she doesn't think—'

'No fear of that, believe me, or she'd not have married
Elwick, God rest his soul.'

'Was he a dear man?'

'Dear?' he said, easing the horses round onto the road with

a turn of his fist. 'Hardly. As dull as ditchwater. She didn't need his title. Didn't need his wealth, either. Can't think what she needed him for, come to think of it.'

'She has two beautiful children.'

He glanced at her, hearing a wistful note creep into her voice. 'So could you, Miss Boyce,' he said, quietly. 'Quite easily.'

So quietly did he say it that she could hardly believe her ears, though she blushed to the roots of her hair.

She would have preferred it if he had allowed her to go into the house alone, but he seemed intent on escorting her into the hall as if he'd known she might need some support. With a glance towards the hall table and its array of top hats, gloves and canes, the footman gave her the news she would rather not have heard. 'Sir Penfold and Lady Aspinall are waiting in the drawing room, ma'am. And Lieutenant Gaddestone and Miss Gaddestone are with them.'

'Then they'll be staying for lunch. Tell cook, will you?'

'I believe cook already knows, ma'am.'

'Good. Lord Rayne, will you stay, too?' She did not think he would.

His reply was unhesitating. 'Thank you, Miss Boyce. I will.'

'Are you sure?' she whispered, darting a look towards the door.

'Quite sure.'

'Then we shall be ten,' she told the footman, 'counting the three boarders and Mrs Quayle.' Removing her spectacles, she tucked them into her reticule, passed her hat and gloves to her maid, and went into the drawing room to meet her guests. With Lord Rayne close behind her, she found she could brave Aunt Minnie's hostile glare with more tranquillity than if she had been on her own.

Chapter Seven

Having met often at Tattersalls, White's Club and at Jackson's Boxing Saloon, as well as at Chesterfield House, Sir Penfold Aspinall and Lord Rayne greeted each other warmly. Letitia received the impression that Uncle Aspinall liked him, though Aunt Minnie could only favour him with a vinegary smile meant to show her disapproval of his appearance here at Paradise Road.

It is doubtful whether Rayne even noticed, being more interested in the appearance of another of Letitia's cousins, Miss Gaddestone's younger brother Lieutenant Fingal Gaddestone, who had been away at sea for almost three years. Rosie Gaddestone's girlish face shone with happiness, her arm linked through his as if to anchor him to her while his other hand held Letitia's. The two cousins had once been close, each of an independent spirit that recognised the need to break the family mould, which both of them had done successfully, but not without some anguish. Old Lady Gaddestone, Lady Boyce's sister, had died while he was away, some said of a broken heart, and Rosie had gone to live with her cousin Letitia rather than stay alone in London.

Disengaging her hand from his, Letitia could see the kind of changes that affected so many naval men: bronzed skin, lines around the eyes and mouth, a lean fitness and a newly assured manner that she assumed he had acquired as an officer. He was now a handsome young man with sun-bleached hair, a friendly smile and a teasing manner that made Letitia change the subject hurriedly and turn to her other guest. 'Lord Rayne, will you allow me to introduce my cousin Fin to you?'

'Certainly,' he said, stepping forward with a slight bow.

Both men drew themselves up smartly, pulling back their shoulders as if an extra half-inch could make all the difference.

'My lord,' said Lieutenant Gaddestone.

'Where are you lodging, sir?'

'Temporarily with my uncle and aunt in London until I can find a suitable place of my own. Then I shall settle down and live a normal life. Did you serve, too, my lord?'

'Briefly, in Spain. Cavalry. A few years of that was enough.'

'So now you're a man of leisure?'

'Not exactly. I train cavalry recruits at Hampton Court Palace. You must come and see, one day. My elder brother is responsible for the Royal Stud there. We shall need every available horse once the celebrations begin next month. It's going to be a busy time.'

Aunt Minnie could not resist asking, with a certain acid relish, 'And will you be escorting Miss Boyce, or her two younger sisters, my lord?'

Blandly, Lord Rayne studied her as if trying to make up his mind, then said, 'Lady Aspinall, as soon as I've made a final decision on that, you will be the first to be told of it. There, how will that do?'

Minnie Aspinall was not so stupid that she could not tell when she'd been snubbed for impertinence and, although Letitia thought she deserved it, she herself quaked at the damage it was doing.

The tension was broken by the arrival of Mrs Quayle and her three charges, and the meal progressed peacefully, the conversation to-ing and fro-ing with ease, neatly bypassing Aunt Minnie's simmering disapproval of her niece's friendship with Lord Rayne, her glowering silence being wasted on the company who had so much to say to each other. Letitia knew only too well that the news would be taken back, post-haste, to Lady Boyce and her twin daughters with predictable results.

However, Aunt Minnie refused to relinquish her role as critic and, as soon as she was able, reminded Rayne that Letitia's *dear* sisters had obtained vouchers for Almack's that same evening and were hoping to see him there. But to her great annoyance, he refused to pass on any message to her nieces except an enigmatic smile. She tried again on a different tack. 'Young Lieutenant Gaddestone and Letitia have *always* had a *tendre* for each other since they were children. He seems particularly interested in her now, doesn't he, my lord?'

'I suppose it's to be expected, Lady Aspinall. They must have plenty of news to exchange after an absence of three years,' he said.

She did not give up. 'Indeed, yes. He's done *terribly* well for himself, you know. Went out to the Americas with pockets to let and came back with a considerable share of prize money. Yes, he'll be a good catch for some fortunate young lady before too long. Of course, the army don't go in for prize money, do they?'

'No, my lady. They don't.' Cultivated through generations

of blue blood, the patronising smile in his voice and the quirk of one eyebrow was quite enough to remind her that her observation had backfired. Cavalry officers, drawn mostly from the wealthy aristocracy, could afford to fight for the sake of adventure and glory rather than for the pay, which was not good. Their colours, kit and horses usually cost a fortune, and few officers emerged wealthier than they were already. After that, Aunt Minnie confined herself to observing the two cousins and making plans for their future.

That evening, while her sisters were at Almack's, Letitia spent several hours writing her notes into her journal and continuing her story about the young Perdita who, by coincidence, was experiencing similar emotions and conflicts to herself.

She took her leave of him, allowing her hand to rest in his a moment longer than was appropriate for one who had only that day insisted they could never be good friends. To humour her, he had cheerily agreed, but the look in his eyes told a different story, and the pressure of his fingers was like a caress around her heart, adding to the slow thaw that had begun with his first disturbing kiss. He would never know what that had done to her. He would not understand how a maid could be melted, insidiously, by a gentle embrace offered that day out of compassion. What was an untutored girl to understand by this, except that he saw her as some trophy to be won? Was it too late for her to refuse him her heart? Had he already claimed it? 'Good day, my lord,' she said. 'Thank you for…'

'For what?'

'For the drive. For staying. For being here.'

He nodded, smiling with wicked brown eyes. 'Progress, Miss Perdita? Are we making some progress at last?'

She watched his two giant strides take him to his high curricle, revealing the length of his steely thighs and calves. Responding like quicksilver to his commanding hands, his team leapt away, leaving Perdita to watch him disappear into the blue autumn haze, already counting the hours before she would see him again.

Lord Rayne, on the other hand, had said nothing about progress to the author, nor had *his* wicked brown eyes smiled as he took his leave of her after luncheon. He had looked sternly at her instead. 'Well,' he said, 'don't be going on any drives with your cousin, will you? Naval officers don't have much practice with horses, and you two together would be a liability.'

'Thank you for your advice, Lord Rayne. Your concern is touching.'

'My concern is mainly for the horses. Good day, Miss Boyce.'

When shall I see you again?

Halfway across the pavement, he stopped and turned as if he had heard her. 'Tomorrow. At church. You'll be there?'

'Yes.' She nodded, startled by his reading of her mind.

His acknowledgement was curt to the point of incivility, his two strides to the curricle seat taken without another glance.

Her intention to be at church next morning, however, was upset by an incident that shocked the adults involved in the smooth running of Miss Boyce's select seminary.

Letitia and Miss Gaddestone were preparing to leave the house, waiting for Mrs Quayle and the three girls to join them, when the three arrived with serious faces, without their chaperon.

'Is she coming?' said Letitia, drawing on her gloves.

'Yes,' said Edina. 'She asks that you wait for her while we go on ahead. Shall we go?'

'Yes. We'll catch you up. Go with Miss Gaddestone.'

Once they were out of the way, Mrs Quayle entered the house through the back door, leading an unkempt Sapphire Melborough, who ought to have been at church in her parents' pew. Sapphire was sullen and indignant, her pouting mouth reddened as if she'd been eating strawberries. Her long fair hair, which should have been braided, hung down on to one muslin-covered shoulder, the fabric of which was loosened by the undone row of hooks and eyes down the back of her bodice. One hand held the front of her dress in place while the other carried her pink bonnet and reticule, and her prayer book.

If Letitia was lost for words, Mrs Quayle was not. 'I think,' she said in her severest tone, 'that this young lady has some explaining to do. First, she may like to tell us why she prefers to spend her Sunday morning in the potting shed rather than at church with her parents.'

Guessing the answer to that, Letitia started from a more obtuse angle. 'Where do your parents think you are, Sapphire?' she said.

'At church or at home, Miss Boyce,' the young woman whispered. 'They're away visiting for the day, but I pleaded to stay behind.'

'So you could come down to Paradise Road while we were at church?'

'Yes.' The blue eyes had lost their merry twinkle, taking on a heavy-lidded tiredness, guarded against probing personal questions.

'To meet the gardener's son?'

'How…how did you…?'

'*Tell* me! Never mind how I know.'

'Yes.'

Bristling with indignation, Mrs Quayle felt obliged to add details she knew Sapphire would not willingly have offered. 'The great hulking lout ran off, buckling his belt up, leaving this young madam—' she cast a jaundiced look at Sapphire's dishevelled state '—to pull herself together as best she may. Down on the bench they were, when I found them, rolling about like a couple of pups, and him with a black eye as big as a cabbage.'

'Yes, thank you, Mrs Quayle. Sapphire, come here and sit down. Did you walk down Richmond Hill on your own? Without a maid?'

'Charity came with me, ma'am, to keep watch.'

'To keep *watch*? For pity's sake, what has it come to? Where is she now? Still out there?'

'I don't know, ma'am.'

'Sapphire, how long has this been going on?' Before the girl could develop her fib, it was snapped off in a sudden burst of anger. 'Don't *lie* to me, young lady. The truth, if you please. How *long*?'

'Not long, Miss Boyce. Since I first hurt my ankle.'

Letitia closed her eyes, seeing the occasion in one quick blink. They had left Sapphire behind in Miss Gaddestone's care to finish off her watercolour in the summerhouse while the rest of them went to the Royal Academy. Gaddy would have dozed off. The gardener's son would have beckoned, offering Sapphire an irresistible alternative. She was not a girl to refuse that kind of adventure, as she herself had done. She would have pushed aside any reservations and taken whatever experience was waiting for her, and she would emerge at the tender age of seventeen knowing far more about a man than Letitia knew at twenty-four, a novelist who wrote about such relationships as if she knew what she was talking about. Sapphire's behaviour could not be excused or condoned, but neither could she be condemned out of hand for wanting to know exactly what would be expected of her in marriage, before committing herself to it.

'With the *gardener*'s son, Sapphire? Is that the best you could do? Could you not have waited for marriage?'

Sapphire hung her head as if in shame, but there was no trace of shame when she lifted it again to look Letitia full in the face. 'I could, Miss Boyce,' she said through swollen lips, 'but Ted's not like the men my parents approve of. He'll keep it to himself, not prattle and boast as others do, swapping details, comparing, laughing about it, giving one a reputation and a silly nickname to match. I wanted to find out what I need to know without everyone hearing about it. He's had lots of girls. He knows what he's doing. Not like some of them. And now I know what it's like. It was *not* what Mrs Quayle says, rolling about like pups. It was good, or I'd not have returned.'

'Have you no shame, Miss Melborough?' Mrs Quayle snapped.

Sapphire did not look her way. 'My body is my own to do with as I please. Yes, I know about bloodlines and all that, but experience with men has not stopped some women from making good marriages, and it won't stop me. The difference is that I shall be going into it with my eyes open. As men do.'

'And have you given any thought to the consequences, young lady?' said Mrs Quayle, unconvinced by the argument. 'Do you *want* to bear the gardener's brat? Will your own father recognise it, if you do?'

'There won't *be* any consequences of the kind you mean.'

'How can you be sure, Sapphire?' said Letitia. 'You run a very serious risk.'

'My father tells me one must be prepared to take risks in life.'

'I don't doubt he did, but I don't suppose he had this kind of thing in mind when he said it. Turn round and let me fasten you up.'

As Letitia might have expected, Sapphire's back was covered by tiny pink scratches that rough sacking would make upon delicate skin. But she was not prepared for the pale grey-blue rows of fingertip marks on the upper arms, shoulders and back as if some violence had been used. Finishing the fastenings, she turned Sapphire to face her. 'Tell me the truth, if you please. Did the gardener's son force himself on you?'

The blue eyes opened wider, astonished and innocent, and Letitia knew she did not lie. 'No, he didn't, Miss Boyce. Ted's not like that. I know it might be best for me to say that he did, but that wouldn't explain why I came down here on a Sunday morning when I told the housekeeper and Mama I'd be going to church, would it? I'd have gone straight there, not to your potting shed. I won't get Ted into any more trouble than he is already. Someone's already beaten him up.'

It would have been so easy for Letitia to tell her, but she held her tongue. This was not the time. 'Do you love him, then?' she said.

'No, Miss Boyce, of course I don't. It's not love we were after.'

'What *was* it, then?' said Mrs Quayle, sharply.

Letitia thought the question unnecessary, quelling Mrs Quayle's curiosity with a frown. 'My concern,' she said, 'is for your personal safety, which has been put at risk. And what on earth am I to tell your parents, when you choose to use *my* property to misbehave on while you were not supposed to *be* here? I shall have to insist that they find another seminary for you, Sapphire. Just when it was all going so well.'

'Do you have to tell them?'

Letitia recognised the plea for privacy, and there was a moment of hesitation before she replied, 'Yes, they must know. Certainly they must. They are responsible for you still, and I cannot pretend not to know what's been happening. That would make me as irresponsible as you. You must see that. I can only be thankful that it's been stopped before it gets any worse, though it will be bad enough if that young man has fathered a child on you. I pray it has not happened.'

'He must be got rid of *immediately*,' said Mrs Quayle.

'He will be. I should have done it sooner.'

'Why?'

'Well…er…because it's his father who's employed here, not Ted. He only helps out when he's needed.' She recalled Rayne's caustic and rather indelicate words about who else Ted had 'helped out'. 'Has he been associating with any of the other girls, Sapphire?'

'No, Miss Boyce.'

'Are you quite sure?'

'Yes, ma'am. Quite sure.'

Letitia sighed with relief. 'Stand up. I'll tidy your hair before I take you home. Turn round.'

'I'd rather stay here with you, ma'am, if I may. My parents won't be home until this evening.'

'Very well, but you must stay upstairs out of the way. I'll have your lunch sent up on a—' Her words were cut off by the insistent clang of the front doorbell, followed quickly by a loud commanding voice. 'Oh, no! That's Mama!' she whispered to Mrs Quayle. 'Quick! Take Sapphire upstairs.'

But it was too late to take Miss Melborough anywhere before the footman opened the door, his announcement obliterated by the loud greeting of Lady Boyce who had come on a mission of some urgency. *'Letitia!'* she bawled, then stopped abruptly to take in the unusual scene of her eldest daughter dressing the hair of a dishevelled young beauty, while her plump brown neighbour looked on with alarm written clearly on her face. With eyes sharpened by years of training, Lady Boyce saw that something was seriously amiss—a minor tragedy that demanded her personal investigation.

The hour that followed was one of the most difficult Letitia ever had to endure while defending Sapphire Melborough against Lady Boyce's embarrassing inquisition, far worse than Mrs Quayle's barbed enquiries. After ignoring repeated invitations to visit Paradise Road, she had chosen that Sunday morning to descend upon her daughter at last, not with smiles of appreciation, but solely to find out more about the relationship with the man she had earmarked for one of her younger daughters. Hoping to arrive before Letitia's return from church, she had intended to do at least half an hour of snooping. She did not enjoy having her plans dislodged, but she *did* enjoy demanding answers to searching questions, regardless of the fact that Miss Melborough's plight was no concern of hers. This kind of detail had never stopped her in the past, and nor did it now.

Usually able to hold her own in an argument, Letitia was this time no match for her mother, particularly on an issue that needed handling with great sensitivity. No amount of protectiveness towards Sapphire would do: that was seen as being on the side of the sinner. And as for Letitia's ideas of a seminary, it had already sunk to a level of vulgarity made worse by the noisy and untimely appearance of Charity, the young lady's maid who, more to save her skin than for any finer feeling, blurted out before anyone could stop her, her own innocent part in the role she had been told to play that morning. With additions.

Letitia's prayer for another unscheduled appearance in the form of Lord Rayne had no effect. If anyone could have dealt with Letitia's mother, he could. But he did not appear and, after Sapphire's eventual tearful departure to Letitia's bedroom, Lady Boyce needed no more convincing that she was right about the seminary being a grave mistake, already being regretted. Having made her opinions clear about the scandal of Melborough's daughter, she was not inclined to take luncheon with her niece, Rosie Gaddestone, or with Mrs Quayle and the boarding pupils. Instead, she launched once more into an attack upon Letitia, demanding to be told what she meant by driving out with her sisters' beau, making it look to the world as if she had stolen his affections. Did she realise what a disservice she was doing by this selfish behaviour? Did she realise the gossip it was causing? And the embarrassment? Did she *have* to wear those silly spectacles to draw attention to herself? Did she know how close Garnet was to being engaged to Rayne? Did she really believe a man like him could be seriously interested in *her*? Could she not see that she was not the kind of female such men married?

'Mama, you've not told me anything I don't already know. There is not the slightest possibility of marriage. Lord Rayne lives here in Richmond at the weekends and, because of my relationship to Garnet and Persephone, he and I are acquainted. Not good friends, Mama, just acquainted. He took me to Mortlake to see his sister, Lady Dorna Elwick, who is a friend of mine. There's no more to it than that. Garnet has nothing to fear.'

'And what about the theatre? I heard—'

'There were fourteen of us, Mama.'

'Well,' she said, looking round at the blue, white and gold décor, the walnut table and chairs, the embroidered seat covers and cushions as if they belonged in a dingy street tavern, 'it's bad enough for you to be doing *this* kind of thing, without trying to take your sister's future husband.'

'Are you not being premature, Mama? You know how Lord Rayne tends to…?'

'Yes, Letitia. I *do* know. That's the problem. And you're not helping matters, are you? And now this *shocking* scandal, too.'

'Which no one need know of, Mama, unless you tell them.'

'Then you must tell Rayne you no longer need his company,' she said, rising. 'That should redirect his interest. Don't ask him to lunch with you again, either. That young Waverley is more your type. Summon my carriage, if you please. It's time I was going.'

'But don't you wish to look round the house, Mama?'

'No time today. I have guests coming this evening.'

'I see. First things first, of course.'

Not being finely tuned to such nuances, Lady Boyce failed to pick up the cynicism. And had not Rosie Gaddestone entered the hall just as she was about to depart, she would have missed seeing her altogether after an interval of eight months. Her quick peck to each of Gaddy's cheeks was both hello and goodbye, delivered to Letitia with the same artificiality.

It was not like Letitia to weep over matters such as this, but the only thing preventing her on this occasion was not fortitude but the gentle clasp of Gaddy's arms around her shoulders and the scent of lavender in an embrace that lasted as the hall clock ticked and chimed over their heads.

'Has Mrs Quayle told you?' she whispered into Gaddy's lace cap.

'Yes, love. We're not having a good day today, are we?'

'No. Was Lord Rayne at church?'

'Yes. He asked about you. I said you'd been delayed.'

'We could have done with him here just now.'

'A change of heart, Lettie dear? That's not like you.'

'I'm not much like me at the moment.' She held her cousin away, her hands buried in the tiers of lace over her arms. 'Oh, Gaddy, what a business this is. Now we may be sure that Mama will tell anyone who'll listen what a mess I'm making of it.' *And unless Lord Rayne stays well out of the way, she will broadcast Sapphire's scandal far and wide. That's for sure.*

The next few days could not be counted amongst the happiest of Letitia's career when pupils, chaperons and tutors felt Sapphire's absence so keenly. Discreet excuses had to be given of how Sir Francis and Lady Melborough had accepted an invitation for their son and daughter to visit an aunt and uncle in Cheltenham during the summer months. Could anything have been more cruel?

The interview had been painful and humiliating, but not hysterically so, for Sapphire had appreciated Letitia's understanding and compassion and had accepted the blame for what had happened. She could no longer expect her parents to foster Lord Rayne's interest in her, such as it was, at least not until some months had passed. At all costs, said Lady Melborough, the disgrace must be kept quiet.

Letitia had agreed completely, but felt it only fair to warn the distraught mother that her daughter's maid Charity was not the soul of discretion, but that to dismiss her for her tactless outburst in front of Lady Boyce would have the opposite effect from the one they sought. If the story came out at all, Lady Boyce and Charity would be the prime suspects. This was not a thought to bring comfort to any of them, and Letitia's farewell to her ex-pupil had been tearful and affectionate. The outings that week were much less interesting without Sapphire's bubbly presence.

Letitia's first task on Monday was to summon Charlie, the elderly gardener, and tell him that his son was not welcome on her property, even though there was still much hard work to be done before Charlie could manage alone. His silent acceptance of the edict suggested that he already knew the reason, for he had seen Ted's injuries. It was time for him to get the come-uppance he deserved.

On Friday evening, Letitia sat before her book of household accounts and a pile of bills spread out under an oil lamp on the parlour table. The fading day was dull and blustery, the fire in the cast-iron grate throwing a soft pink glow over the skirt of Letitia's pale day dress, dancing between the deep frills of the hem. Her hair had begun to come loose from its pins due to the relentless twiddling of fingers while sums were added and columns scanned, and now a delicate veil of silver fell over her page as she wrote.

The light tap on the door produced only a murmur as the pen continued to scratch. 'Lord Rayne, ma'am,' said the footman.

'Oh!' The quill poised in mid-air. 'My lord?'

As always, Rayne's expression was hard to read, though his appearance at this late hour suggested that his visit was more business than social. 'Miss Boyce. I find you well, I hope?' His bow was formal, and he brought with him the fresh cold tang of the evening breeze and an energy that seemed to fill the room. His riding boots showed a film of dust.

She guessed what might lay behind the visit. 'Well enough, I thank you, my lord. Have you come directly from Sheen Court or from Hampton? Will you be seated? May I offer you a drink? I can send for some—' She pulled herself up short, remembering that she was not supposed to be offering him anything, not even the usual hospitality.

'No, I thank you,' he said, flipping up his coat-tails as he sat down. 'My visit will not take long. I've come from Sheen Court where I found a note awaiting me.' The hand that delved into his coat pocket pulled out a folded piece of paper, which he undid and passed to her. 'Perhaps you'd care to read it and tell me what it means.'

Feeling that she was being spoken to rather like an errant schoolgirl, she smiled, ignored the request, and sat down against the green-figured bolster on the sofa. 'I make it a rule never to read other people's letters,' she replied, sweetly. 'And if *you* don't know what it means, how can you imagine I shall do any better? Who is it from?'

He lowered it on to his knee. 'From Sir Francis Melborough. He sent it this morning by hand.'

'Then wouldn't it have been better to ask Sir Francis himself?'

'That is what I shall be doing when I've heard what you have to say about it. I prefer to be in full possession of the facts.'

'Would you care to summarise it? I cannot promise to have

anything at all to add, but I'll do what I can to help. I'm not at my best at this time of the day.'

'Very well. Sir Francis tells me that his daughter is no longer one of your pupils and that she's been packed off to Cheltenham with her brother. Do you have any comment to make on that?'

'No. Why should I? He's at liberty to do whatever he wishes…'

'With his daughter. Yes. So why has he withdrawn her from your seminary so soon after a very successful soirée at his home, and why did he go to the trouble of asking me to purchase a new horse and help her to get used to it only a week or so before sending her off to Cheltenham? Obviously there has been a sudden change of direction. Or is there a conflict of interests here that you could explain? Sir Francis tells me my services as riding master are no longer required.'

'Well, I'm sure you'll manage to find some other young ladies to occupy your spare time, my lord, as soon as you can find suitable mounts for them.'

'That is not the point, Miss Boyce, as you well know.'

'Oh, dear, then I've missed it. I told you I'm not at my best in the evenings.' A yawn behind her hand followed quite naturally.

'Don't try to bamboozle me with that flummery, ma'am. Your tongue and brain are as sharp in the evening as they are at any other time of day, or you'd not be doing your accounts, would you? Why have the Melboroughs withdrawn their daughter and sent her to Cheltenham?'

'I'm not at liberty to discuss the reasons with you, Lord Rayne. If Sir Francis gave you no reason, you can hardly expect that I will do so.'

'I see. Then I shall be obliged to draw the conclusion that you, ma'am, have devised some excuse to get rid of her because she's been occupying an occasional hour of my time lately, and that's your only way of making your displeasure felt. Or could it be some kind of retaliation for what happened in Sir Francis's library? You don't care for the Melboroughs much, do you, Miss Boyce? Are you gunning for the mother next, or have you done enough with this?'

'Lord Rayne, your imagination is working overtime. I will not stoop to answer your ridiculous allegations, but perhaps when you've had a good night's sleep you'll see that people *can* actually make decisions that have nothing whatever to do with you. Now, if you've said all you came to say, I suggest you go to the Melboroughs with your complaints and ask *them* for an explanation. And if that doesn't satisfy you, then you'll have to accept the situation, won't you?'

'Is this to do with your sisters? Have they told you to get her out of the way?'

Letitia came to her feet and waited for him to do the same. 'My lord, I have now heard every silly interpretation you can put upon the subject, including my apparent pique in expelling Miss Melborough from my seminary in order to punish her father for a tiny incident that didn't upset me in the least, except for a few bruises. After all, it was not the first time I'd been manhandled, was it? I happen to like Miss Melborough. She was an able pupil, and popular with all of us, and there is nothing my sisters could, or *would*, have said to make me do anything as irrational as what you suggest. Your insinuations do you no credit, my lord, and I urge you once again to abandon the puerile quest you and Lord Elyot discussed, if you have not already done so, and stay well away from

Paradise Road altogether. I shall no longer acknowledge you when we meet, and I shall instruct my staff not to admit you to my house.'

She ran out of breath on the last few words as she reached over to pull on the bell-cord, the clang of which could be heard above the howl of the wind in the chimney. In the silence that followed, the two antagonists stood without looking at each other, wondering who was being hurt most by this short, censorious exchange.

'There is surely no need—' he began.

'There is *every* need, my lord. I bid you good evening. Please don't come back. And rid yourself, if you will, of the notion that my sisters have any influence over me. You may like to suppose that there is some sisterly rivalry between us, but you'd be wrong. There is none, and there never has been. We have the greatest affection for each other. One of them will make you an excellent wife.'

'It won't do, Miss Boyce. You are not going to be free of me.'

The door opened. 'Yes, I am,' she said with a curtsy. 'Goodbye.'

Having been helped into his caped greatcoat and taken possession of hat, gloves and whip, Lord Rayne was about to pass through to the outer hall when the drawing room door opened and a voice whispered his name.

He turned. 'Miss Gaddestone. Good evening, ma'am.'

'Shh!' she said, sidling through the gap. 'Can you spare me a moment of your time, my lord? Please, just a wee moment?'

Without hesitation, Rayne followed her into the drawing room and closed the door quietly. A tall silver oil lamp spread a pool of light on to an open workstand bearing a pile of

mending, with a needle-and-thread jabbed vertically into it.
The armchair by the fire bore the hollow imprint of where
Letitia's cousin had been sitting to do her sewing. Still with
one finger to her lips, she indicated the opposite chair where
he should sit. 'Keep your voice down,' she whispered, poking
at the air in the direction of the wall adjoining the parlour. 'I
dare say my cousin will not like it much my telling you this,
my lord, but she could have done with you being here last
Sunday morning. Oh, yes,' she said, seeing his eyebrows pull
together in doubt, 'she told me so.' She smoothed the woollen
stole over her knees.

'Why, ma'am? Has something happened?'

'She's not told you about Lady Boyce's visit?'

'Not a word. Is that not what she'd been hoping for?'

Rosie Gaddestone shook her head, bouncing the brown
curls that spiralled around her face. 'Not *that* kind of visit. No
indeed. Her ladyship can be very intimidating, you know.
I've never known Lettie to be quite so upset by her. I took the
three girls to church, as you know.'

'Yes, you told me Miss Boyce and Mrs Quayle would
be delayed.'

'Then I came back here in case I could help, and when I
got here Miss Melborough was with them. Then Lady Boyce
rolled up, of all times to choose, when she must have known
we'd all be at church.'

'You mean Lady Boyce arrived while Miss Melborough
was here?'

'In this very room. That's why Lettie wished *you'd* been
here, my lord. Such a to-do it was.'

Rayne sat back, his frown deepening. 'Can you tell me
what happened, Miss Gaddestone?'

She looked doubtfully at the pile of mending. 'If Lettie has not told you of it herself, I suppose I ought not to be doing, either.'

'If it would ease your conscience, I've had a letter from Sir Francis telling me that Miss Melborough and her brother have gone to Cheltenham.'

Her face brightened. 'Yes, I suppose she'll have to be kept out of the way for a few months at least, won't she? Such a foolish featherbrained girl to throw away all her chances of a good marriage. Perhaps if she'd not been allowed to read all those romantic novels, she might not be so full of ideas. I cannot think it's good for—'

'And did you hear what Miss Boyce's reaction was?'

'I heard what her *mother's* reaction was,' she said, stoutly. 'I should think everyone in the house heard Lady Boyce bellowing at the poor girl while Lettie was having a time of it trying to get a kind word in edgeways. Not that she was approving, you understand, but that was no way to set about the girl when she'd just been found… Well!' She took her fan out of the work-table drawer and fluttered it across her bosom. 'With the *gardener's lad*, as I heard later. Tch!' She took a deep breath, fanning frantically.

'Where, exactly?'

'In the potting shed. There's one in the kitchen garden, you know.'

'By Miss Boyce herself?'

'It was Mrs Quayle who found them, just before church. Lady Melborough turns her back for just a few hours and this is what she gets up to. Lettie was handling it all so well, as I heard, but once my Aunt Euphemia arrived and saw that there was some kind of problem that was *no* concern of hers… Well, it was that young maid…Charity…that spilled the beans, otherwise they'd no doubt have made something up. After that, poor Lettie didn't stand much of a chance, nor the girl, either. Then Aunt Euphemia gave Lettie a good set-down. They must have heard it in the *kitchen*, my lord,' she whispered, leaning towards him. 'Wouldn't even look round the house. Wouldn't stay to lunch. Didn't even exchange two words with me, her own niece. Tch!'

'So you heard what she said to Miss Boyce?'

'We all did. I told you, Lady Boyce doesn't do whispers.'

'She was still angry about Miss…?'

'About *you*, my lord. Seeing Lettie, to put it plain. She don't like it above half. She don't like it at all. I think that's what she came for.'

He nodded, pressing his fingertips together, beginning to understand. 'No, I gathered as much, but I didn't think she'd go that far.'

'Oh, she would, my lord. Aunt Euphemia doesn't like having her plans upset, you see.'

Without warning, the door suddenly opened very wide. 'Lord Rayne,' said Letitia, 'I have already asked you to leave. Would you mind respecting my wishes?' She stood to one side, leaving a gaping hole of escape beyond the room.

Rayne stood up, bowing to Miss Gaddestone. 'Ma'am, this is highly unconventional, but I wonder if you would mind allowing me a few moments alone with Miss Boyce?' He held out a hand to help her up.

Throwing a questioning glance towards her cousin, she accepted it. 'If you don't mind, Lettie dear? Or would you rather I stayed?'

'No, Gaddy,' Letitia said, wearily. 'It's all right, love. Just a moment or two, that's all. There's a nice fire in the parlour.'

Chapter Eight

Rayne closed the door and came to face Letitia across the hearth, this time with a kindlier expression. 'You should have told me,' he said, softly. 'Why didn't you tell me?'

'Because it concerns no one but those involved, my lord. And I wish my cousin had not discussed it with you.' Icily, she turned aside as he moved towards her. Passing the work-table, she jabbed the needle hard into the white linen. 'And if you have any more accusations to make, you had better make them in writing so that I can show them to my lawyer.'

'Lettie!'

'I am not Lettie to you,' she snapped, whirling to face him again. 'I am Miss Boyce, and I do not *ever* want to—' The words her mother had demanded stuck in her throat, refusing to emerge as the lies she knew them to be. She *did* want to see him again, but not at the price of her mother's revenge or her sisters' unhappiness. 'Lord Rayne,' she said, attempting to stay calm, to think rationally, 'I told you once before that this has gone far enough. Now I must ask you yet again to abandon this foolish game of…of chase…whatever you like to call it…and leave me alone. Your opinion of me cannot be so high if you can believe that I would expel one of my own pupils to spite you or her father. I am not in a position to break a confidence, but you had no right to draw such mischievous conclusions, and I want nothing to do with a man who finds it so convenient to put me in the wrong. I can do that for myself quite easily, but I don't deserve it from you, Lord Rayne, however much you wished to goad me.'

'And I deserve that set-down, Miss Boyce. That, and more. You are right to be angered and hurt, but may I say in my defence that, if I'd known Lady Boyce was here last weekend, I would have put quite a different construction on Sir Francis's letter. Miss Gaddestone did not divulge to me what the whole house must have heard, but I can guess well enough how your mother must have upset everyone, particularly you. Well, now you have said what she told you to say, using my unfair criticism as an excuse. It was quite unforgivable but, even so, I beg you to accept my unreserved apology. I admit that I have, in the past, taken some pleasure in trying to goad you, but never to earn your disgust.'

'You do not disgust me,' she whispered.

'I am relieved more than I can say. My conclusions do *not* reflect my high opinion of you, Miss Boyce, but rather the unusual tangents of my mind these days for which, like it or not, I hold you responsible. But if you think I intend to take the slightest notice of Lady Boyce's demands, then I must warn you again that no one dictates to me who I visit. I am well able to make my own decisions there.'

'I must interrupt you. I can understand your determination not to be dictated to, particularly by Lady Boyce, but have you stopped to ask yourself what this is all about, my lord? To insist on going against her wishes just to prove a point at my expense is hardly fair, is it, when I made it clear from the beginning that we have nothing whatever in common?'

Her heart lurched at his quick frown. Was it irritation, or pain?

'You think that's what this is all about?' he said. 'That I have no other purpose than to thwart a middle-aged matron, through you? Is that *really* what you believe? That I'm playing some kind of devious power game with you and your sisters in the middle?' Scowling, he dug his hands deep into the pockets of his greatcoat and hunched his shoulders. 'I don't know what Lady Boyce has told you about my friendship with Miss Garnet and Miss Persephone, but you may take it from me that I have *never* given them any reason to think that I have serious intentions towards them. Ask them yourself. They will tell you as much.'

'You may think that answers every question, my lord, but I'm afraid it doesn't. There's more to it than that.'

'What more?'

'Miss Melborough's indiscretion. Had Mama not arrived just then, it would have remained a secret. I would not have made it public at any price. She's made a foolish mistake but, at seventeen, she doesn't deserve to lose her reputation over it. My mother, naturally, doesn't see it like that. She will use what she knows about Miss Melborough to force me to do what she wants and, if I refuse, Sapphire's affairs and the good name of my seminary will be the latest gossip.'

'Blackmail? Heaven help us, she doesn't do things by halves, does she? Would she be so vindictive?'

'She's a very determined woman, my lord. I dare say she's been waiting to find a way to make me conform, and now she's found it.'

'She may lead a horse to the water, Miss Boyce, but she cannot force it to drink. I am not obliged to fall in with her plans.'

'Perhaps not, but I wish for my sake that you would. She is quite determined that, if anyone diverts your interest from my sisters, it will not be me. I am to keep you at a distance, though, after your earlier condemnation of my actions, that may not be too difficult.'

'For which I have asked your forgiveness.'

'I dare say Gaddy thought she was doing me a favour in telling you what happened. It would have been better if she had not, I think.'

'And I think that the sooner you are removed from Lady Boyce's influence, the better. Something will have to be done.'

'Oh, it will be. You can help by doing what I suggested earlier.'

'I heard what you suggested earlier, Miss Boyce. I have not the slightest intention of abandoning what you call my puerile quest.'

'Not even though I plead with you?'

'No,' he said, almost soundlessly. Taking his hands out of his pockets, he came towards her, moving her backwards, holding her at bay against the long velvet curtain. Tenderly, he moved aside a wisp of hair that hung untidily down her face, not knowing how the touch of his fingertips wiped her mind as clean as a slate. 'No, my beauty. Your pleading would have a hollow ring to it, wouldn't it, when I know as well as you that it's not what you want. You are not so hard to read, Lettie Boyce.'

'You are arrogant, my lord. Talking nonsense, too.'

'Sure of myself, you mean. Sure that your mama will not have the last word in my affairs. I've fought more devious foes than her, and won.'

Angrily brushing aside his hand as it came up to hold her chin, she dodged to one side, bumping into the overloaded workbox on her way to the door. 'Oh yes,' she cried, slightly breathless, 'this is all about men fighting the foe, isn't it? Winning at all costs. Don't spare a thought for those who are injured on the way, will you? For Sapphire. Or me. Or my pupils and tutors who depend on me. And for what? To prove a point? Is that all, when the relationship you seek to protect doesn't even exist?'

'You're wrong. It *does* exist.'

'No, Lord Rayne, it doesn't! It never has. You talk about knowing what I want, but what I want is to be left alone to get on with my life. I don't need any kind of relationship with a man of your experience, and I have no interest in boosting your notoriety by becoming your latest mode. A blue-stocking, no less. Rayne's latest excess, they'll say. His latest bright idea.'

His eyes narrowed, dangerously angry, and she knew she had overstepped the mark with her outspokenness. 'Enough!' he said. His many-caped greatcoat seemed not to hinder him as he reached her in long silent strides, and she was unable to evade the hands that took her by the shoulders in a firm grasp that bit through her fine sleeves. Turned roughly, she was propelled forward to stand before the gold-framed mirror above the white marble fireplace with no choice but to face herself and him, scowling and quarrelsome, lit by a halo from the lamp behind.

'Look!' he demanded. 'Look at yourself, woman, and for pity's sake stop this damned self-deprecating twaddle, will you? Once and for all, recognise what's there. Be honest with yourself, for a change.'

Before she could see what he was about to do, he had pulled the last two pins from her hair, loosing it over his hand and her shoulders like a shower of molten silver. She tried to turn away, but he made her stand, still gripped by his hands, her hair falling in a pale sheet across her face, obscuring what little detail she could just make out.

'Look there!' he demanded again. 'Tell me that's not beauty, if you can. Tell me that's not a sight to turn any man's head.' His voice was quiet but harsh with exasperation while he watched the reflections, his hand lifting her chin and holding it up, cupping it in his warm palm. 'Who gave you this absurd notion that you cannot be my woman?' he whispered through her hair. 'Mama, was it? Well, my beauty, if she thinks she knows more about what I want than me, she's mistaken, and blind, and jealous, and resentful that you're beyond her control. Unconventional and rare are the words for you, Miss Boyce, not blue-stocking. Intelligent and independent, stunningly beautiful, sharp-tongued, quick-witted, imaginative and talented, loyal, compassionate—'

'Stop!' she muttered, trying to remove her chin.

'And I don't care a damn how many pairs of spectacles she wears or where she chooses to wear them, this is the woman I have chosen, this snapping snarling vixen with the body and face of an angel who believes her mother's opinion to be more valid than her own. But this has little to do with silencing her, or about my personal dislike of being told what I can't have when I know otherwise. It's about what you and I both want. She lost you soon after your father, and now she's trying to control you from a distance because she needs to be needed. Well, that's too bad. I found you, Lettie Boyce, bawling me out in front of my own men like a vixen protecting her cubs, spitting and fighting when I cornered you, flaying me with your quick tongue. And that's when I wanted you. That's when I laid claim to you. And that's when you first responded to me.'

'I did no such *thing*,' she cried, wrenching herself out of his grasp at last. 'My response was to take a swipe at you, and it was no more than you deserved. I only wish it had connected.' Pacing away from him, she reached the other end of the room, fuming with indignation. Throwing the mane of hair over her head, she continued. 'And my mother is *not* controlling me, Lord Rayne. I am a free agent. I do as I please. I am not answerable to anyone, and I can find my own way out of my problems.'

'At my expense? No, Miss Boyce, that won't do. I shall not allow you to ditch me. You may prefer not to remember exactly how, but respond you did, in spite of your anger.'

'You are indelicate, my lord,' she whispered, holding a hand to her cheek. 'You have no right to remind me of that shameful episode. I shall not swoon because I am not a swooning kind of woman, but I must ask you to leave me. Your memory is severely at fault.'

'Then perhaps you could help me to restore it.'

'Perhaps you should go. I am very tired. I cannot…' She made a vague gesture with one hand as if to fend off an invisible enemy.

'Lettie,' he whispered.

'No…no, don't. Just go.'

From the kitchen below, there was a crash as if someone had dropped a tray. Then silence.

'Have you been into the garden today?' he asked, quietly.

She shook her head, wearily.

'Then I think we should go and take a look. Come on, my

beauty. The air will make you sleep better.' Slipping off his greatcoat once more, he held it for her to put on, adjusting its flopping capes. It was much too wide across the shoulders and the hem touched the floor. Warm with the faint aroma of horses and leather, it seemed to wrap her in its protection, as intimate as his embrace.

With an arm across her back, her ushered her through the dimly lit hall towards the back of the house and out through a door, past the new beds of gillyflowers and lilies of the valley, lavender and ferns. The light had almost gone, the wind swaying the trees above them, lifting the loose ends of Letitia's hair like a ruff of silver lace.

A few moments ago, she thought, she had been wrangling with him yet again, each of them wanting the upper hand, determined not to yield an inch, yet taking a certain pleasure from knowing that after the wrangling would come a period of calm to lift them to another level of friendship. He had been right, of course. She *had* responded, briefly, before she was able to stop herself, before her fury had returned. She could forgive herself for that, but it was most ungentlemanly of him to remind her of it.

Their feet crunched along the pathway, sending next door's cat leaping away to rustle the distant shrubbery. Ahead of them, enclosed on two sides by pink rhododendron blossoms, the summerhouse was closed for the night. Yet it was towards that sanctuary that their unhurried steps led them, as if to recapture that precious moment when she had accepted the comfort of his arms. The memory of it was still fresh in her mind, contradicting all she had said to him earlier about not needing him. She did need him, even when they were at daggers drawn.

Responding to some unspoken signal, they came to a halt where they had stopped before, where the conflict in her mind was plain to see as she held her hair aside and looked across at the house, at the curtain-drawn windows, the conservatory shining with black and silver reflections, at the lights winking from the basement kitchen. Rayne took her by the hand, making the decision for them both. 'Come inside,' he said.

It was so much what she wanted him to say.

The summerhouse was still warm from the afternoon sun and, with the door closed behind them, the wind's roar softened to a whisper, muffling them in the quiet darkness of evening. Cares and quarrels faded into the shadows, heightening her anticipation. She thought he was about to take back his coat when his hands turned her to him, but they slid around her, easing her into an embrace as soft as thistledown, holding her against him as he had done before. This time, his fingers combed into her hair, grasping it lightly and tilting her face to receive his kiss that played over her lips and kept her spellbound with delight, fondling them with his sweet warmth. Unlike those first derisory kisses at Hampton Court, intended to humiliate and bring her to heel, these were offered with care and sincerity, received at first with a little hesitancy and then with a wonder that stirred something deep inside her like a suddenly discovered hunger.

There were things she needed to say to him, mostly negative, about how she must be left alone to sort out her problems, about how she had so far managed well enough without him. But they remained unsaid, banished like bad memories to the furthest reaches of her mind, overtaken by the physical needs of her body, disciplined for so long. The sheer luxury of surrendering herself to this man's arms, to his authority and care, seemed to her like the most dreamed-of boon she could imagine, and the hunger she had ignored for so long now raged within her, filling her with an ache to yield to him, allowing him to take over. After all she had striven for, stridently proclaiming her independence, setting up her own household, managing her own affairs, becoming a published author, all it took was such a man to show her how incomplete she was.

She might have wondered if, with his experience, he would take advantage of her extreme innocence as Ted had done with Sapphire. But she had nothing to fear, for Rayne knew better than anyone how not to force the pace with a woman so full of contradictions, and when he drew her towards the cushioned bench along the back wall, it was not to lay her upon it, but to sit her beside him in the close circle of his arms with his hand beneath the soft woollen greatcoat.

Even now she felt the confusion of her emotions acutely. 'What am I doing?' she whispered, breathless after his kiss. 'We can scarce find a civil word to say to each other, unless others are there. You came here on purpose to quarrel.'

'There are some things that have to be put straight,' he said, speaking into her hair. 'I cannot have you thinking that my first attempt to make love to you was the best I can do.'

Squirming, she tried to extricate herself, to no avail. 'Lord Rayne, if *that's* the only reason—'

'It isn't,' he said, laughing softly, holding her fast.

'You are indeed the most—'

'Odious man. Yes, I heard that before. Hush now, my beauty. You are not used to being teased, are you? So stop trying to find reasons for everything. Some things *are* unreasonable, and to you this looks like one of them. To me, it doesn't look that way at all.'

'Oh? Then how does it look, my lord?'

'Perfectly natural. You've had a disturbing few days, and when you needed me I was not here. Now I am, and I can give you the comfort you need. And more, if you want it. There's nothing to be ashamed of in wanting a man's comfort, sweet-heart, especially when that's what he's wanted to do since he first saw you.'

'It may not do much for my good reputation, though.'

'There's a lot of nonsense talked about reputations, Lettie Boyce.'

'I know that women rise or fall by them.'

'Those who don't know the rules, yes. You believe that Miss Melborough's good name will be lost for ever if word gets round about her little peccadillo, but it won't be any such thing. She'll have a string of gouty old dukes dangling after her at Cheltenham, and she'll come back home as a duchess. You'll see. It'll take more than Lady Boyce to damage that one. After that, she'll probably take young Ted back into her service.'

'She wouldn't do that, would she?'

His laugh was low and husky. 'For a woman of your pro-fession in charge of young ladies only a few years younger than yourself, Miss Boyce, you are remarkably ill informed about what they get up to. Did you have a governess, you and your sisters?'

They had, but Garnet and Persephone had socialised more than she had. The heroines of *The Infidel* and *Waynethorpe Manor* had not been typical of any young female she knew. She was trying to make Perdita more worldly, full-fleshed and rather extrovert, if anything, more ready to fall into adven-ture with a splash. Could her own preference for solitude be one of the reasons why Perdita was struggling with her image? Apart from her own ignorance of men, did she also need to investigate the real day-to-day behaviour of women, too? A seminary of seven privileged young ladies was hardly going to help much, with the exception of Sapphire.

'Yes,' she said. 'Then we were sent to Miss Wood's seminary.'

'That must surely account for it.'

'For what?'

'Lettie, I shall have to kiss you again,' he said, smiling. His hand had been roaming as they talked, challenging her mind to stay on course and to ignore what slow explorations were taking place under his greatcoat. Now, as he kissed her again and held her head upon his shoulder, the hand came to rest beneath the fullness of her breast, fitting it perfectly into the cupped palm. His timing was exact, for what would certainly have been a protest became instead a soft low moan of desire under his skilful lips.

Her hand covered his, pressing it even closer, directing all her senses towards the caress, to his kiss, and to his nearness. At once, the kiss deepened, luring her into a world of sensations about which she had yearned to know since she had started writing her first imaginative novel.

It had been an uncomfortable week, dragging its heels under the dark cloud of Lady Boyce's unreason. Letitia had felt particularly vulnerable, neither dependant nor free. Worse than that was what had happened to Sapphire, conveyed in one glance through those heavy-lidded eyes, not triumphant but fulfilled and knowing, confident and womanly. Mrs Quayle had been angered by the change, but Letitia had been moved by it, guiltily envious, sympathising with the girl's longing to discover what happened between a man and a woman in private without the fuss and publicity of marriage. It was exactly what she herself needed to know. Sapphire had taken matters into her own hands just as the heroine Perdita would do. Letitia would record it without a shred of evidence to go on except that look on Sapphire's face. Why could she not do as *she* had done and allow an expert to teach her here, in her own place, with no questions asked?

The answer was not far away: the risks were too great and too numerous. Courage was one thing, but experience of the sort she needed would cost too much, if a child should be the result of it.

Like a freezing mist the warning covered her, shrouding the enticing new world from view. Her hand closed over his and eased it away from her breast, clinging to it like a manacle. Her lips turned away from him with refusals littering his shoulder, whispering denials she could hardly expect him to believe. Shaking with the effort, her body stiffened and drew away, gathering strength to stand, distancing herself while drawing the greatcoat around her with a shudder. 'I'm so sorry…I led you on…it's my fault…I should not have…' she whispered.

He came behind her, placing his hands over her arms, smoothing her with his comfort. 'Hush, lass, it's all right, hush now. This is not about taking the blame for something we've discovered together. We have to talk about it, Lettie.'

'No, it's best to say no more.'

'That's foolishness. Come and sit with me for a while. Come. Side by side, over here.' Steering her, he lowered her into a basket chair and pulled up the other one near enough for him to lean over and take her free hand in his. 'It's no good walking away from this as if it wasn't happening,' he said, gently. 'We have to accept that there is something between us.

Yes,' he said, squeezing her hand as another protest began, 'there is, otherwise we'd not *be* here. And I can understand your reservations perfectly.'

'Can you?' she whispered. 'This cannot be what you're used to.'

There was a warmth in his voice as a smile entered it. 'Nothing about you is quite what I'm used to. Which is why it would be a great pity if you were to retire into your safe shell like a threatened oyster rather than face the situation with your usual courage. No, hear me out,' he said, stopping yet another protest at the unflattering analogy. 'You are known, Lettie Boyce, for being unconventional, independent, and too uncomfortably intelligent for most men. But I am not most men. I can accept all the reasons why you have chosen to remove yourself from Lady Boyce's contempt to a place where you can quietly get on with the business of being yourself and doing what you do best. But, sweet lass, I also believe that if you truly had the courage of your convictions, you would—'

'Are you suggesting that I lack courage? After what—?'

'I am suggesting that you are so concerned with what you may *not* do, that all those things you *could* be doing are passing you by. For a woman to defy convention is not such a crime these days, you know, and it can be made so much more enjoyable if she has someone to help her to do it.'

'In my mother's eyes, it *is* a crime.'

'And is your mother's opinion always regarded in such matters?'

'She would like it to be, but, no, it isn't. Not by a long way.'

'Then we are agreed that we need not take her into account. Which means that there are some things you would like to do which at present you are suppressing. Like taking a lover, for instance.'

Coming so soon after the last few wonderful moments in his arms, that struck a chord in her with more than usual force. 'It's not so much Mama's opinion on *that* which prevents me, my lord. You must know that the main reason for rejecting that option, if it should ever become one, is that the risks are too great. I stand to lose too much, as an independent woman.'

'In fact, they are not nearly as great as you suppose, but since you are not in the right frame of mind to hear about the alternatives to celibacy, you may like to hear about a different idea that would cause no loss of face. Indeed, it would be much more entertaining than dancing to your mother's tune whenever she calls it. Which is what you're doing at present.'

'I can't deny that. What are you suggesting? And what is it I'm not in the right frame of mind to hear about?'

'Since you ask, it's about the possibility of being my mistress.'

'You're right, my lord. I'm not ready to hear about that.'

'No, I didn't think you would be. Not yet. Nevertheless, Miss Boyce, I do not believe you're going far enough to present yourself as a woman of consequence, either here in Richmond *or* in London. Appearing occasionally with your brood at various public venues is all very well, but you could be singular in so many more ways, as I suspect you would quite like to be, if you were to have me beside you as your escort. Yes, I recall your earlier concern about being known as my latest eccentricity, but I believe it would be seen as the other way round, with some careful management. Besides, we are both secure enough in our habits to rise above silly remarks of that kind. What is more important, Lettie Boyce, is for you to take back the reins into your own hands, stop being controlled by your mother, and show the world that *you* have what other women lack. Uniqueness, style, wit and beauty. I was not entirely funning when I said that you could start a new rage by wearing your spectacles in my company.'

'You make it sound as if I secretly crave a wild social life, my lord. I don't, you know.'

'Not at all. Almack's is not the highlight of my week, either. But how many times have you been able to attend the evenings at the Misses Berry on North Audley Street since you left London? They still hold their evenings for intellectuals, and they still ask after you.'

'Not once since I left. But do you go there, Lord Rayne?'

'Whenever I'm invited. I could escort you and, if you prefer not to stay with your sisters at Chesterfield House, you'd be welcome to stay with my parents and me at Berkeley Square. My brother and sister-in-law would be glad to make up a party to the theatre or the opera. Or if you wished to attend a lecture, my brother and I would escort you, and Bart, too, if he's interested. You could take the town by storm, Miss Boyce, if you chose to.'

'Are you not forgetting that I have pupils to attend to?'

'No, I'm not forgetting. I'm seeing them as an addition to your image. They have their tutors and chaperons. They could all come, too. Just think, they'd make a perfect foil, and they'd provide a perfect reason for you all to be seen out and about, visiting, sightseeing.'

'I don't know what their parents would say.'

'The parents would love it. You'll have new ones begging to enrol with you. I can see you now with a bevy of well-mounted young ladies riding on Rotten Row. They'd all meet eligible men within days, and remember, they were not sent to you because you're like all the rest, but because you're different. You'll not lose any pupils by showing them more of the world than Richmond has to offer. But more to the point, *you* have nothing to lose by showing the world what kind of a woman you are, rather than trying to hide it.'

'And Mama? Can you imagine what she'll say to discredit me?'

Lifting her hand, he kissed her knuckles one by one. 'What do *you* imagine she'll say, sweet lass, when all her acquaintances are raving about the very exclusive and singular Lettie Boyce who rides a superb grey Arab mare, wearing the most divine Hussar habit made by Weston, and gold spectacles, with Rayne beside her, too, and a crowd of handsome *gels* and heaven only *knows…*' his voice took on the yelp of Lady Boyce's rhetoric '…how many chaperons and tutors, all of them Top o' the Trees, you know. You should just *see* them, my *de…ah*!'

'Stop…stop!' Letitia begged him, laughing.

'She'll not be tempted to disown you, believe me. If I know your mama, she'll be the one to claim it was all her doing.'

Still laughing, Letitia was bound to agree. 'I like the idea of taking all the tutors, too. We could take Mr Chatterton. He'd be in his element.'

'We could take Dorna, too. She loves a good show.'

'We could attend some of the celebrations next month.'

'All summer. My parents will be holding at least one ball and several dinners. I'd be honoured to partner you, Lettie.'

'You mean…as your…?'

'As my personal guest, my partner, my woman, whatever would make you feel safest and protected. That's something you've missed since you lost your father, isn't it?'

She nodded. 'Uncle Aspinall has been very good to me, but it's not quite the same. Aunt Minnie is…'

'Yes, but with me beside you, she poses no threat, does she?'

Memories of the lunch came to mind where Rayne had silenced the woman's sour-faced disapproval. 'No, none at all,' she said.

'Then allow me to be your escort, Lettie. I cannot take your father's place, but I could be as protective. I could also be something else to you, if you'd let me get closer.'

'As you did just now?' she whispered.

'As we did just now. Do you need some time to think about that?'

The last of the light had all but disappeared, leaving Rayne's head and shoulders in solid black silhouette against the window, with the smooth planes of cheek and brow just visible beneath a thatch of dark hair. Even in the darkness, she thought, his handsome features had the look of an aristocrat, regular and distinguished. How could she not want such a man by her side for all to see? How could she not feel protected and safe, even after their disastrous first meeting? The idea *did* appeal to her, for if her mother was unlikely to be silenced by simple disobedience, she would certainly be non-plussed by a stylish show of patronage from the Marquess and Marchioness of Sheen, no less. Whether the twins would forgive her remained to be seen.

'I *would* like to think about it,' she said. 'Yes. Thank you, my lord. I can see the advantages but, as a woman, I can also see the risks.'

'That particular risk,' he said, singling out the one in her mind, 'need not keep you awake at night, sweet lass. If it happened, you would marry me.'

'Oh.'

'That surprises you? Do you *still* think I'm playing games?'

'Well, as to that, my lord, I don't quite know what to think except that I'm more used to hearing about the women you've been seen with and then dropped, than those you've offered to marry. I cannot see in what way I shall differ from the rest in that respect. I'm not doubting your sincerity for one moment, only my own inability to hold your attention longer than any other woman. I have to say though,' she continued, warming to the theme, 'that the idea of being a little more…er…audacious…does appeal to me because I don't believe Mama will have a leg to stand on once she saw that I had your family's approval and that I chose to stay with them instead of with her. That would certainly give her something to think about. And I love the idea of taking the whole seminary up to London to mix their education with pleasure. Perhaps we could hire some riding horses from Mr Hall's Livery Stables, could we? I could even *rent* somewhere for us all to stay. Now, why did I not think of that before? That's a perfect idea. And I might even drive my phaeton again, if you were to sit with me. I usually ask Bart, but he's not—'

'Miss Boyce.'

'Yes?'

'Am I to deduce from that, that you have decided to allow me just a little further into your life? On trial, so to speak?'

'It does sound rather like that, doesn't it? I feel sure that if I were to take up your suggestion of being more adventurous and, dare I say it, a little more…er…*extravagant*, I could then…'

'Stylish and glamorous.'

'…begin to dazzle.'

'The audacious Miss Lettie Boyce and her dashing escort, her brilliant tutors, her strikingly lovely and talented pupils.'

She clapped her hands. 'That sounds rather like fun to me. What a pity Miss Melborough would not be with us. It's just the kind of thing she'd—' She stopped suddenly, responding to the capture of her hand, both of them struck by the same ingenious idea.

'She *could* be,' Rayne whispered.

Letitia agreed. 'She could. We'd only have to wait… well…a few weeks perhaps, and then if she's not…oh, dear…I *do* hope she's not.'

'If she's perfectly well, you could ask for her to return. Surely her parents would not insist on her staying all summer in Cheltenham?'

'Bringing her back to join us would let it be seen that all my pupils are of the highest *ton*. Mama would be utterly confounded, and she'd not be able to use Sapphire's disgrace against me if she wasn't *in* disgrace, would she?'

'Indeed she would not, Miss Boyce.' Reaching across through the darkness, he took hold of the greatcoat collar and pulled her towards him, meeting her mouth to take the kiss that awaited him.

'Oh, dear,' she said. 'Surely we cannot have solved all my problems at once, can we? Does this mean that things are beginning to sort themselves out?'

'Oh, I doubt it,' he said, caressing her cheek. 'No, this is just a hiccough. We'll soon find some more complications to make life more exciting, if we look hard enough. Are you ready to go in now?'

'My hair! What did you do with my pins?'

'Left-hand pocket.'

'Oh, so they are. Now, how am I going to see, I wonder?'

'What do you need to see? You know where your hair is. Here, give them to me. Turn round.'

Once again, but this time in almost complete darkness, Rayne acted as lady's maid, raking and twisting her long hair into a tight coil which he pinned up using the pins held between his lips. 'That will cost you another kiss, ma'am,' he said, turning her to face him. 'I'm expensive.'

Swooning in his arms, Perdita tried in vain to remember what she had been told about the impropriety of physical contact, apart from the assistance of a firm hand under her arm. But this was different, and both of them knew it, and these kisses were sweeter than anything she had imagined in the seclusion of her curtained bed. She did not believe any woman, unless she was heartless and cold, could have resisted his demands, but...

Wait a moment, Letitia thought. *Is* she going to resist his demands? Surely she's not going to leap into bed with him after a few kisses, is she? Is that what happens? Is that what I would do?

The quill pen was laid aside as she sat back to watch the lamp-flame's sinuous dance. Yes, it probably is what I would do, she told herself, but perhaps Perdita had better hold back until I know more about it. With a secretive smile, she re-read what she had written about those kisses. The idea of becoming Lord Rayne's newest mistress was by no means as far from her intentions as she had allowed him to believe, but for that to happen so soon would hardly provide her with the body of information she required about the lengthy art of wooing. No, he must be kept waiting until his patience wore thin;

meanwhile, she must not allow him to know how useful he was being in contributing to her literary talent.

It had been a stroke of genius, however, for him to offer help with her new image, a more daring Lettie Boyce whose lights need no longer be hidden under a bushel, whose pupils and staff would be seen and sought by society hostesses, as her sisters were. Now, she would have Lord Rayne's protection against anyone who felt threatened by her intellect, giving her the confidence she needed to wear her spectacles like an unusual fashion accessory and to see where she was going, at last. A small detail, but so very important.

Picking up the pen once more, she dipped it thoughtfully into the satin-black ink, thinking what a pity it was that her mother was more likely to be put out than delighted by the new development. It was a pity, too, that she would never be aware of her eldest daughter's literary achievements, though it was debateable whether that knowledge would embarrass her or make her proud.

The pen began to scratch. If she was going to wait, then so must Perdita. *'No…no,' said Perdita. 'This must not continue, sir.'*

Chapter Nine

At breakfast the next day, Letitia's announcement that they would be spending a few days in London as soon as things could be arranged was greeted by some very ungenteel squeals of excitement, though the reaction of Miss Edina Strachan was quite the opposite. With one look of sheer horror, she pushed back her chair, begged to be excused, and rushed out of the room before anyone could ask her about the problem.

Maura and Lucille, the other two boarders, appeared to have run out of sympathy for their Scottish friend. 'Oh, she *cannot* still be homesick,' said Lucille. 'Not after all this time.'

'It's only been a term and a bit,' said Maura, more reasonably. 'Does she not like the idea of London? I wish she'd tell us what the matter is.'

'I'll go to her,' said Mrs Quayle. 'But don't you two go off to Mrs Price's without me. I want to take another look at her satins, and I have a mind to that brown grosgrain, too. It's just my colour.'

By mid-morning, the Saturday shopping spree into Richmond, one of the week's highlights, resulted in a small mountain of parcels and boxes, each one opened to smiles of approval and admiration: silk stockings at twelve shillings the pair, pink satin evening shoes at five and sixpence, a blue pelisse at seventeen shillings, though the fur trim had cost an extra ten, a matching velvet hat with a turned-up brim, a length of best Lyon velveteen at fourteen shillings a yard, and some of the pretty Pekin striped silk. Edina, who had consented to go, too, could not be persuaded to spend more than one shilling of her weekly allowance. Mrs Nest, the milliner, had been the main source of ribbons and lace, artificial flowers, feathers and beads with which to remodel and beautify bonnets and, as soon as the chocolate pot and cups were returned to the kitchen, the three girls arranged themselves around the parlour table with the contents of workboxes spilled across it.

Letitia left them with the two ladies. She had asked Mr Waverley to call on her to explain why Mr Lake, her publisher at Mercury Press, still had not paid her what she thought was her due. This had been an irritant to her for well over a month for, having begun her third novel, no contract had been sent, nor any sales money for the second.

'What's the problem, Bart?' she asked, waving him to the chair beside hers at the dining-room table. 'Is he losing interest?'

Mr Waverley's good-natured smile was meant to reassure her, but lately Letitia had begun to wonder whether he was negotiating firmly enough with Mr Lake or whether he was simply accepting whatever the man proposed on the basis that she was fortunate to be in print at all. Sitting down, he spread out a sheaf of papers before her. 'No, of course he's not,' he said, 'but the longer he can hold on to any money, the better he likes it. Any business is the same. I've brought the new contract that I collected yesterday, and I'll take it back to him next week to be countersigned. But I have to warn you, Lettie, that his costs have increased.'

'What, without any warning? Poppycock!'

'I'm afraid it's true. The sales from *Waynethorpe Manor* are very healthy, but out of that you have to pay for—'

'For paper, printing, advertising, and anything else he can think of. Yes, I know that, Bart. Have *all* those costs gone up?'

'That's what he tells me. Not including his ten-per-cent commission, which he says, as a goodwill gesture, he will hold down just for you.'

'Hah! How very kind. And what kind of profit is *he* raking in from my success?'

'I don't know. But he reminded me that you'll be liable for any shortfall if the income from sales doesn't cover the pro-duction costs of the next one.'

'Well, I *know* that. Does he think it might not, next time?'

'He didn't suggest as much. I think he wants to remind you not to spend all your profits, in case…well, in case it's needed.'

'Typically patronising. What's the man playing at? I think we should go elsewhere if he's going to be difficult.'

'Don't fly off the handle, Lettie. Look, I've brought you the new contract to sign.'

'More to the point, I want to see a list of these higher expenses so that I can see exactly what he's deducted. He did pay you, I suppose?'

'He did, at last.' Producing a brown paper parcel tied with string, he laid it upon the table with a smile. 'Two hundred pounds for one thousand copies. That's a very tidy sum, Lettie, by anybody's standards.'

'If it had been two hundred and fifty, I'd have been more

impressed. Personally, I think he's making a tidy sum out of it, too.'

'Doesn't he deserve to?'

'No,' she said, indignantly, 'he doesn't. And I shall not be signing this immediately, either. I'll read it first and then decide. After my success, I can sell my new one to anyone I choose. He can simmer for a while.'

'Phew!' Blinking like an owl, Bart dipped his head to study her from beneath his brows. 'This is a newly sharpened Lettie Boyce indeed. Who's been coaching you? Rayne, is it?'

Her first impulse was to deny any such thing, but Bart was a good friend, and more than once she had wondered if he might offer to introduce her to some of the tender moments she would like to have experienced. He was clean, well presented and attractive, good-natured and obviously fond of her, yet never once had he given her the kind of look that made her heart beat loud and fast, as Rayne had done, nor had he ever spoken a private word of affection. Now, she felt the inclination to try him out. 'Would you mind if it *was* Rayne?' she asked.

To her relief, he did not pretend to misunderstand her meaning, but nor did he pretend to flirt, as she had given him the chance to do. 'We are good friends, Lettie,' he said, 'and I like Rayne. Always have done, even at school. But you and he make a much better pair that you and I would. Don't take it the wrong way, but you'll always be like a sister to me, nothing more.' He spoke with such sincere gentleness that Lettie was neither surprised nor embarrassed when he picked up her hand, took it to his lips and placed a kiss upon her fingers in a gesture of simple chivalry.

A brisk knock at the door gave no warning, no time to say either enter or wait, and as Lettie snatched her hand away, her snappy retort for the overeager young footman reached the ears of the man close on his heels.

'I *told* you we were not to be disturbed, Sam. Oh…Fin! Good morning.' As she rose to meet her cousin, Mr Waverley hurriedly gathered together the papers and then stood, hugging them close to his chest.

At the same time, it was clear that Lieutenant Fingal Gaddestone had witnessed the tender looks, the hand being snatched away, and the private nature of some business between them. 'I beg your pardon. I am intruding,' he said with no obvious intention of withdrawing. His startled frown quickly changed to a smile by which he hoped to lessen the seriousness of the interruption. Lettie was more concerned that her private papers should be collected than with welcoming him.

'Do come in,' she said, frowning. 'Mr Waverley is just about to leave. Have you two met?'

The introduction was brief and already suffering from the construction put upon Mr Waverley's friendship by her cousin. In the circumstances, Letitia was relieved to see that Uncle Aspinall and her sisters were entering the hall as Mr Waverley left, their noisy greetings soon covering her confusion. She was also relieved to see that Mr Waverley had the presence of mind to take with him the brown paper package.

Assuming that Cousin Fin had come primarily to visit his sister, she detached Miss Gaddestone from the amateur milliners and left them alone to walk round the garden, arm in arm. Uncle Aspinall's intention was to visit the stables. 'Talk to you later,' he whispered to Letitia, with an added wink.

Smiling, she squeezed his hand. 'After lunch?'

'Something light, Lettie. No shellfish. My gout is bad today.'

'I'm sorry, love. Shouldn't you be resting?'

'Yes,' he said, twinkling, 'but your mother thinks you have too many horses, so I'm going to take a look, then I can tell her she's talking rubbish.'

'What does Mama know about my horses? Has she been snooping? Three of the hacks belong to the girls, anyway. She's never shown much interest in my finances before.'

'Don't be hard on her, Lettie. She cares for you, in her own way.'

Letitia's refined grunt implied that she remained unconvinced. But the thought of her mama remaining completely ignorant about her elder daughter's tidy income soothed the irritation of the continuous interference. She joined her sisters in the sunny garden where their murmurs of delight at the planting made her realise how much she had missed their company. Hugging them both, she came close to tears, thanking them for liking her attempts at homemaking.

They laughed, of course. 'Why d'ye think we keep on turning up like bad pennies most weekends?' they said. 'We love it. If only Mama would redecorate in this style, Lettie. Chesterfield House is so *heavy* compared to this lightness.'

Laughing with them, she drew them towards safer ground. 'Now tell me about the latest beaux,' she said. 'Who are they this time?'

She had not expected to elicit anything particularly new on this subject, but in the space of two weeks it appeared that the twins had put Lord Rayne out of mind and replaced him with two extremely handsome, well-connected, well-bred, wealthy and available young men only recently returned from the Peninsular Wars ahead of Marquess Wellington. Amidst giggles, expostulations, descriptions and contradictions, Letitia gained the impression that the twins, already madly in love, had been in their company every day and every evening, and that Mama thought they were quite heavenly, their manners perfect, their credentials faultless, at least in England.

With some understandable trepidation, Letitia asked, 'So you've not seen much of Lord Rayne?'

'Rayne doesn't get a look in,' said Garnet, dismissively.

'To be more accurate,' said Persephone, 'we haven't seen him at any of the assemblies for ages. Mama insists that his interest is still on us, but we know it isn't at all. He's only ever been a friend, never a serious contender. He's never been known to keep a woman for very long, so it's silly of her to get up hopes for us. We never did.' For Persephone, the quieter of the two, that was quite a long explanation. So long, in fact, that it left both her sisters temporarily without words.

Letitia took a deep breath, her fingers pulling at the fringe on the edge of her shawl. 'Then if that's really the way of things,' she said, 'I have an admission to make.'

'Oh, we know about *that*,' said Garnet, kindly, removing the fringe from her sister's fingers. 'We were not going to speak of it until you did because we know how annoying you must find it to be told you must not show any interest in him. As if Mama could insist on *that*, indeed.'

'Mama told you not to speak of him?'

The twins nodded, but Persephone went on. 'We both know Rayne is more interested in you, so if you think you may be treading on our toes, you can take it from us that you're not. You may be treading on Mama's, but—'

'But that wouldn't be difficult, would it?' said Garnet, giggling. 'You are in the safest place here, Lettie dearest, where she can't get at you.'

Letitia understood by that, that the twins knew nothing of

their mother's controversial visit last Sunday, so she said nothing to contradict their belief. She saw no harm, however, in telling them how Lord Rayne had taken her up in his curricle, how she found him good company, how she was on friendly terms with his Richmond family and how, if she were to stay with his parents in Berkeley Square quite soon, they must not take it amiss, in view of Mama's opposition.

'Not a bit of it,' Persephone assured her. 'That would be further than *we* got with him. He never invited *us* to Berkeley Square.'

'Is he going to ask you to be his mistress, Lettie?' said Garnet, unable to keep the excitement out of her voice.

'You've been reading too many novels, love,' said Letitia, laughing. 'But what would you say if he did? Would you be shocked?'

'Envious!' said the twins in one voice. 'Is he going to? Will you accept him? Will he buy you another house? Do tell us. Mama would *explode*!'

'That's what bothers me,' whispered Letitia.

There was a pause. 'He's asked you?' said Garnet.

'No. Mentioned it, that's all. Just a mention.'

With affection, they watched the blush creep into her cheeks, brightening her eyes. Garnet leaned forward, speaking intensely. 'What we said just now about him not staying with any woman for long, well…forget it. He'll be looking for a wife at his age. That's our guess. And he's not stupid enough to let someone as good as you slip through his fingers, Lettie. Men must play the field, you know, before they find what they're looking for, and if Rayne wants you, take no notice of Mama. We are bound to toe the line because we're still under her wing—'

'Who's mixing her metaphors?' murmured Persephone.

'But you're not. You can please yourself. We'd just *love* to be somebody's mistresses, but it's not likely to happen.'

'Not with two of us.'

'Unless we shared,' said Garnet, dolefully.

'So,' said Letitia, 'if I were to rent a place in London for my tutors and pupils, and Gaddy and Mrs Quayle, would you come out with us?'

'Of course. Anywhere you like. Is that why they're remaking their bonnets? For a London visit?'

Letitia nodded.

'Then you should tell Uncle Aspinall. He'll find you a place, but you'll have to hurry, with all the celebrations planned for summer. The rentable properties will soon be snapped up if you don't get a move on.'

It occurred to Letitia then that perhaps she ought not to have spoken so soon about her plans, for now Gaddy would be sure to tell her brother, who would mention it to Aunt Minnie, who would rush to Lady Boyce with the news. And then Mama would not only wonder how she was able to afford all her horses and carriages but also how she was able to purchase the lease on a house in the middle of town at a time when everyone else was doing the same. Could she look forward to yet another meddlesome visit?

Although the twins knew nothing about Lady Boyce's visit to Richmond, her elder brother Penfold Aspinall certainly did. After checking her horses and stables as her father would have done, and after a lunch of cold tongue, baked ham, pigeon pie and salad, he took Letitia into the garden for a private chat. Telling her she must not take too seriously any of her mother's threats concerning Sapphire Melborough or the seminary, he reminded her of how his sister made a great deal of fuss and noise to get her own way. She had been that way from birth, he told her, adding that he should know about that better than anyone.

Having been on the receiving end of the set-down, Letitia was not wholly persuaded by his encouragement. How could he be so sure?

'The real reason she doesn't want you seeing Rayne is because of his reputation with women, and you being here on your own, unprotected and—'

'Independent, you mean.'

'No, unprotected, love. That's what concerns her. She still looks on you as a green girl, unfamiliar with men's ways.'

'Then why has she encouraged him to see the twins so often?'

'Tolerated, not encouraged. Because they're there with her, under her eye. And because there are two of them, Lettie, each looking after the other. She knows he can't have them both, and you know how they stick together like glue. They're safe enough. She also knows that the louder she shouts about Rayne being close to making one of them an offer, the quicker he'll back off. You're not safe, in her eyes. She doesn't want what happened to her to happen to you, too.'

'What? What *did* happen to her?'

'Oh, Lord, I've said too much, as usual.'

'No, you haven't. Tell me. I need to know.'

'Well, keep this under your bonnet, Lettie,' he said, lifting a straggling briar for her to pass beneath. 'It was while she was engaged to your father. I took her to a house party at the Listermans' down in Sussex, and she was miffed that your father had not gone with her. Some excuse or other…'

'He hated house parties.'

'Well, she jumped the gate and got into another man's bed. That's just like her. Cut off her nose to spite her face. She was a virgin, too.'

'Mama took a *lover*? To spite my father?'

'Not exactly to spite him. He knew nothing about it. But you know what she's like. Acts first, thinks later. I didn't know exactly what had happened until afterwards when the man began to pester her for more. Then she asked me to go and keep him quiet. So I did. Peacekeeper Penfold. I took with me a pretty young lass of very good lineage who is now the present Lady Melborough. Diverted his attention, you see.'

'The one who lives here, up on the hill?'

'The very same, love. Sir Francis is quite a bit older than her. More your mother's age. He's still frisky, too, by all accounts. Anyway, Euphemia married your father soon afterwards, so no one was any the wiser except Sir Francis Melborough. Certainly not Sir Leo Boyce.'

'So you don't think…?'

'Ah, I know what you're thinking. But, no, love.' He stopped beside the large cold-frames and stared inside. 'No, you were born a full year later. No connection whatever.'

'I see. Then could that be the reason why she doesn't care to visit Richmond, for fear of a chance meeting?'

'It sounds a bit extreme, but it could be. Her first visit was on a Sunday morning while everyone in Richmond was at church, wasn't it?'

'Except the Melboroughs, as it happened. But it might explain why she refused to attend our concert at their house.'

'And why she was *so* furious with the Melborough girl.'

'She told you what she'd said to her?'

'Yes, and expected me to agree. But I didn't. I reminded

her instead of a certain young lady at a house party in Sussex. And I told her it was your business and that of the Melboroughs, not hers.'

'Thank you, Uncle.'

'Cucumbers are doing nicely, Lettie.'

'Yes, we're growing tomatoes, too. Somewhere. Is what you've told me the reason she doesn't want me to live here, Uncle Aspinall?'

'Aye, lass. That, and living without proper protection.'

'And I suppose she would not regard Lord Rayne as proper protection?'

'You're old enough to know your own mind,' he said, 'and that's what I've told her. There's nothing wrong with Rayne that a good wife won't put right. Show me these tomatoes of yours, Lettie.'

'Over here,' she said, thinking that what he'd divulged to her about Sir Francis Melborough might help to explain why he'd been foolish enough to put his arm around Euphemia Boyce's daughter.

Before they rejoined the others, Letitia sounded her uncle out about available properties in London to rent for the summer season. He promised to help, though it was his lack of curiosity about who was to pay for an establishment large enough for upwards of fourteen people that made Letitia suspect that he must have come to his own conclusions. She saw no reason to query them, whatever they were.

Her conversation with Lieutenant Gaddestone, however much she had hoped to keep it both public and brief, was more to be endured than enjoyed. His untimely, and unnecessary, interruption that morning had confirmed a sneaking suspicion that he had returned from naval duties more full of himself than when she had known him as a youth, and this was not a side of him with which she felt comfortable. Nor did she appreciate it when he assumed the role of elder brother to a rather unworldly orphan.

She tried to curb her impatience, not to let it show. 'Mr Waverley,' she told him in answer to his remark, 'is our accounts and mathematics tutor as well as being my good friend. In those capacities we often have private business matters to discuss.'

'Oh, don't for one moment think that I disapprove of a young lady in your position accepting help when it's offered, Lettie. But one must observe the proprieties even *more* strictly when there are other young ladies in your care, and—'

'Cousin Fin, thank you for your concern, but I assure you it is entirely unnecessary. I am perfectly familiar with the proprieties, as all my staff are, and I have not given a single thought to your approval or disapproval of what I do. Now, shall we return to the others?'

'Oh dear, I see I have offended you.'

'Not at all, cousin. I shall not be in the least offended as long as we both respect each other's need to conduct our own affairs as we please. I am not quite the green girl I once was, you see.'

'Nevertheless, I would be failing in my duty if I did not try to warn you about single young men who try to make themselves indispensable…'

'To people like me? Then consider me warned, Fin. There, now you've done your duty. Feel better?'

'It pleases you to make light of my concerns, Lettie, but I would feel better if you were to come to me for help.'

'I don't need any more help, thank you, cousin. Uncle

Aspinall is the one to whom I turn for advice, and I shall continue to do so.'

'And Lord Rayne?'

'What about him?'

'Is he in your confidence, too?'

'Cousin Fin, I don't know what the navy years have done to you, but they seem to have given you leave to probe into matters that are not your concern. Now, if you're ready, we'll go and join the others. Uncle Aspinall will want to be going soon. He and Aunt Minnie are expecting guests this weekend.'

'I'm sorry you see it that way, Lettie. I have only your best interests at heart, and I have seen something of the world, you know.' When he saw that she was not about to reply to that, he continued. 'Before we rejoin the others, may I ask a favour of you on behalf of my sister?'

'Of course. Whatever can it be? Does she require a holiday?'

'Not that. It's her room, Lettie. I believe she has only one.'

'She has a bedroom, and free access to all the other rooms, as I do.'

'Yes, that's what I thought. Then I wonder if I might ask if she could be given a private room for her own personal use. Her own parlour, you understand. It would make such a difference if she could have a space to call her own. To entertain a guest, perhaps?'

'Has Gaddy asked you to speak to me?'

'No, indeed she has not. She would never complain.'

'Probably because she has so little to complain of, cousin. Sadly, I do not have any spare rooms, since we use them all every day. Of course, if you were to feel the need to contribute something towards Gaddy's upkeep, or help her with a little pin-money, perhaps? That would be much appreciated, and I'm sure she'd not refuse a small donation from time to time. Nor would I, as soon as you're in funds.'

'Ahem! Er…yes, indeed. As soon as my prize money is made available to me, I shall certainly begin to contribute towards her expenses. Gladly. You may depend on that, Cousin Lettie.'

Yes, she thought, you were not left penniless, either, when your parents died, and dear Gaddy would not be in need of my charity if you had made better provision for her before you went away.

Given a captive audience for the better part of an hour, Lieutenant Gaddestone relieved his failure with Letitia by regaling them all with an account of his successes, promotions, commendations, and future plans to buy a house here in Richmond for himself, his servants, horses and carriages *and*, he assured them, looking directly at Miss Gaddestone, for his dear sister, too.

Gaddy beamed back at him with gratitude and continued to stroke the lace edging on her sleeve. Letitia, on the other hand, was not inclined to join in the polite applause that greeted this announcement, being suddenly overtaken by the uncharitable thought that an extra room for Gaddy might easily be used for an entirely different purpose whenever the worldly Lieutenant Gaddestone needed a bed in Richmond. The more she thought about it, the more she was convinced that there could be more to his request than Gaddy's comfort, especially when he had shown so little interest in her welfare until now. As for expecting him to make a financial contribution, she was just as highly sceptical, and the small crease in her brow that had watched the departure of the carriage down Paradise Road took quite some time to disappear.

* * *

As if by arrangement, a diversion occurred to steer her thoughts away from the serious business of the morning when Lord Rayne arrived to say that two new riding horses were waiting at Sheen Court for the approval of Miss Lucille Ballantyne and Miss Maura Derwent. Already dressed in preparation for an afternoon ride, the four ladies accompanied Lord Rayne across the park, with Miss Edina Strachan looking distinctly out of sorts. Assuming that this might be because her old mount was not to be replaced by a more showy creature, Letitia had lent her the hunter to ride, though she was still visibly subdued.

The two new horses had arrived only that morning. One chestnut mare of fourteen hands, the other a dark bay gelding, both with excellent manners and breeding, as well as an interest in discovering whether their new owners would be as overweight as their previous one. 'Lady Enslack is an excellent horsewoman,' Lord Rayne told them, 'and these two are very well schooled. But they're not up to her weight, so she's letting them go. I thought you might like to try them out in the paddock. My brother and his family are eager to see how you like each other.'

Rarely had a trial passed so amicably as in those next two hours when the Elyot family joined in, and Edina, too, to practise over small jumps in the parkland beyond Sheen Court, to gallop and canter, and to accept all the help they were offered by two masters of the art. Not entirely to her liking, Letitia was guarded zealously by Lord Rayne for, without her spectacles, she was not aware of dangers in time to avoid them. Although she understood the reasons for his cautions as she leapt over hurdles and logs only a stride or two behind him, she found it both unusual and galling to be given constant warnings. What was worse, the three young Elyot children, all of them good riders, were beginning to think she was inexperienced, which was far from the case. Five-year-old Augusta loudly commiserated, having only recently been freed from the indignities of a leading-rein.

While Lord and Lady Elyot took the three young ladies back to the house for refreshments, Rayne escorted Letitia towards the stable where the two redundant mounts had been unsaddled. Stable lads and grooms carried buckets and rugs across the yard with only cursory glances in her direction, turning deaf ears to the snappy exchanges between the two as if they'd heard it often enough from Lord and Lady Elyot.

Holding her palm level with the ground, Letitia scolded. 'I've been riding since I was *so* high and I can count the times on the fingers of one hand when I've fallen off at a jump. There was simply no need for…what…where?'

Wasting no words on an answer, Rayne guided her without ceremony into the deep straw of the nearest loose box, closing the door upon the scene outside, enclosing them in the warm aroma of horses and the shadows of high barriers. She swayed against him, her feet hampered by the straw, her eyes straining to find any detail that would help her to focus before she was pulled roughly into his arms, her next spate of protests stopped.

Her mind whirled and steadied, then slowly closed down, sinking into the deep sensual place inside her that responded like fire on dry tinder at the first touch of his lips. It was not like that first time, fraught with anger and discomfort, nor was it like last night's kisses in the summerhouse, carefully regulated towards her inexperience. This time, it was as if both of them recognised the spontaneous and uncontrollable hunger for which the quarrelling was no more than a temporary release, a need that had perhaps grown during the night, directing every moment since then towards an excuse, any excuse at all, to satisfy it.

No explanations were asked or given, nor was there any time for pretence of maidenly reticence, the tenderness of the summerhouse kisses having wakened her to a vision waiting just beyond her reach, and now she was willing to be led to it without delay. But delay was inevitable in the meagre time allowed to them, and both felt the seething frustration of wanting more when their lips parted at last, leaving them trembling with the shock.

Letitia, to whom nothing like this had ever happened before, was ready to believe that Rayne would think little of it. But as in so much else regarding her knowledge of men, she was mistaken in this, too. And if she had expected some sort of flippant remark to put her at her ease, she was to make the surprising discovery that their fiercely passionate encounter had done nothing to moderate his impatience with her. Quite the contrary. Taking her by the wrists, he held her back against the high side of the loose box in an unnecessary show of restraint, as if she were an adversary instead of a lover.

'Saints alive, woman!' he whispered, harshly. 'You bring out the worst in me as well as the best. Heaven knows, I could put you across my knee. I was trying my damnedest to protect you out there, to keep you from injuring yourself. Little goose-cap!'

'I know,' she whispered. 'I know. I'm sorry.'

'And now I want to…no…no! That won't do.' Releasing his grip on her wrists, he drew them to his chest. 'That won't do at all. I'm losing my head, Lettie Boyce, and it's all your fault.'

'Tell me,' she said. 'Tell me what you wanted to do.'

His reply was slow to emerge, seeking a way. 'No, I cannot. It would not be fit talk for an innocent young lady's ears. You'd be disgusted.'

'Would I? I think I've moved on in the last few days, you know. But then, if you think I would not like it much, you're probably right, my lord. You know so much more about this kind of thing than me.' Even in the dim light, her coyness did not escape him; the tilt and turn of her head, the flutter of lashes and the untypically meek tone of voice.

'Yes, I do, minx. And when I share my *boundless* store of knowledge with you, it will not be in a stable or a summer-house, nor will there be a time limit. It will be in a bed. A large bed. And I did not say that you would not like it much, I said you would not approve of the *talk*. Once I have you in my bed, we shall be doing very little of that.'

'Oh, I see. May I be allowed to put my hat straight, please?'

Taking a step away, he watched the sinuous curve of her back and the outline of her high breasts under the habit, the reflection of light on the silvery hair resting on the collar, the graceful hands adjusting and pinning. Reaching out, he took her narrow waist in his hand, drawing her close again. 'Wayward, top-lofty creature,' he said. 'Still balking at my attempts to help, aren't you? Eh? Could you be a little less intense about protecting your independence now, do you think? You'll lose nothing by it. I want to be seen as your pro-tector, and I want *you* to be seen as my woman. Is that too much to ask?'

'No, my lord. I must try a little harder. Forgive me, I'm unused to it. And I *would* like to be seen as your woman. In fact, I think I may quite get used to the idea, in time.'

'Do you mean that?'

'Yes, really. Shall we begin again?' Meekly, she placed her hands upon his shoulders, learning to bend herself like a bow.

In view of the readjusted hat, his kiss this time was gentler. Yet in that short space of time, Letitia realised once again that the behaviour of the romantic heroes in her novels was based on imaginings with no more relevance to fact than fairy-tales, and that perhaps the reason for their success was because of her understanding of women's emotions and her ability to express them convincingly. Men, it seemed, were not as straightforward or predictable as she had believed them to be, if Lord Rayne was anything to go by.

After taking tea with the Elyots and riding back to Paradise Road with Rayne and the girls, Letitia's demeanour was so compliant and appreciative in every respect that he suspected her of intentionally overdoing it. Which she was. She had not, she told him on parting, quite got the hang of it yet. To which his reply fell some way short of the gentlemanly or the indulgent lover, though Letitia was quick to hide her smile.

Her writing that evening flowed as never before. Page after page was covered like parched ground after rain, soaking up her newest experiences, luscious with words and emotions as if her heart had slowly begun to blossom, promising fruit for the future and making her more eagerly impatient for the harvest; the next episode.

Sunday morning brought her back to earth with a crash and its usual measure of drama from Mrs Quayle next door, who came rushing round to Number 24 before Letitia had finished dressing to say that one of her charges was missing. It was Miss Edina Strachan.

'Her clothes and portmanteau are gone,' she wailed, 'without a word to anyone. How could she *do* such a thing?'

'Has her bed been slept in?' said Letitia, pushing her bare feet into slippers.

'She put a pillow into it,' said the plump little lady. 'Everything else is tidy. She's taken all her allowance, too. Where would she have gone?'

'She may have decided to go home.'

'To Guildford? To her grandparents? Oh, I don't know about that, Lettie. Why could she not have said?' Mrs Quayle's white lace morning-cap bobbed and fluttered, her face crinkled in distress as she took the artful deception as a personal affront to her hospitality.

The additional arrival of Lucille and Maura, with hair hanging loose, went some way to solving the vexed question of Edina's whereabouts. Clutching a small grey square of newsprint, they laid it down upon Letitia's counterpane and smoothed out its folds. 'We found it down by the side of her bed,' said Lucille. 'On the floor.'

'Torn out of Friday's *Morning Post*,' said Maura, with finality.

'We think it may be where—'

'Yes,' said Letitia, frowning at it. 'Thank you, girls, but we're—'

'Please read it, ma'am. We think it's quite possible she's gone to Portsmouth. Look, it gives a list of the ships that have returned to harbour in the last few days, and those that are expected.'

'And one of them is underlined. There, see? The frigate, *Centaur*.'

'Edina knows about frigates, ma'am. She told us.'

'Lots of times,' added Maura, under her breath.

Letitia took up the scrap and read it closely, her face visibly paling. 'To Portsmouth?' she whispered. 'Does she have a brother in the navy?'

Lucille was convinced otherwise. 'No, ma'am. A *lover.*'

'Oh, don't be…*what*? Would she? Could she? Surely not.'

'She doesn't have a brother,' said Mrs Quayle, 'but this could be why she's been so upset recently. Someone in the navy?'

'Yes,' said Maura, 'and she's gone to find the *Centaur*…'

'To seek the man she loves…'

'And then they'll have to elope, and…'

The story was moving too fast for Letitia. 'Thank you, girls. You've provided us with some good information here. Now you go and finish dressing for church, have your breakfast, and Mrs Quayle will join you in a few moments. Thank you for your help. We'll soon find her.'

The door closed upon the two satisfied sleuths, and the echoes of their excited chatter floated downstairs, leaving Letitia and Mrs Quayle to stare blankly at each other in some astonishment for the second consecutive Sunday.

'What's happening here?' Letitia said. 'Are we going to start losing one pupil a week? What's the matter with them? First Sapphire, now Edina. I'm not doing terribly well at keeping them, am I?'

For all her initial fluster, Mrs Quayle could see how much her friend was affected and was quick to assume her more usual practicality. 'Nonsense, dear,' she said, 'they're young girls with heads full of romance, aren't they? Now let's just sit down and think this through.' Settling herself upon Letitia's *chaise longue*, she took a deep breath. 'Today is Sunday, so she's not going to be on a stagecoach to anywhere, is she? Even if it passed through Richmond, which it doesn't. So the only thing she *could* have caught is last night's mail that picks up at Number 9 King Street after dark. That'll be the long-distance that goes from London down to Portsmouth, you know. Edina went up to bed early last night, complaining of a head. You know how off-colour she was all day yesterday. I was not too surprised. She took a cup of hot chocolate with her.' Her wide eyes expressed concern as the events began to link up.

'You didn't look in on her later?'

'Yes, I peeped in. It was dark. I saw the lump in her bed.'

'And you heard no sound? No door closing?'

'Nothing.' Mrs Quayle's lace cap flapped as she shook her head.

'Then if that's what's happened, she must have bought her ticket beforehand. As you go downstairs, tell Sam to run down to the posting office and find out who got aboard the mail to Portsmouth last night, and get them to look in the ledger for her name. I want to know what time it arrives, and the route it took.' The last few words were called out as Mrs Quayle disappeared onto the landing. 'Orla, we're going down to Portsmouth. Find us both something suitably grand and comfortable to travel in, and pack our portmanteaux for overnight.'

'Yes, ma'am.'

'But first, run down to the stables and tell Mr Benjamin that I need to speak to him immediately, if you please.'

'Yes, ma'am.'

'I'd better tell Mrs Brewster, too. See if Miss Gaddestone is about.'

'Yes, ma'am.'

'She'd better *not* be eloping,' Letitia muttered, kicking off the slippers. 'Underage and without her parents' consent. Little idiot.'

Chapter Ten

Tucking the torn-out square of newsprint into her reticule, Letitia heaved a small sigh of annoyance and turned for relief to the window of the coach where trees and hedges flew past, and approaching coaches seemed to disappear before she could see them. At least, she thought with a guilty satisfaction, this was sure to be a more comfortable ride than the one poor Edina must have endured in the mailcoach, squashed between two others, faced by three more, all probably snoring, grumbling or chattering noisily. In the darkness, there would have been nothing for her to see and only the briefest of stops to change horses.

Her own reticule, a kid bag with long straps for security, bulged with five- and one-pound notes, sovereigns and crowns, for every journey had its price. Edina's saved weekly allowances would be scarcely enough to see her through this adventure. Was that what it was? Just an adventure?

No, whatever Edina was, thought Letitia, no one could call her adventurous. Quiet and introverted, obviously unhappy, she had performed well at the concert, playing a medley of haunting Scottish airs to do with love, and the loss of it. Why had none of them seen the problem? Who was this naval man she was expecting to join? And where in Portsmouth would they be now? Or would they already have moved on? That she herself ought to have taken time to talk to Edina gave her no room for complacency, for she had been bound up in her own affairs to the detriment of her pupils. She had not noticed the smallest signs in Sapphire, either, to her shame.

'Why are we stopping?' she said to Orla.

'It's a tollgate, ma'am.'

A small thatched building appeared by the side of the road where a stout gate barred the way. Touching his cap in deference, the tollgate keeper approached the window. This was a superior conveyance, its occupants sure to be gentry with a pair of high-stepping greys like those.

Letitia let the window down. 'Good morning. How much?'

'For a town coach and pair, m'lady,' said the man, casting an eye over the gleaming panels and shining brass lamps, 'that'll be ninepence.'

'That will take us through the next one, too, will it?'

'Through the next two, m'lady,' he said, scribbling the details of the transaction on to his pad of tickets. 'Going far, are ye?'

'To Portsmouth,' she replied, passing him a handful of coins. 'Give the ticket to my groom on the rumble-seat, if you please.'

'Very good, m'lady. Not a lot of traffic today. Pleasant journey to ye.' With a wink at Letitia's pretty maid, he passed the ticket to the groom and went to open the gate, watching in admiration as the chariot swept past at a smart trot.

Letitia sat back against the soft upholstered seat and packed a cushion under her elbow while Orla pulled the window up with the leather strap. There were no seats opposite, only a slatted blind through which they could just make out the shape of the coachman's high box-seat. The large side-windows were curtained, fringed and tasselled, the floor carpeted and clean, a far cry from the functional crowded mailcoach. With so light a load, the pair of greys would make better speed than the team of six needed to draw the heavy mail with its many passengers and all their luggage. Although it would pay no toll, its horses were changed every ten miles or so. Edina's man, whoever he was, must be worth it for her to suffer willingly so much discomfort for his sake, Letitia thought.

Earlier, Sam had returned from the posting office in Richmond bearing the news that Miss Strachan's name was in the ledger and that her ticket to Portsmouth, bought on Saturday morning, had cost her twenty-five shillings, which she must have saved for weeks, if not months. How, Mrs Quayle had asked, was Edina going to pay for any accommodation except of the meanest sort? Miss Gaddestone did not think Edina would have thought that far ahead. Nor did Letitia.

Nevertheless, in spite of the concern, the guilt, and the sympathy that invaded Letitia's peace of mind, there remained the more unsentimental prospect of being able to observe Edina's determination and courage to join the man she loved at any price, and to use those observations in Perdita's story. One way or another, Letitia did not intend this experience to be entirely wasted on a wild goose chase to rescue a young lady who would probably not thank them for rescuing her.

A large part of the journey was taken up with thoughts about her own gradually mellowing relationship with Lord Rayne, the man she had been quite adamant she could never grow to like. There was no doubt that she was playing a very dangerous game by allowing herself to respond to him, for although she had intended it to be a device by which she might regain control of a difficult situation, the truth of the matter was that her heart had already begun to take the lead, leaving her head to catch up as best it may.

Asked if she was becoming addicted to the need of him, she would have refuted the suggestion hotly. Asked if she was falling in love, she would have scoffed at the idea. Wasn't love supposed to be deliciously comfortable, and weren't lovers supposed to be starry-eyed and agreeable? No, this thinking of him, past, present and future, could not be love, for the two of them had rarely agreed on anything except during those magically intimate moments.

The journey that would have taken the mail about six hours took the competent Mr Benjamin less than five, including two stops to change horses and to refresh herself and Orla. The first stop was at the Kings Arms at Godalming where Mr Moon the proprietor bowed and scraped, giving orders that only the soundest pair be put to the splendid town coach with the black-and-yellow wheels. Likewise at the Dolphin at Petersfield where the ostlers vied for the honour of harnessing the new pair and for pocketing Letitia's generous tip.

The long five-mile drag to the top of Butser Hill was fatiguing even for fresh horses, and Letitia insisted on a rest at the top from where they could see beyond the steep sloping sides as far as Portsmouth harbour, the Isle of Wight, and the open silver sea in the furthest distance. Ten more miles took them downhill to Horndean and another rest before the last eight miles to Portsmouth itself by mid-afternoon.

Larger by far than Richmond, the town had expanded as a port and naval base beyond the old fortifications that surrounded the old parts like a girdle. In the town centre, the narrow streets thronged with navy men of every rank, with merchants and suppliers, dock labourers and shrieking women, rumbling wagons, yapping dogs and the incessant cry of seagulls wheeling over masts and rooftops.

Mr Benjamin drove the coach straight down the High Street to the town's best hotel, the George, where Lord Nelson had stayed briefly in 1805. Hardly had Letitia's feet touched the cobbled courtyard before the innkeeper and his white-aproned wife were there to greet her, offering their best room and a private parlour, and a meal as soon as she was ready. One glance at the equipage, at her fur-trimmed pelisse and matching grey silk bonnet, not to mention the liveried groom and pretty maid, told them all they needed to know about the status of their guest.

The enclosed yard swarmed with ostlers and stable boys, horses and carriages, echoing with the clank of buckets, shouts and whistles, the clatter of hooves. Inside the comfortable low-beamed inn, the warmth was heavy with wood and tobacco smoke. The aroma of roast beef reminded the two women that they had missed Sunday lunch at Paradise Road that day. Housemaids and bootboys scurried past, doors opened and closed, bells rang, voices called, porters staggered over luggage and waiters swayed under trays held above their heads. Up a flight of polished stairs, they were led along a creaking passage to the door of a sizeable panelled bedroom, where mullioned windows looked out across the peaceful vegetable garden at the rear of the house next door.

'It's much too noisy at the front, ma'am,' said the landlord's wife, opening a small door in the corner of the room that gave them a glimpse of a small chamber with a narrow bed by the wall. 'Here's your maid's room and a closet for your clothes,' she said, beaming, proud of the extra facility. 'Your parlour is downstairs, ma'am, and the lad will be here with your bags at any moment. Shall I have a tea-tray sent up?' Nothing, it seemed, was going to be too much trouble.

A cup of tea was all there was time for, however, Letitia being determined not to waste a moment on creature comforts while Edina was adrift in a place like Portsmouth at the weekend, with dangers from every quarter. It was one thing, she said to Orla between sips, for them to be snugly protected in the town's best hotel, but it would be quite a different story for a lone young woman with very little money in her reticule.

Edina's parents and grandparents would have been frantic with worry, if they had known, but Letitia had decided that for them to be told at this stage would not help matters, since there was nothing that either set of relatives could do that she herself could not do more efficiently. Besides, it would take days for a message to reach her parents in Scotland.

Their first duty, she said, was to go out and search while there was still enough light before sunset, and a message was sent to Jamie, the groom, to meet them downstairs. He was a Portsmouth lad and would know where to go. He also had a soft spot for Orla.

Letitia had anticipated this moment, if not with dread, then with no pleasure, either, never having put a foot over the threshold of a tavern in her life, but having a fair idea of what to expect. With this in mind, she saw an advantage in changing from her elegant fur-trimmed pelisse to a very plain ser-viceable brown one with a straw poke-bonnet that would help to shield her face from insolent stares. Tying a long scarf round her bare neck, she regarded herself in the mirror, hoping to see nothing remarkable that would attract anyone's attention, yet respectable enough to show a woman of breeding with her maid and manservant. The plain gold spectacles, which would have been so useful to her on this occasion, went on and came off twice before being stowed away with most of the money she had brought. If she wished to avoid attracting attention, the spectacles were definitely not the accessory to wear.

The next two uncomfortable hours opened Letitia's eyes to the seamier side of Portsmouth life as she trawled through one inn after another, and some of the many boarding-houses, too, that were situated along the waterfront and in the narrow back streets. At this time of the weekend, the town appeared to be overflowing with guests come here to meet people off the ships or to deliver them, and although Orla and Jamie did much of the visual searching for her, the enquiries were left to her. But no one remembered seeing a young lady answering to Miss Edina Strachan's description, and while some replies were politely sympathetic, others were suspicious and rude, or asked a deal too many personal questions that had more to do with Letitia herself than with Edina. Verbally, she was well able to hold her own, but the relentless innuendo, intimidation and sly suggestions began to take the polished edge off her natural good manners, and she could hardly wait to sit a while and regain her temper.

After the first disappointing hour, Jamie had a suggestion to make. 'Do we know for certain whether the *Centaur* has arrived yet, ma'am? Has Miss Strachan's man actually signed off, or is he still expected?'

'I don't really know,' she replied, turning her head away

from the lewd remarks of a passing bunch of sailors. 'I'm assuming it will have docked. How do we find out for sure?'

The intrepid Jamie had the answer and, after disappearing into a noisily crowded tavern across the road, came bounding out a few minutes later with his hat in his hand and his hair ruffled. 'The *Centaur* came in last Thursday, ma'am. All the young midshipmen are in there.' He tipped his head towards the screams of laughter and the screech of a fiddle. 'But there's one who's gone off with a woman.'

'Gone? Missing, you mean? Absconded?'

'They won't know for certain until tomorrow, ma'am. But the woman he's with is a local lass, so he's probably not Miss Strachan's young man. Of course, her man might be a lieutenant or some other rank, but these chaps don't know much about what lieutenants get up to while they're ashore.'

'Then it looks as if we shall have to keep on searching, Jamie. Now, which of the inns have we not seen yet?'

'It's getting late, ma'am,' said Orla. 'Would you not prefer to eat and take a rest, and continue at first light tomorrow?'

'There's still some light left,' said Letitia, looking across at the dark shapes of boats and masts swaying gently on a mirror of apricot pink. Deeply troubled, she did not see how she could abandon the search knowing that Edina would face a night in this dreadful place, probably alone. 'Let's just walk up here. Where are we now, Jamie?'

'This is Broad Street, ma'am. It leads up to The Point.'

'One last try, then. We may just be lucky.'

Jamie and Orla exchanged a troubled glance, neither of them daring to suggest that Portsmouth Point was not the place for a respectable woman to be seen on a Sunday evening. Certain taverns were where men were paid their week's wages and, in spite of the laws against Sunday trading, those wages were all too easily liquefied, gambled away, stolen or paid to prostitutes. The Point was a curved spur of property-covered land from where the watermen ferried husbands and lovers to their ships after last farewells. To Letitia, it seemed to be worth her making another effort before darkness fell, for the idea of abandoning a genteel young woman to her fate might be the stuff of romantic novels, but had little to do with reality.

Predictably, the narrow street was already crowded, every door spilling out bawling women, children, dogs and drunks, rollicking and rolling towards the gap between buildings where could be seen the tall sails and the rigging of ships, rocking and rattling in the breeze. Small boats swarmed round them like flies, their occupants waving to children weeping in their mothers' arms and to women clutching at their bonnets.

'Surely this is not where she'll be, ma'am,' said Orla.

'She may be,' Letitia insisted. 'I have to go and see.'

The Ship Tavern was on one side, Moses Levy the Money-lender on the other, between the two an open space where a wooden-legged man scraped a fiddle for a jolly couple to dance to, porters heaved trunks, and a young woman was being carried out by two sailors in white trousers and blue jackets.

'That's her!' Letitia cried, making a dash towards the group.

But it was not her, only an unconscious girl of the same age.

'Where are you taking her?' she asked the one whose hands were hooked under the girl's limp arms.

'Home, ma'am,' he said. 'She's me sister.'

Letitia turned away, not knowing whether it was the truth or a lie. 'Will you take a look in there, Jamie? Or shall I go in? I will, if you prefer to stay here with Orla.'

'Lawks, no, ma'am, you ain't going in there. Here, you sit on this barrel, both of you, while I go inside.' Confidently, he strode off.

Sitting in the doorway of a fruit and vegetable shop, a woman smoking a clay pipe held their attention for a while before a loud burst of laughter from the door of the Ship made them turn in alarm. A crowd of sailors tumbled out on to the cobbles, each of them supported by women whose state of undress left Letitia and Orla in no doubt of their profession. Before either of them could move away, the boisterous mob surrounded the barrels, using them as convenient couches upon which to fall back with screams of delight, one couple landing across Letitia and using her lap as a pillow.

Furiously, she struggled to extricate herself, shouting in anger at the stinking half-naked woman and her cursing mate, tipping them off on to the floor in a tangle of limbs over which she had to clamber to be free. Sickened by the stink and obscenities, she kicked out at the grasping hands and turned to see Orla being wrestled backwards on to the barrel by a leering drunk whose stained white trousers were being hauled down by one of his mates. Hurling herself at the man, Letitia knocked him easily off balance, giving Orla just enough time to straighten up and roll away, clasping at the bodice of her gown. Then, holding hands, they hared down the street the way they had come, just as Jamie emerged from the tavern.

That experience was enough to convince them that their search would have to be resumed in daylight hours, for there was no more they could do that night. Edina was nowhere to be found on Portsmouth Point, nor did they encounter anyone who had seen her. It was hardly surprising in a town so packed with people intent on spending their Sunday in a state of self-induced forgetfulness.

By the time they reached the George Hotel, the shallow bay windows were ablaze with light, and the aroma of cooking and pipe smoke wafted out and mingled with the cool evening air. Even now, more guests were arriving, arguing over rooms, tripping over baggage, shouting orders, bumping into each other, some good-humouredly, others less so.

Exhausted and upset, despondent, hungry, worried and unsure about how best to proceed, Letitia was not even certain that Edina was actually in Portsmouth at all. Sending Jamie off with thanks and a hefty tip, she told him to go and eat with Mr Benjamin in their lodgings and to return in the morning for instructions, after which she followed Orla wearily up the stairs to their room, where the lure of a strange bed and an evening spent in her own sad company was strangely unappealing.

In the shadowy passageway opposite her door, a tall man stood with one shoulder leaning idly on the oak panelling, reading a newspaper. With a flutter of irritation, Letitia knew that they would have to speak to him to pass, and had just begun to wonder if they could sneak like children underneath the expanse of newspaper without setting fire to it when it began to lower, very slowly, revealing a tall beaver hat and then the face of the reader.

For one heart-stopping moment, she thought her eyes and the shadows must be playing tricks as a result of her tiredness. Disbelieving, she moved closer, seeing Orla dip a quick curtsy before unlocking the door, glance back at her mistress, and disappear inside. The shadowy face was exposed as the hat was lifted, his eyes lighting with laughter as the newspaper dropped to the floor, his arms reaching for her across one long ground-covering stride. 'Lettie!' he whispered.

'Oh! It *cannot* be. Can it?'

Without a single thought for either plans or propriety, she clung to his shoulders, curving into his hard comforting embrace as if he was the ultimate solution to every one of her cares, the one on to whom she could unload all she had carried since that morning, and before.

'Rayne…my lord…you're here,' was all she could manage to mumble as her mouth lifted to seek his, to take like a hungry fledgling all he had saved for that moment. Clinging, laughing, breathless with relief, they swayed gently like reeds, completely blocking the passage and quite oblivious to the clearing of throats that denoted a shocked disapproval. Eventually, Rayne's shoulder was tapped, turning him abruptly with an apology at the ready.

But this time the outraged expression behind them was too close for the shadows to hide, the tall feathers in the turban, the trembling feather boa around the shoulders too distinctive to cause any uncertainty. The voice yelped with malice.

'*Letitia!*'

'Aunt Minnie? Oh!' Letitia rested a hand on Rayne's arm for support.

Aunt Minnie yelped again, glaring at him, at her niece's possessive hand, then again at his face. 'Lord Rayne! What *am* I seeing here? Am I to believe my eyes?'

Coolly, with a slight lift of one eyebrow, Rayne placed a hand deliberately over Letitia's. 'Well now, Lady Aspinall, that would depend very much upon what your eyes have told you, wouldn't it? Are you staying at the George, too, or have you come especially to see us?'

Aunt Minnie gasped at the insolence. 'Young man,' she scolded, 'I did not come here to be questioned. You, however, have some answers to provide, and they had better be satisfactory, for it seems to me that this is just the kind of vulgar behaviour that only—'

'Aunt Minnie!' snapped Letitia. 'Lord Rayne and I have no intention of discussing anything with you in a passageway. If you will oblige us by stepping inside our room, we can perhaps speak in private. I've had a long and tiring day.'

The large hand squeezed hers, taking over. 'And Miss Boyce needs to rest and eat. After you, my lady.' Opening the door, he stepped aside and allowed her to sweep past him like a schooner in full sail. 'Leave it to me,' he whispered in Letitia's ear. 'You said *our* room.'

'I know I did,' she whispered back.

'She thinks we're…' He closed the door.

Aunt Minnie had not a moment to lose. Although turned fifty, she knew what she had seen, and heard. 'There can be absolutely no shadow of doubt,' she said, taking the centre of the room after a glance at the large double bed, 'that you have completely overstepped the bounds of common decency, Letitia, and you must now both—'

'Just a minute!' said Rayne in a voice that owed much to his years of commanding unruly young men. 'There is no one, I repeat, *no one* who will tell either of us what we must do. Or what we must not do. I hope that is clear, Lady Aspinall. Whatever you may think, we do not owe you an explanation for the greeting you saw just now. Miss Boyce is quite exhausted, having spent several hours looking round the town, and her relief at seeing me is perfectly understandable. It may not be what you are used to seeing, but times change.'

'And I suppose you are about to tell me that you're simply the best of friends, and there is no understanding between you.'

'None whatsoever,' said Rayne, emphatically.

'None whatsoever,' repeated Letitia, ignoring the quick squeeze on her captured hand. 'Between a mistress and her lover there is no requirement for an understanding of the kind you mean, Aunt Minnie. Lawks, but you're sadly out of time with such matters, you know. You'll be expecting me to wear a ring next, I suppose?' She felt Rayne's reaction through the briefest tightening of his fingers but, to his great credit, not even by the flicker of an eyelid did he betray the slightest astonishment at her unexpected announcement.

'You appear to be lost for words, Lady Aspinall,' he said. 'Is this a sudden affliction, or have we said something to cause you embarrassment? Surely there were such things as mistresses and their lovers amongst your ancestors, were there not? There are amongst my own, even in my generation. Let me see now, my brother *and* sister, father, mother, countless uncles and—'

'Stop! This is not a boasting matter, Lord Rayne. It's *outrageous*!'

'Of course it's not outrageous, Aunt Minnie,' said Letitia, crossly, finding that Rayne's solid presence beside her gave her the courage to speak her mind as she had never quite dared to do before, not even with Uncle Aspinall standing by. 'It's no good you telling me how different I am, how I never conform, how I don't fit in, and then getting all upset when I run true to form, is it? Will you and Mama never understand that you have forfeited any right to tell me how to run my life? When have *you* ever offered me support and approval instead of criticism and predictions of failure?

When have either of you ever sought my company just for the sake of it, as Lord Rayne has? Uncle Aspinall has, but not you, nor Mama, either. If ever I need any help, it will not be to you I turn, but to my lover, the only one apart from my sisters and a few others who would come to my aid even before I asked it.

'I didn't know Lord Rayne was coming, but he came, and I was overjoyed to see him. That was what you witnessed, Aunt. You would not know much about joy, would you? You would mistake it for outrageous behaviour. Well, call it what you like. I've had more kindnesses from Lord Rayne in one month than I've had from you since I was born. I had almost forgot how to tell kindness from interference, would you believe?' Her voice shook and wavered on a rising note close to hysteria that reflected the pressures of the day, the dreadful hours of searching, and now this. Suddenly, she felt weak and overcome by exhaustion, almost on the verge of tears.

'Enough, sweetheart,' said Rayne, placing an arm around her as only a lover would. 'Come and sit over here. Shall Orla order some dinner now? Is it not time we were eating?'

Letitia nodded, croaking a 'yes'. Orla curtsied and left the room.

'May I ask,' Rayne said to the dumbfounded aunt, 'whether Sir Penfold has accompanied you to Portsmouth, my lady?'

His question was redundant, for Orla had doubled back to knock on her mistress's door and to admit the gentleman in question. 'Sir Penfold Aspinall, ma'am,' she said, wishing she could stay to hear the rest.

The benevolent uncle took in the scene at a glance, his wife's high colour, her rigid posture, her most unusual silence and Letitia's sparkling eyes, a sure sign that she was up on the high ropes. 'Lettie, love,' he said. 'My lord, how d'ye do? Minnie, is it not time you were in our room preparing for dinner? I shall be ready to eat in a matter of minutes. Come on.'

Aunt Minnie thought there was something he should understand first. 'Aspinall,' she said. 'Letitia has had the impertinence to inform me that she is now Lord Rayne's mistress. There. What d'ye have to say to *that*?'

'What do you expect me to say, woman?' Holding out his hand to Rayne, he shook it in hearty congratulation. 'Well done, m'boy. Lettie needs a man of your ilk. Lettie, m'dear, you'll do well enough with Rayne. He's had plenty of practice. We'll talk tomorrow, eh?'

'Thank you, Uncle,' Letitia whispered, choosing not to comment on the practice Rayne had had, compared to her own. 'I'm glad *you're* not shocked.'

'Not a bit of it, love. Your aunt and I have to go and meet some friends off the *Primrose* tomorrow, as soon as she docks. They're coming back to London to stay with us a while, but we won't return home without seeing you again. Come on, Minnie lass. You're not needed here, and my stomach thinks my throat's been cut. Goodnight, you two.' Herding his very vexed wife like a stray sheep, he left as suddenly as he had arrived with a last smiling nod at his niece and a wink at her new lover.

Letitia discovered that she was trembling as she recalled the many times she had longed to speak to Aunt Minnie like that, but had never been able to summon enough courage. It would not have been worth the censure that would have come her way. With Rayne's support, that did not seem to matter.

'What have I done?' she whispered. 'What must you be thinking of me? That was a most unladylike thing to say.'

Rayne knew she was not talking about Lady Aspinall.

'You wonder what I think of you, Miss Boyce?' he said, moving away from the door. 'Well, first, that you are a never-ending source of delightful surprises, and second that you look all in. Come here, my splendid creature.' He leaned towards her and hooked his hands under her arms more lovingly than the sailor with his sister, easing her up to him, supporting her, feeling her unsteadiness in his arms. 'Straight from the heart,' he said, softly. 'There's nothing fake about you, is there, my beauty? Eh? You came straight to me like a bird, didn't you?'

'I've put you in a very difficult position,' she said, smoothing the lapel of his dark blue coat. 'It seemed to be the best way of avoiding all the dust she would have kicked up. But if you think I should not…'

'I think you should have said it sooner,' he said, laughing, 'but better late than never. I *did* mention it before, you know. Only two days ago.'

'Yes, I know.'

'And I said then that it was probably the most effective way of keeping the relatives quiet. Look what happened to your aunt just now. She was struck dumb. Have you ever seen that before?'

'Only with you there. Do you know, I think it might work. Would it be too much of a nuisance to you, my lord? You don't have to *be* my lover in every sense, you know, just because I said that. I really didn't mean… Oh, dear, this is so indelicate.'

'Lettie Boyce, listen to me. Between a man and his mistress there is nothing too indelicate to talk about. That's one of the advantages. There are no obligations or constraints that cannot be discussed, and I'm certainly not about to throw you on the bed and make violent love to you. That's for when you tell

me you're ready, in your own good time. It was my recom-
mendation, remember, that we should place you on a different level of society where you can be yourself more fully. And
that's exactly what this will do. What's more, I'm going to
enjoy helping you to stay there. We're going to see a more
confident Miss Boyce, a woman of distinction. That's what
I've been searching for, for years. A woman of distinction.'

As fleet as a hare in the night, the thought crossed her mind
that this was what she also had been searching for since she
began writing, not only for a way to rejoin society without her
mother's constant carping to spoil it, but also to provide her
with the kind of intimate experience that the heroines of novels
acquire when they take lovers. Which they always do. Whether
she agreed with him about wanting to make love at that precise
moment was a question that caused a slight hesitation. She had
never seen him more handsomely dressed in skin-tight
doeskins and matching waistcoat, and his hands warmly en-
circling her bodice left a memory behind of how once, just
once, they had strayed to more private places.

'Then that is what I shall endeavour to be, my lord, since
you have been good enough to come to my aid more than
once. It was true, you know, what I said to her.'

'About the kindnesses? Then she must have been excessively
uncivil to her lovely niece. But no matter. We don't need her.'
Taking her by the hand, he led her to the window-seat and sat
beside her. 'Now, I think you'd better tell me all about this pupil
of yours who is so eager to escape. Where have you searched?'

As concisely as she could, she told him of the fruitless enquiries, omitting the fracas outside the Ship, which she knew
would only earn her a scolding. She might have known that
he would look for her at church, and that Gaddy would tell

him, but she had not expected him to follow her in his own post-chaise, or to find her so quickly. He really was, she thought, proving to be the kind of stuff of which romantic heroes are made, even if the rather excessive dominance was more comfortable on the written page than in reality.

An hour later, with Orla's help, Letitia was refreshed, clean, and looking more her usual self in a pretty white muslin gown under a pale blue sleeveless pelisse for extra warmth. A Paisley shawl was thrown around her shoulders as she went down to the private parlour, which she had offered to share with Lord Rayne.

'Do mistresses float about in dressing gowns?' she said, mischievously. 'If so, I shall be a sad disappointment to you. I've rarely had any cause to float.'

Rayne led her to the table and pulled out a chair. 'Invariably,' he said. 'Floating while in a state of undress is one of the prime requirements of a mistress. You have my word on it. I shall overlook it on this occasion, however, since the new position has taken us both unawares, but I shall expect you to practise your floating, in or out of a negligee, as soon as we return.'

'Very well, my lord,' she said, demurely. 'What's for dinner?'

He reached across the white linen tablecloth to take her hand, making her look at him and to see in his eyes a very personal answer to her question. Roaming over her, they rested on the pile of pale hair bound with blue ribbons and caressed the creamy skin of her neck and bosom, returning to her own flint-grey eyes framed with long lashes, the perfect half-moon lids, the fine arch of her brows. She could hardly fail to understand his silence or the gentle pressure of his fingers.

But he knew, as she had expected him to, how concerned

she was for her missing pupil and the dangers she would be facing, and that for them to rest here in comfort while Edina was still at large was not why they had come. They had already agreed on that.

'I shall take no more than a bite before I go into town. You will stay here and finish your meal and, if it grows late and I have still not returned, you will go to bed. When I find her, I'll bring her straight to you, whatever time it is. Don't wait up for me.'

'Come and tell me when you return, even if you return alone.'

'If it will make you more comfortable, I will.'

'Thank you. We can start looking again tomorrow.'

He smiled. 'Talking about looking....' He reached for a package that lay on the table. 'I think you may find this useful.'

It was wrapped in brown paper. 'A telescope? Like Lord Nelson's?'

'Not a telescope. Better than that.'

Inside the wrapping were two cases, one of engraved silver and mother-of-pearl, the other of green snakeskin edged with bands of gold. She knew instantly what they contained, for they were just of the size to hold folding spectacles, one pair of silver oblong-framed glasses with adjustable sliding arms, the other pair of gold with folding arms and diamonds set on the outer edges. Both of them were pretty enough to be worn with evening dress, delicate, modish and expensive.

'Oh, my lord! These are truly the most *beautiful*, the prettiest...'

'For the new Lettie Boyce. For indoors and out.'

'Yes, oh, yes *indeed*.' Putting on the silver pair, she stared at him with an innocent twinkle in her bright eyes. 'Is this distinctive enough?'

'Stunning. Are they going to fit? I can have them altered.'

'They fit perfectly. Now the others.'

The gold pair were oval and, with a movement of her head, caught a flash of blue-white light across the diamonds, creating the opposite effect from the plain steel frames she had worn before in public. These were quite unique, speaking of high fashion that only a few would be able to emulate.

'They're *very* good,' she said. 'I can see much better than with my others. I shall wear them all the time. Thank you, my lord. You are the kindest of men.'

'Not odious now?'

They rose and came round the table to meet each other and to melt in an embrace, which appeared to be all he wanted by way of thanks, though Letitia suffered a pang of guilt at the strangeness of it all. 'No one has ever given me anything like this before. Ought I to be accepting gifts of this nature?'

'If my mistress wants to see what she's doing,' he said, 'I would say she ought. Otherwise she's going to miss half the fun.'

'And if she wants to see what her lover is doing?'

'Then of course she should remove them and place them somewhere safe, until later. And while we're about it, I remember that we were rudely interrupted.'

Their kiss, continued from the one in the passageway, was destined not to be allowed to run its course, for the knock on the door had to be answered, and the waiters had to set the steaming dishes upon the dinner table.

Chapter Eleven

It was well past midnight when Letitia heard the tap on her door for which every nerve had been straining for the last six hours. She was at the door in one bound, tying her robe and peering into the dim passageway with a gasp of relief. 'Come inside,' she whispered to the two dark figures, one swathed in a pale greatcoat, the other leaning heavily on his arm, wearing a shawl over her crumpled day dress and spencer.

She might still have been taken for a young lady of quality, but the ravages of the last twenty-four hours were easily definable, especially on the drawn face. Even so, a glance from the expressive brown eyes showed how much she had longed for this moment.

'You should not have waited up,' Rayne said, closing the door.

'I had to. Where did you find her?' Letitia drew Edina forward and untied her bonnet. 'Come over here, love. Orla, go down to the kitchen and have a bowl of soup sent up. Some bread, too. And a jug of hot water. Is there any luggage?'

'I have her portmanteau here, luckily. Two women were trying to part her from it. I had to pay them to let it go.'

'Sorry,' Edina's voice wavered. 'I never meant this to happen.' Her eyes welled with tears, and Letitia felt the exhausted weight of her in the homecoming embrace. Then, remembering her dignity and Lord Rayne's presence in a lady's room, Edina turned and held out her hand to him. 'Thank you, my lord. I shall pay—'

'Miss Strachan, I *am* paid back, just to see you safe again. I shall leave you to tell Miss Boyce what happened, but first you should allow her to tend you. This is the moment she's waited for all day. I shall see you downstairs at breakfast, ma'am.' The candle flame shone across his features, showing Letitia the rather impudent lift of one eyebrow and the smile mingled with tiredness, the meaning of which went far beyond the formalities. 'Goodnight, Miss Boyce,' he said.

'Goodnight, Lord Rayne. We are both so very grateful to you.'

'Glad to have been of service, ma'am.'

'Eight o'clock breakfast?'

He bowed, catching her eye with a smile before he left.

Aware that a volley of questions would be inappropriate, nevertheless she allowed herself just two. 'Where were you?' she said, removing Edina's bonnet. 'Did you find a place to stay?'

'When Lord Rayne found me, I was at the Dolphin just a few yards up the High Street. I didn't have a room there. I was looking for…' The explanation faltered as a sob caught in her throat.

'The Dolphin? But that's a respectable inn.' Quickly, Letitia realised that the surprise in her voice was giving the wrong impression. 'I mean, did you expect to find somebody there?'

'It was a last resort,' Edina sobbed, with tears rolling freely down her face. 'I'd looked everywhere else. I found his mates in one of the taverns. They said he'd gone off with a local girl. I couldn't believe it. He must have known I'd be here to meet him. It's been six months, ma'am. So I went looking for him. All day, all night.' She seemed to assume Letitia would know that a young man was involved.

'Even though he'd found someone else?' Letitia knelt in front of her, taking the cold hands into hers. 'You wanted to find both of them together?'

'Yes, I wanted to see what she had that I lack. It's just as well that I didn't, or I might have torn her to *pieces*! Him, too.' The Scottish burr seemed somehow appropriate to the unlady-like threat of mutilation on such a scale, the rolling R's and the cutting *pieces*, the fierce Scottish passion. The poor girl, whoever she was, would have stood little chance against Edina in this mood.

To Letitia, this was a revelation. The quietly mannered Miss Strachan had not whimpered off like a scolded pup, but had scoured the town from end to end, angry, unhappy, and not willing to let go without a fight. All that, after weeks of despair. How terrible was this thing called love. What pain it could cause. Taking Edina into her arms, she rocked her like a mother and was mildly surprised to find how she softened before the storm of weeping overtook her, shaking the sixteen-year-old body with rasping sobs. 'Hush now, shh…!' she crooned. 'You're safe and unharmed, and what's done is done. We'll talk more about it later. Have you eaten?'

'Not since the last coach-stop. My money ran out.'

'And no sleep last night, I suppose. Come on, love. Take off these clothes. We'll soon have you comfortable again.'

Hot water and clean clothes, food, warmth and rest were plied within the next hour, at the end of which Edina lay like a child deep within half of the great bed, fast falling into sleep. Instead of adding to her wardrobe as the others had done, she had saved her allowance week by week, with this scheme in mind. During the previous hour, it had emerged that the errant young man was a naval recruit she had met while staying at Guildford with her grandparents. On parting, they had promised to write and eventually to go across to France where they could be married without parental consent, apparently not seeing England's hostilities with France as any barrier to this plan. It was this illicit correspondence that had kept Edina's spirits up, but when it was discovered, she was sent off to Richmond to get over her infatuation.

Letitia was slow to fall asleep, her mind buzzing uncomfortably with thoughts of Edina's unhappiness and how it ought to have been recognised before it came to this. On a more positive note, she had not understood until now how such a tangle could affect a young woman of Edina's calibre, a sturdy no-nonsense Scot whose heart was both wounded and insulted by a man's treachery, who could turn that affection so immediately into a furious energy great enough to sustain her through hours of humiliation and searching. She had shown a passion and courage none of them had thought her capable of, and now it remained to be seen whether she would stumble into John Bunyan's 'slough of despond'. Meanwhile, Letitia decided on some therapy.

* * *

Over breakfast in the cosy parlour, Lord Rayne supplied more details of his search that had taken him into every stinking tavern, only to end at the upper-class Dolphin Inn because, like Edina, he believed it to be a last resort.

Removing the top off her boiled egg, Letitia dipped a finger of toast into the yolk. 'I wonder if we might stay another day here,' she said. 'I have a mind to take Edina and Orla shopping for a few things.' The winsome smile indicated that this would include a tour of the local haberdashers and milliners.

'Of course. We can return tomorrow, if you wish.'

'What about your obligations at the barracks?'

'That's not a concern. There are others to take over while I'm away. I saw your uncle just now. He asked me to go with him to the Crown this morning. It's known here as the Navy House because the officers go to eat there. It's where he's arranged to meet his friends.'

'Aunt Minnie will probably spend the morning in her room. Do you know, I think we've shocked her so badly she may never recover.'

'Your uncle, on the other hand, feels quite the reverse. He thinks I am exactly what you need.'

'Uncle Aspinall is *usually* right,' she said, frowning at the toast before she bit at it, 'but not *invariably*. Still, I have his approval so I shall not be too concerned about anyone else's. Particularly now that I can see what I'm doing.'

'They look enchanting, Miss Boyce.'

'Thank you, sir. Orla likes them, too. And Miss Strachan.' She had already received several admiring stares on the way down to breakfast, and the thought of being able to see the entire contents of a shop instead of a blur of colours made her as excited as a child at Christmas.

After taking her breakfast in bed and borrowing some of Letitia's clothes, Edina and her two chaperons stepped out of the George into the High Street. Her parents and grandparents, she told Letitia, would have punished her severely instead of taking her out shopping. Although her pride had taken a battering, the previous day's fury had abated and, after some discussion, she was ready to accept that plans made at sixteen were not always the most permanent.

With her heroine Perdita in mind, Letitia observed with some interest the phases of emotion through which her pupil passed, noting how they were never far from the surface even while out shopping. Walking out of the Fabric Emporium after choosing dress lengths for all three of them, Letitia was stopped abruptly by Edina's hand on her arm. 'There…look, ma'am! Over there. Those two at the back.'

Through her new spectacles, Letitia could see across the promenade to where a young sailor was running to join a chastened group of midshipmen being jollied along by two lieutenants towards the place where a boat was moored at the wall steps. The sailor was trying to fend off a dishevelled girl, who clearly had not appreciated that her role had become redundant at the Monday-morning round-up. The young man bawled at her and she fell back, and Letitia saw the anguish on Edina's face at the public rebuff, as if it had happened to her, too.

The girl appeared to be the same age as Edina, and as pretty. 'That's him, ma'am. Shall I go to her?' Edina whispered, clutching at Letitia's arm, the previous intention to tear her limb from limb having, in that single moment, changed to compassion. Now, her only thought was to comfort her.

'I think it might be best,' Letitia said, 'if you did not. She may be even more hurt to know that there was someone else, or that she's being pitied. She will have friends somewhere. Look there. Behind. Two others are going to her.'

'Yes, but I wonder if—'

'Let it go, Miss Strachan,' said Orla from her other side. 'She'll not thank you for interfering. And there's better young men than that.'

It was not the usual way of things for a lady's maid of Orla's years to offer advice unasked, but nor was the relationship in the usual way of things, either, and Letitia was glad of her maid's support at a time like this. 'Shall we go to that art emporium next to our hotel?' Letitia said, gently drawing Edina away. 'You need some more brushes and paints, and that place is much better stocked than the little one in Richmond.'

Half an hour later, they emerged with smiles of satisfaction and several parcels carried by Jamie, for Letitia knew that Edina's watercolour box was a shabby old hand-me-down, not one to be proud of. Finding one with compartments for everything, wrapped cakes of paint, squirrel-hair brushes, pencils, palettes and water-bottles, Letitia bought it for her grateful pupil with a brief show of tears that were for pleasure, as well as pain and pity. Guilt, too, on Letitia's part, for she knew that this indulgence was partly to make amends for her previous neglect. In addition to that, Edina's artistic ability was superior to any of the others.

* * *

That evening, when Edina was in bed, Letitia and Lord Rayne were able to spend some time together in the parlour where they could decide what to do about her. 'She has pleaded not to be sent home,' Letitia said, snuggling into the angle of his arm. 'What am I to do?'

'Respect her wishes. It's hardly likely to happen again, is it?'

'The mailcoach ride alone was enough to determine that.'

'And neither parents nor grandparents are likely to find out.'

'No.'

'And she doesn't want to call at Guildford on the way back?'

'No, that would invite questions. She wants to return to Richmond.'

'With her box of paints and dress lengths and heaven knows what else. Was that a reward for her, or conscience gifts for you?'

She plucked at the black hairs on the back of his wrist before answering. 'Oh, you're right. I should take them off her and put her on bread and water for a week. Then I should be amazed if she doesn't run off again next weekend.'

'Minx,' he said, laying a hand over her wrist. 'I'm not suggesting you should punish the lass, but nor is there any need for you to fall over backwards to admit that you've failed her. You haven't. She appears to have begun this correspondence well before she came to your seminary, so she's been planning to make a run for it for months. What's more, she *chose* to save her allowance rather than spend it. She can't have it both ways. And what kind of message is this going to give to the others? Are you going to do the same for Miss Melborough, too?'

'Are you quite devoid of compassion, my lord?'

'No, nor am I quite devoid of common sense, either. You're getting emotionally involved in this and there's no need to. Miss Strachan is not a china doll, she's a—'

'She's a young lady of *sixteen*, which is beyond your experience, I might add. You think the rejection will do her no harm. Well, you may be right, but at this moment she feels the pain very acutely, as I have seen for myself, and since her parents are not on hand to help, I'm doing what I can to ease it. A lot is happening to her, my lord, and I believe she's feeling rejection from all sides, not only from the young scamp who promised her friendship. A few gifts are not going to turn her head.'

'You think not, eh?' he said, softly.

Then, before she could decide what he might mean by that, his arms swung her sideways, placing her across his lap, unable to move. Scooping her legs up, he set them on the cushioned seat and held them until she had stopped protesting, finally taking her wrist in his grip. 'So,' he said, 'if a few gifts are not going to turn her head, Miss Mother Hen Boyce, what will? In my experience, it usually works quite well.'

'That's not what I mean, my lord. You know it's not. Your gift to me was not given for that purpose, was it? Because you feel sorry for me?'

'Miss Boyce, I may feel some exasperation from time to time. I may even feel like taking you in hand, but pity for you has never been on my list, as it happens. To feel sorry for a woman who has everything, as you appear to do, would be a complete waste of time. I don't even feel sorry that you need to see better. Irritation, perhaps, that you have steered yourself on to the wrong social track, but that's something we can rectify, between us. The gift of spectacles was merely to begin that process.'

'Then why should you think differently of my gifts to Edina? She has a talent for painting, yet her parents have equipped her ill for it. I wanted to begin her healing. It was neither a bribe nor a reward.'

He studied the rebellious eyes, dark in the candlelit room and showing a trace of fear for her vulnerable position. Her lips had trembled as she spoke of healing. 'You feel her pain, too, don't you? That's it, isn't it? The rejection?' He traced an outline of her pointed chin with one finger. 'Caring woman.'

Tears rushed behind her eyes and brimmed over into the corners. ''Tis what all women feel,' she said.

'No lass. Not all women. Some would feel nothing, believe me. You feel things very deeply, don't you? Too deeply for your own comfort.'

'Too *fast* for my own comfort. I think I may have galloped into something I had not prepared for. This must be the first time you have ever been *told* by a woman that she's your newest mistress instead of waiting to be asked. But it's not too late to undo what I said last night, my lord, if you feel you've been rushed…'

'Oh, yes, it is,' he said, bending his head closer. 'Don't imagine you can wriggle your way out of it now, my beauty. I'm not letting go. You're netted, Lettie Boyce. Well and truly netted.' Releasing her wrist, he slipped his hand possessively into her underarm to fit snugly against her breast while his lips closed over hers, preventing any further discussion.

Letitia did not expect him to accept her offer, having already gone so far down a road of no return. Intuitively, she had sensed that it was her innocence that attracted him, and a kind of artlessness he was not used to. Fresh, responsive and smart, she was eager to learn and to bring to it a piquancy that previous amours had not. What other motive could he have for wanting her to be his mistress? To a man like him, what could be more enticing than that? she wondered.

His voice was thick with desire as the kiss ended. 'If we had privacy here,' he said, 'I'd be tempted to go further, but we cannot risk being discovered like this, sweetheart. Besides, as I've already said, I want you in bed for your first time. With all the trimmings.'

She could not resist a smile at the image, for she liked the idea of being in a more romantic place than this. It would fit more happily into her story, for one thing and, when the time came for them to part, he would be just as gentlemanly and considerate, she was sure. Men so hated it when women made a fuss.

After a fond farewell to Uncle Aspinall, the journey back to Richmond next morning was taken in convoy with Rayne's smart post-chaise leading the way, the front window of which gave them a view of the road ahead, and the liveried postilion. 'Tell me,' Letitia said, looking down at the gloved hand holding hers upon her lap, 'what did you and Uncle Aspinall do at the Crown yesterday morning?' Her shoulder was tucked warmly beneath his, though there was plenty of room for two on the seat with padded elbow-rests.

'Waited for Sir Penfold's guests to arrive. Chatted to several captains and admirals. One of them, a Captain Blair, knows your cousin, Lieutenant Gaddestone. He was surprised to find that Gaddestone was Sir Penfold's nephew, and staying with him.'

'Well, there's a coincidence. Did the captain like Fin?'

There was a slight hesitation before he replied. 'Oh, I don't know that captains and lieutenants need to *like* each other, exactly. But your uncle was very interested to hear what the captain had to say about him.'

'He would be. He'd be able to compare it with what Fin himself has to say, which is a great deal too much. Did I tell you he's asked me to give Gaddy an extra room? I'm convinced he'll ask to use it for himself.'

'You must not allow it, sweetheart. Not under any circumstances.'

'The only spare room I have is below stairs.'

'Keep it like that. I intend to be around more, Lettie. The plans for the Allied celebrations are being finalised, and I've done all I need to do for the present. The recruits are being sent to their regiments, and that leaves me free until the next batch arrives in the autumn. I'm ready to take some leave.'

'That means you'll be more…available?'

'From now on, I shall be very…available.'

'But I shall not. Have you given any thought about how this is going to work? It will be several weeks before we can go and stay in London.'

Rayne's voice was impassive, his eyes focussed straight ahead as if he knew she was stalling. 'It will work. Leave it to me.' When she made no reply, he looked down at her. 'Afraid?' he whispered.

'No. Of course not.'

Smiling, he squeezed her hand and turned his attention to the view.

Edina's homecoming on Tuesday afternoon was similar in many respects to that of the prodigal son without the fatted calf. Happy to see her back home, the girls bore her away, expecting to be given all the details of the adventure. But the discovery that Mr Waverley had not turned up for his usual mathematics lesson that morning was most disturbing, as was

Miss Gaddestone's news direct from his housekeeper. 'Attacked by highwaymen yesterday on the London Road,' she said once the girls had disappeared upstairs. 'I sent round a nice piece of beefsteak for him, so he can put it on his cuts and bruises or eat it, whichever he prefers. Poor Mr Waverley. She said he was quite poorly.'

'Highwaymen?' said Rayne, with barely concealed scepticism. 'In broad daylight? I'd be very surprised. I'll go round and see him, Lettie.'

'I'll come,' she said. 'Bart is a personal friend.'

'I suppose it's no good me telling you you can't, is it?'

'None at all. Shall we walk?'

'Very well. Might as well let the gossip start sooner as later.'

'Gossip?' said Miss Gaddestone. 'What gossip would that be, dear?'

'I don't know what Lord Rayne is talking about. Won't be long.'

Immaculately preserved, Mr Waverley's beautiful early Georgian house on The Green, almost next to the theatre, was a reflection of Bart himself: rose-toned carpets and walls, white and gilded woodwork, and delicate pieces of furniture perfectly arranged.

The housekeeper led them up the pale polished staircase, her worried frown preparing them for a disconsolate patient, but not for the sorry sight that lay swathed in bandages upon the ghost-white sheets of a four-poster bed. His upper head was turbaned with bandages, one arm was bound inside a sling, the other was covered with weals and bruises, his chest strapped across revealing triangles of mottled skin. One eye was completely closed, the other open just wide enough for him to see.

His mouth was cut and badly swollen, making it difficult for him to speak or to show his pleasure at seeing them.

Mr Thomas, the Welsh elocution teacher, rose to his feet as they entered, touching Bart's hand to say farewell. 'I'll call in later,' he said, articulating musically. 'Miss Boyce…my lord…'tis a sad business.'

Letitia went to kiss Bart's cheek.

Rayne wanted to know, 'Were you with him, Mr Thomas?'

'Monday morning, my lord, is when I'm at Number 24 with the pupils. Mr Waverley was riding on his own. One should not ride alone on the London Road, you know. I never do. Good day to you.'

They sat beside him, talking low, listening to his difficult whispers. He had been going to London, quite early, intending to take some papers to Mr Lake on Leadenhall Street. He had been set upon only a few miles out while the road was still deserted except for three men riding towards him. They had returned his greeting, then had turned and dragged him off his horse, beat him up, kicked him senseless and left him in the ditch. His horse had run off, but had been caught by a passer-by and brought back to him, and that was how he'd returned to Richmond, more dead than alive. Yes, he had told his housekeeper and doctor they were highwaymen, but of course they were not. He looked at Rayne with great sadness at that point, his swollen bloodshot eyes filling with tears.

'It's all right, old chap,' Rayne said, gently. 'Don't grieve. This kind of thing happens, and at least you're alive, fit and healthy. You'll make a good recovery. You have good friends and, in future, you won't go out alone. Were you not wearing your sword?'

'No.'

'Then you must. You know how to use it. Were the papers stolen?'

'No. In my saddle-bag. Safe.'

'Money taken?'

'No, nothing.'

'*Nothing*? Did you recognise any of them?'

Bart shook his head. 'Hired, I expect.'

'For what?' Letitia asked. 'To kill Bart? Why? Who would want to?'

Rayne laid a hand over hers. 'Perhaps we'll go into that when he feels a bit stronger.' He made as if to leave, but Bart signalled him to stay.

'Need to see Lake,' he whispered. 'Important.'

'Who is this Lake on Leadenhall Street?' Rayne said, giving nothing away. 'Can I help? I know where it is.'

Bart and Letitia looked at each other, sharing the secret, but not knowing how to proceed. It was time, Letitia thought, to accept some help; if that meant letting Rayne into it, then they must trust him. 'It's for me,' she said. 'The papers are mine. Mr Lake is a publisher. Mercury Press.'

'A publisher. I see. And you have papers for him. Well, that should be easy enough, if you will trust me with them.'

'It's a contract,' said Letitia. 'It needs to be discussed. Bart was going to bargain with him.'

'I see. You want him to publish something for you.'

Bart made a sound of impatience. 'Lettie,' he croaked, 'is an *author*, Rayne.' His mouth worked his swollen lips around the words, '*The Infidel.*'

'Good grief!' Rayne stared at Letitia, but found her eyes hostile, even suspicious. 'That's very interesting. Are you really? Those best-sellers that my mother reads? Well, then,

I'd be glad to help. I'll go and bargain with your Mr Lake. I'm quite good at that.'

Letitia frowned at him. 'You're not shocked?'

'No. Just tell me what you want from him and I'll fix it in no time.'

'It's not as easy as that. Bart has already spoken to him once. He's making things difficult. He doesn't know me. We've never met. That's the problem.'

'Nego…tia…ting through an inter…' Bart mumbled.

'Through an intermediary, yes. But it's always best if you can talk to these people personally, I think,' said Rayne.

'I can't do that,' said Letitia. 'That's why Bart does it for me.'

'Of course you can. You can come with me, can't you?'

Bart mumbled again. 'Are you and Lettie…?'

'Yes, old chap. We've come to an arrangement. D'ye mind?'

'Course not. Glad.'

'Good. I'll take care of her. I'll take her to Lake. He'll not get anything past me. Of course, I may not do as good a job as you, but I reckon it's time he spoke to the author herself now, don't you? This is a good opportunity.'

'We shall come and see you again before we go, Bart dear. And thank you for going. I'm so *very* sorry it's cost you this.' Letitia put a hand over his.

''Tis nothing,' Bart whispered. 'You go with Rayne, Lettie.'

'Yes, love, but while we're here, may I take the papers and that package with me?'

He pointed to a desk over by the far wall. 'In there.'

Lifting the veneered lid, she removed the contract and money and gave them to Rayne. 'Will you carry it for me, my lord, if you please?' She kissed Bart again before they left, holding back the tears for his dreadful injuries as the housekeeper showed them out. A few steps further on, however, she stopped.

'Forgotten something?' said Rayne, stopping with her.

'No. You're not such a good actor, are you, my lord?'

'What?'

'In there. You knew, didn't you? Don't deny it. You couldn't act the dunce to save your life. I could *tell* that you knew. "Good grief! That's very interesting,"' she mimicked. '"Are you really?" As if he was telling you I have two arms and two legs. You're supposed to be utterly *astonished*, not mildly surprised.'

'Oh, dear,' he said, attempting a look of remorse. 'I don't do astonishment very well, do I?'

'No, you don't. That's what comes of being one of the worldly "I've-seen-it-all" types, I suppose. How did you find out? Have you made enquiries?'

'Not at all, Miss Boyce. I found out quite by accident, though I don't think it was very clever of you to use your own initials for a pseudonym.'

'That was Bart's idea.'

'That doesn't surprise me. I don't know why you need a pseudonym at all. What's wrong with your own name?'

'Do you really need to ask that, after knowing my mother?'

'Take my arm. We can't stand here arguing. There, now let's get this straight. You are my responsibility now, and anything you want to do, you can do without seeking anyone's approval but mine. And I say you should be proud of your achievements and put your name to them.'

'It's not done.'

'It *is* done. Miss Austen lets it be known that she writes for a living. Maria Edgeworth does. So should you, as part of your new image. In fact, that would be a perfect way to re-invent yourself when we take London by storm.'

'Yes. Right. Have you actually *read* my novels?'

'Yes. Both of them. I could hardly qualify for the title of Worldly-I've-seen-it-all if I had not, could I?'

'And do you seriously believe that I would be accepted in polite society as the author of *that* kind of novel? It's not exactly Miss Austen's cup of tea, you know. Nor Maria Edgeworth's.'

Rayne halted as they reached the black railings outside Number 24 Paradise Road. 'Are you ashamed of them?' he said, turning her to face him.

'No, of course I'm not.'

'I should hope not. With the kind of success you're having, you should be proud to own them, not determined to remain anonymous. They're good.'

'You liked them?'

'I liked them, yes. And I can see why they're so popular, but it's quite clear that the author is inexperienced. If she's going to write a third, she'll have to think up something a bit more convincing and adventurous for the bedroom than the first two. All very nice, but not quite accurate, you know.'

'Not…accurate?'

'No. Imaginative, romantic, but lacking authenticity. She needs some first-hand experience.'

'Who does?'

'Well, the heroine for one, and the author for another. Quite soon, I would say.' They passed into the front hall, aware that this was hardly the kind of conversation to hold in front of young Sam. Nevertheless, the disguising of the topic was something that afforded them both a frisson of excitement.

'What kind of time did you have in mind, my lord? Within months? Or weeks, perhaps?'

Rayne handed his gloves and silver-topped cane to Sam and removed his hat, raking his fingers through his hair with a glance at the mirror. 'Hours,' he said.

Miss Gaddestone came gliding into the hall to meet them. 'Ah, you're back. How is dear Mr Waverley? Why, Lettie dear, the walk has put a bloom in your cheeks.'

Letitia swept past her. 'Shall we have tea and cakes in the drawing room?' she said, holding a hand to her neck.

The surprises of that day were not over, however. Taking Mrs Quayle with her in the town-coach, Letitia drove up Richmond Hill to the gracious home of Sir Francis and Lady Melborough, neither of whom had been far from her thoughts since the revelation that her mother's high-flown morals were not as pure as she pretended. For her to put pressure on both Sapphire and herself to toe her line was, Letitia thought, extremely hypocritical. It was time to put matters straight.

Unsure of the reception she would receive, she was glad of Mrs Quayle's bright bird-like chatter that complemented Lady Melborough's delight at seeing them. Within moments of hearing their voices echoing in the hall, Miss Sapphire Melborough herself came down the winding staircase, her arms open wide in greeting, her expression bright with joy. With a yelp, she flung herself into Letitia's arms in a manner not taught at the seminary for young daughters of gentlefolk, but which affirmed the news that Letitia had been hoping for without a single question being asked.

As soon as she was sure—only a matter of days—as it turned out, Sapphire had thanked her Cheltenham relatives for their kind hospitality, borrowed their old carriage and dismissed herself, and now she was ready to be given a second chance, if only Miss Boyce would allow it. Which was exactly why Letitia and Mrs Quayle had come.

With a certain knowledge on her side, Letitia's meeting with Sapphire's father was by no means as strained as it had been before she knew the reason for his previous over-familiarity. Now, she could put it into context, and the man was no longer a threat, and she could forgive his effusiveness instead of being offended by it. The meeting went better than expected. Sapphire would rejoin her friends at the seminary, having already forgiven Lady Boyce for her harshness on that particular Sunday. It was, Letitia told them, the overreaction of a mother to the foolishness of a daughter. Catching Sir Francis's eye at this point, she was reasonably sure that he understood the message: Miss Letitia Boyce was not another Miss Euphemia Aspinall.

Excusing herself immediately after dinner, Letitia went to her room to catch up with her writing, eager to commit to paper all that had happened to herself, to Orla and Edina and, indirectly, to Bart, too. At frequent intervals, the writing was suspended, pictures and words overpowered by other more personal developments and their significance to her future as a headmistress, as a writer, and as Lord Rayne's mistress. Was it all moving too fast for her? Had he already guessed her purpose in accepting the latter position with much less resistance than he might have expected, given her earlier hostility? Had his offer of help, both off the page and on it, been made in the knowledge that this was a role for which she had already selected him? He had, after all, gone straight to the heart of the matter during their walk home from Bart's house. He was no fool. Yet hardly had a day passed when she had not needed his help in some way, and not an hour had passed without thinking of him, and now a new question sneaked under the others about whether she needed him for her own sake or for Perdita's. Her eyes closed. The ink on the pen dried, and Perdita was left to her own devices as the wick burned lower.

On Wednesday morning, while the girls were upstairs in a French lesson, Mrs Brewster the housekeeper took delivery of a large item brought by the Ackermann's wagon from London to Miss Letitia Boyce. The white-aproned delivery man who carried it into the hall could not tell them the name of the donor. He accepted his tip and went on his way. Taking scissors to the string and copious brown paper, Letitia and Orla unravelled the mysterious package to find that it contained an exquisite portable writing-desk, the kind of thing she had promised to buy for herself as soon as she could justify the expense.

By its silver handle, Orla carried it into the dining room and laid it upon the table where Letitia smoothed its sides of tulipwood inlaid with ivory, running her hands over the silver mounts and hinges. 'Who is it from, ma'am?' said Orla. 'There's no card nor message, nothing except Ackermann's Repository, Strand, London.'

'There might be a message inside,' said Letitia, turning the key in the tiny lock. The lid opened out to make a velvet-covered writing surface that sloped towards cut-glass containers for ink and pounce, a place for pens, letters and papers, compartments, secret drawers, a space beneath for a manuscript book that closed with a conspiratorial click. But there was no clue as to who had sent it.

Letitia left it upon the table to be admired. Naturally, it caused a lot of interest.

Later in the morning, while she was arranging a vase of flowers, she heard someone enter the hall through the front door with a very loud and cheery greeting for Miss Gaddestone, followed by an imperious command for Sam to bring a bottle of wine from Miss Boyce's cellar. Then, marching towards the garden room while throwing over his shoulder the information that the phaeton was back in the—

The visitor didn't finish the sentence. 'Lettie! Good God! You're…you're back!' Lieutenant Gaddestone stopped in the doorway as if struck by a thunderbolt.

With hands fluttering like moths, his sister appeared behind him. 'I tried to tell you, Fin,' she whispered. 'Lettie came home yesterday.'

Poised like a miniature javelin in Letitia's hand, the sharp stem of a rose hovered over the vase. 'Good morning to you, too, Cousin Fin. The phaeton is back where? In the coach house, is it? My very expensive bay, too, I hope? Sam!' she called. 'We shall not need the wine, I thank you.'

'Er…well, you see…' he said, clinging to the brass doorknob.

'No, I don't think I do. Did someone give you permission to take my phaeton?'

'I didn't think you'd mind, Lettie. I came by on Monday morning to ask you, and Rosie said—'

'No, I did *not* say it would be all right, Fin,' protested his sister. '*You* said it would be all right and that you'd bring it back before Lettie returned.'

'Which you hoped would be later rather than sooner,' said Letitia, dropping the rose-stem into the water. 'So now you've brought it back in the hope that I shall be none the wiser, and you walk into my house as if it were your own, and then you order my servant to supply you with my wine. Is there anything else you would like to take advantage of, while you're here?'

'Oh, Lettie, don't go off into a pet about it. I wanted to ask you—'

'Like you asked about the wine? Really, cousin, are these the manners the navy has taught you?'

'I'm sorry, Lettie. I really didn't think you'd mind.'

'Unfortunately, I do. You could have hired a phaeton in London if you needed one so badly.'

'Short of funds, Lettie. That's the long and short of it. Pockets to let until they send me my pay and prize money. Shouldn't be long now, then I can buy my own. Sorry, old girl. Forgive me?' His boyishly handsome face relaxed into a winsome smile that had doubtless been tried on many a woman with unqualified success. This time proved to be an exception. His Cousin Lettie was furious. Not that this prevented him from asking a favour of her. 'You couldn't lend me a bit o' blunt, could you, Lettie? Just until it arrives? Pay you back, of course.'

'Will you excuse me for one moment? I've forgotten to ask Sam something.' Letitia went into the hall where Sam was straightening the pink Axminster. Straightening up, he received his mistress's message and went off to the stables as fast as his legs could carry him.

Curious, Lieutenant Gaddestone followed Letitia into the dining room. 'Are you going to ask me to stay to lunch, now

I'm here, Lettie? I had thought of taking my sister out strutting for an hour this afternoon.'

'I thought you understood, Cousin Fin, that Gaddy lives here in return for chaperon duties. This is a seminary, you know. Some of my tutors are gentlemen, and your sister stays in the room at all times. Quite often Mrs Quayle and I do the same. This afternoon, she will be with Mr Dimmock's class.'

'Can't you do it instead, this time?' His eyes were drawn to the portable writing-desk on the table. 'Oh, this is nice. Just arrived?'

Anxious to pour oil on troubled waters, Miss Gaddestone saw the change of subject as a godsend. 'Yes,' she twittered, 'half an hour ago, from an unknown admirer.' Her hands patted it lovingly.

'Oh, Gaddy! What nonsense,' said Letitia.

'Well, it *must* be, dear. Who else would do such a thing with no message to say who sent it? Isn't it a lovely mystery, Fin?'

There was a gleam of mischief in his eyes as his hand wiped across his mouth, pinching his nose as it passed. 'It is, *indeed*, sister dear. Now you know why I'm skint. Stumped the last of my pewter on gifts.'

His sister and cousin stared at him, open-mouthed. 'You?' they said in unison.

He swung his head like a pendulum, smiling broadly. 'Why not? Lettie's always been keen on writing, hasn't she? Just a token of my regard.'

'But, cousin, this must have cost a fortune. Is this really what you've spent the last of your money on? And now you're asking me to help you out? That doesn't make much sense, does it?'

'Trying to stay in your good books, Lettie. Thought this

might help to oil the wheels. By the way, I like the eyeglasses. They new? Must have cost a pretty penny.'

Angry and deflated, Letitia felt the joy drain from her. She had harboured her own thoughts about who the gift might be from, especially since he'd known for some time that she was a writer and that, for a stay in London, she would need to take her work with her. But for her *cousin* to spend money he did not have on such a thing was quite out of the question. It must be returned. 'It must go back,' she said. 'Gaddy, be a dear and ask Mrs Brewster for that wrapping paper, will you?'

Miss Gaddestone knew better than to argue. For her brother to buy gifts for his cousin was not at all the thing. Turning to go, she almost bumped into the tall gentleman who was just entering the room. 'Oh! Good morning, my lord.'

'Good morning, Miss Gaddestone, Miss Boyce, Lieutenant. Of course it must be returned,' said Rayne, looking sternly at the desk. 'Tell us where you bought it, sir, and we'll pack it up again.'

'Oh, you! Bought it…er…in London. If you think it was not a good idea, Lettie, I'll take it back myself. Look here, I never meant to embarrass you. My lord, are you not being a little high-handed here?'

Letitia breathed a very quiet sigh of relief, for Rayne had obviously heard the previous exchange and would know how to handle it. What was more, she now had a suspicion that Cousin Fin was not telling the truth.

'No, I don't think I am, my friend,' Rayne said, good-naturedly. 'But it's interesting to see that our tastes are so very similar. So similar, in fact, that I bought one exactly like this only last week, thinking that it was unique. I must say I'm not best pleased to find that there are others like it. Where did you say you bought it?'

Cousin Fin frowned. 'Oh, it was some time ago. I cannot quite remember.'

'Ah, of course. So many gifts. Confusing, isn't it? Well, Miss Boyce, we can soon settle the problem. If you were to lift up the little wafer compartment next to the pounce jar, you may find the answer. That's it, lift it right out and look underneath.'

'There's a card. One of yours, my lord.'

'Turn it over, if you please.'

'It says, "With highest regards from Seton Rayne to Lettie Boyce." There, I don't think there can be any doubt about that, can there?' She smiled, shyly.

'A mistake,' Lieutenant Gaddestone muttered, turning very red. 'Easily made. Must have forgotten…meant to…thought I had done…lot on my mind, you know. Yes, saw one just like it….lovely piece…ah, well, I suppose I'd better be making tracks. Has Rosie gone? I wonder if I might have a quick word with her? Er, you couldn't let me have the use of one of your horses, could you, Lettie?' The request was given in a hushed tone, which he hoped would not catch Rayne's ear while that gentleman studied the hinges of the desk.

Rayne's ears, however, were in good working order. He straightened, favouring Lieutenant Gaddestone with a long hard stare. 'That would put Miss Boyce in a difficult position, sir,' he said. 'The horses in her stable belong to the young ladies here, except for the carriage horses. You surely didn't have the grey Arab in mind, did you?'

Cousin Fin coloured even deeper. 'I can see my timing is at fault, Lettie. I shall take my leave of you. Where will I find my sister?'

From the open door came the sound of voices and the patter of slippers on the staircase as the French lesson ended and laughter was released like a peal of bells. The girls would want her attention. Letitia knew that Cousin Fin would ask his sister for money for his return to London on the mailcoach. She also knew that, if she had not been here, he would have helped himself to one of the horses without Mr Benjamin to prevent him.

'Come with me, cousin,' she said, with a glance at Rayne. 'Don't go, my lord. I shall only be a moment. Please excuse me.'

Chapter Twelve

'Yes, you're quite right,' said Letitia, closing the dining-room door. 'I know I shouldn't have lent him anything, but the alternative was quite unacceptable, my lord. I could not have him taking money off Gaddy, nor could I allow him to walk all the way to London. Even though I do have a spare horse in my stable, I would not let him use it after he took my…' She sighed, walking over to the window to look out upon Paradise Road.

'Your what? What's he helped himself to?'

'To my phaeton and the bay.'

'Without your permission? The man's a bounder.'

'It was Monday morning and we were still in Portsmouth, and so was Uncle Aspinall. Poor Gaddy, she's so cut up about it. But thank you for coming so quickly to answer my call.'

'I was only at the end of the road. I'd been to see Bart. He's quite poorly. I told him I'd take you to see Lake tomorrow. I thought we could stay at Berkeley Square with my parents. Will it be convenient?'

'Yes, I believe so, but it means two more nights away.'

'You needn't be concerned. I've taken the liberty of hiring a butler for you.'

'But I've got Sam.'

'As a footman, yes, but he won't manage to keep the likes of Gaddestone out, will he? You need a large imposing adult butler, sweetheart, especially when there are young ladies to be protected. Parents will appreciate it.'

That small detail had escaped her. 'Right again,' she whispered.

'I'll never get used to it. Come here, woman.' He opened his arms, enclosing her with warm hands on her back.

'No,' she said, pressing herself against him, 'it cannot be good for a man, can it? Shall you be getting devilish righteous now, my lord?'

'Unless you can suggest a better reward.'

'Thank you for the beautiful desk. I could not have accepted it from anyone else, and I *did* so want to. It's the loveliest, most perfect thing I've ever seen. Shall we take it to London with us?'

'It can go anywhere with you, so I cannot be accused of taking you away from your writing.'

'Expensive gifts. I am already indebted to you.' She raised her head to meet his lips, drawing from him both comfort and excitement.

'And I intend to make sure it stays that way. Now, later today the new butler will arrive. His name is Mr Beck, and he knows exactly what his duties are. Perhaps you'll get Mrs Bruin to—'

'Mrs Brewster.'

'To show him round, have his room ready. Tell him who you want kept out, then be ready for me to pick you up at about ten tomorrow, and have your papers ready for Lake so that you can tell me about it on the way. We'll go straight to

Leadenhall Street. Then there's an evening soirée at the Misses Berry. They'd like us to go. Shall we? After dinner?'

'My lord, you think of everything,' she said, caressing his cheek.

'Yes, and there is one particular everything I think about almost non-stop. But now I must go, and you must tend your flock. Don't allow thoughts of your cousin to disturb you. I have his measure.'

'Do you, my lord?'

'Oh, yes, I most certainly do.'

No sooner had he taken his leave of her than she went straight away to find Miss Gaddestone, whose pretty room overlooked the garden, though it was obvious from the red and watery eyes that the view was not the occupant's focus of attention. Letitia took the frail creature in her arms. 'Oh, dear, please don't weep, dear Gaddy. I don't blame you in the slightest. Not in the *slightest.*'

'I should have told you, but he told me not to, that he'd get the phaeton back before you knew it and that I was not to worry. It was very wicked of him to put me in such a position, Lettie, because he must *know* how much I owe you, and how loyal I am, and now he's spoiling it by this *dreadful* behaviour, and lies about the desk, too. Oh, how *could* he do that? So…so humiliating, Lettie.'

'Gaddy dearest, you don't have to change one bit. I know how loyal you are. Fin is in a difficult position until his pay arrives.'

'Well, I don't know how he's going to make an offer for Number 20 when he has no idea how much he'll be getting.'

The hair along Letitia's arms stood on end. 'Gaddy dear, what did you say about Number 20? That's where old Mrs Sawbridge and her King Charles's spaniels live.'

Gaddy's hand flew to her mouth, her red-rimmed eyes like saucers. 'Oh, good heavens!' she said. 'He told me not to say anything about that, too. I'm not very good at deception, Lettie. I never have been, have I?'

'Thank goodness you're not. Please tell me. I think I ought to know.'

'That's what I said, too, but Fin said he'd tell you himself. Old Mrs Sawbridge is looking for a private buyer, Fin says, because she doesn't want people traipsing all over the house and upsetting the dogs, and she's going to live with her sister in Mortlake. She has a huge place by the—'

'Yes, love. I'm sure that will be best, but has Fin made her an offer?'

'He wants to look round it first, and that's why he was going to suggest to you that, while we're in London next month, you might let him stay here to look after things for you.'

'So he can pester Mrs Sawbridge to sell it to him? But as you said, he doesn't have any money yet. Is he expecting Uncle Aspinall to help him out, until he's in funds again?'

'I don't know, dear. He was in a rush to get your phaeton and go. He asked about Mr Waverley and then dashed off.'

'Just a moment. This was on Monday. Did you know then about Mr Waverley's accident?'

'No, not until Tuesday when he didn't turn up for his mathematics lesson. I was surprised Fin should have asked me about him, because they're not particular friends, are they? I just told him he was well, as far as I knew.'

'Did he ask you anything else about Mr Waverley, or me?'

'Only how long you'd known each other. I said several years, but I didn't think it was any of his business, and I have to say, Lettie dear, that I'm not too happy about him wanting to stay here while we're away, or about him buying Number 20. Do we want him living so close? And do I *really* want to live with him? He'll have his navy friends to stay, you know, and expect me to keep house for him, and then he'll get himself a wife and I shall be a nuisance to her, and…oh!' The tears spilled down her cheeks as the future spread itself before her like a bleak landscape full of pitfalls.

Once again, Letitia comforted her, telling her that she need never live anywhere she didn't want to. Besides, she was very much needed. How else would they manage? And, by the way, Lord Rayne had appointed himself their champion.

Gaddy sniffed and dabbed. 'That's not really a surprise, Lettie dear. I knew you and he were getting on well when I heard raised voices. That's always an indication of high regard, isn't it?'

If that was heartening news, Gaddy's disclosure about her brother's plans was quite the opposite, as was the news that Number 20 was up for sale. The ideal solution would be for Letitia herself to bid for it, to expand the seminary, but if the girls' parents objected to the idea of her writing books and being someone's mistress, the future would take a more unexpected turn. Ideally, she would like to take in more boarders and give Gaddy more space, but of such things were dreams made.

Taking written messages from the girls, flowers, a freshly caught trout, some new spinach from the garden, a book of poetry and an embroidered bookmark, Letitia paid a visit to Mr Waverley and stayed with him half an hour to tell him of her plans to go to London with Rayne. Not wishing to disturb him with Cousin Fin's devious activities, she kept well away from that subject, but told him instead of Edina's happy return to the fold and of the courage she had shown, and how she herself had made good use of the experience at second-hand for Perdita's story, which, she said, was likely to be the best of the three. Although Bart's attempt to smile was rather grotesque, it showed that he knew why she expected to improve.

By the time they reached London on Thursday morning, Rayne was in full possession of the facts about Letitia's writing and Mr William Lake's publishing of it, including the price of every volume, the number printed, the costs incurred and the fee paid, which he said was derisory in view of her success. If necessary, Rayne told her, they would give Lake the unsigned contract back and tell him that, in future, Miss Letitia Boyce's books would be offered to Egerton, Miss Austen's publisher, or John Murray in Albemarle Street. There were others, he said, who would jump at the opportunity.

But Rayne was in determined mood, and once Mr Lake had recovered from his initial astonishment at seeing, after two years, what his most famous author looked like, not to mention the aristocrat who brought her to his offices, he seemed not to resemble Mr Waverley's description of hard-bitten businessman as closely as all that. On the contrary, though Letitia said very little on her own account, Mr Lake responded to Rayne's amazingly fluent grasp of the business with obvious admiration.

While not for one moment implying that Mr Lake had been exploiting the anonymous author and her gentle well-bred mediator, Rayne picked up and renegotiated every single clause in the brief contract, including publication at Lake's own expense, a larger print run with a doubled cover price of six shillings for each volume, and a much increased payment for the copyright of the third book, to be renegotiated for subsequent ones. This, Rayne said, Miss Boyce would prefer to receive in advance. She would also want a bigger percentage of all sales and, for Mr Lake to make the best of these new arrangements, he would have to increase his subscription list to defray costs, find some more prestigious sponsors and employ some better marketing techniques. It was a pity, Rayne said, that one had to chase all round the London libraries to get copies of Miss Boyce's novels when they ought to be available from every bookshop. Libraries and borrowing from friends did not bring in the money.

However, Mr Lake brightened considerably when Rayne told him that, from now on, the author's name would appear on the book, for the name of Boyce would undoubtedly be good for publicity and, it went without saying, for Mercury Press. A new contract would be drawn up immediately, said Lake.

'To be delivered, by hand, to Number 24 Paradise Road, Richmond, within seven days, if you please,' said Rayne, 'for my client to check the details, and sign.'

'Of course.' Mr Lake blinked like an owl at Letitia, who smiled.

'It will be returned to you for your counter-signature within the next seven days, after which you will promptly return her copy and her fee. By hand. We do not expect to have to traipse all the way to London to collect any monies due to my client in future. This is to be written into the contract, sir.'

Again, Mr Lake blinked and scribbled furiously, slightly reddening around the jowls. 'As you say, my lord. We shall not delay. Anything else?'

'Miss Boyce?' said Rayne. 'Does that cover everything?'

'My two free copies to be increased to six?' she said, trying not to laugh.

Lake scribbled again. 'Certainly,' he mumbled. 'Six free copies.'

'And I would like the quality of the paper to be the same as the others, if you please, Mr Lake, and the covers, too. I like the gold tooling. Could we have blue covers this time, do you think?'

At last he smiled. 'I don't see why not, Miss Boyce. What will it be called, so that I may enter it in the contract?'

'*Perdita*, sir.'

'Ah, the lost one. And is she lost, this young lady?'

'She starts off lost, but…' she glanced at Rayne, feeling his eyes upon her '…she then begins to find herself. With help. Quite a lot of help, really.'

Lake nodded as if he understood perfectly. 'I look forward to seeing the manuscript. Do you have a date in mind, Miss Boyce?' He dipped his quill in the inkpot, ready to write.

'Probably the end of July. Shall we say July the thirty-first?'

Laying the quill down, Lane sat back to look at her over the top of his steel-rimmed spectacles. '*This* year? You have already started it, then?'

'Yes, it's well under way.'

'Splendid! Perdita will be found by July thirty-first. Excellent.'

By the way he looked at her, Letitia was left with the notion that Mr Lake believed Perdita's story to be vaguely autobiographical. But he was far too astute to say so.

Walking down the dingy wooden stairs from the office into the bookshop-library, Rayne made the remark for her ears only that, if he had anything to do with it, Perdita would be found well before the end of July.

It was no wonder that Lake was impressed, for Letitia had donned her most fashionable day dress and a three-quarter-length midnight-blue velvet pelisse with silver buttons and some very clever lattice work on the sleeves, the collar and around the crown of the matching brimmed hat. This might have been a severe ensemble but for the elaborate frill on the hem of the white dress that appeared also on the cuffs and neckline. If she had been concerned by the reception of Lord Rayne's parents, however, she need not have been for, although she had met them once or twice as a girl, they could not be expected to remember her as Lady Boyce's eldest blue-stocking daughter. Nor did they know from one month to the next who their youngest son's current mistress was, though their welcome was warmer by far than anything Letitia's mother offered her, these days.

'We've been in Berkeley Square only three years,' the Marchioness told her as they walked past portraits of ancestors in their best clothes. 'St. James's Square was becoming a little down at heel, and a bit too close to the high-class bawdy houses,' she confided with a grin. 'Some of them even spread into the square.'

Having met Lady Dorna Elwick several times, there could be no possible doubt about the relationship, for not only did mother and daughter share the same blonde prettiness, but their taste in clothes was remarkably similar, too, glamorous, diaphanous and cut daringly low over voluptuous curves, yet entirely suited to their characters, concealing little except their age. It was hard to guess how old Lady Sheen might be, though Rayne had told her that she had been the Duke of Ashen's mistress before she met his father, but had still been only twenty when she had had Nicholas. As he had said, mistresses were not new to the Sheens.

In the huge house, Letitia's room was along a gold-carpeted corridor hung with oak-garland wallpaper punctuated by white-painted doors. A green-liveried footman held one of them open. 'Here we are,' said Lady Sheen, passing through in a cloud of silk chiffon and swansdown. 'Seton says you must have the best Blue Room, and I can see that it's your colour, my dear. Your maid can have the little closet next door, and I've instructed mine to look after her, so if there's anything you require, she will get it for you.'

'You are so kind, my lady. Thank you. I didn't know quite how you would receive me when my own home is only a walk away. It must look rather…'

'Mothers and daughters don't always get on as well as they might,' said Lady Sheen, taking Letitia's hand. 'I'm fortunate, but I dare say if Dorna and I lived any nearer, we'd fight like terriers. Too much the same, you know. I don't think anything about you being here instead of with your mama, but I *do* want to hear all about this exclusive seminary of yours at Richmond. Ah, here's your maid and the luggage. Come down when you're ready. I think Seton wants to take you shopping.'

Seton, she discovered moments later, was more like his father and elder brother with the same lean fitness and graceful bearing, the Marquess's snow-white hair predicting how theirs might look in another thirty years. Letitia had dreaded some remark about her appearance as Rayne's lady friend, but the elegant Lord Sheen greeted her only with a genuine interest in the eldest daughter of the late Sir Leo

Boyce, the architect, who had flown the nest at such an early age. That showed courage. If you knew what you wanted from life, you should go and get it, he said. Then, laughing at his own moralising, he added, 'And it helps to know what you *don't* want, too. Eh, my lad?'

'Yes, sir,' said Rayne, pulling out Letitia's chair. 'Indeed it does.'

'As long as you don't spend all your best years finding that out,' said Letitia, 'before discovering that your standards were perhaps a little too unrealistic.'

'Then I must be one of the fortunate ones,' he replied, seating himself beside her, 'to have my high standards met before I reach my dotage.'

'Well said, lad,' said his father. 'You certainly aimed high this time. Now, my dear Lady Sheen, do you want me to carve this ham, or shall we see what a mess young Seton makes of it?'

Rayne stood up again. 'It is well known that no one but yourself can make a mess of a ham, sir. Pass me the carvers and I'll show you how to cut it into slices instead of doorsteps.'

'Tch!' said Lord Sheen. 'I was carving ham before you were born, lad. But here you are. You'd better get some practice in before you have your own lunch table. Eh, Miss Boyce?' He winked at her, fatherly.

Letitia smiled at her plate, at the gold rim and the crest upon it.

Replacing the smooth lid of her writing-desk, Letitia locked it. She had decided that, despite her good intentions, her thoughts on the past hours would have to wait until daylight. Now, it was time to prepare for a completely new experience, one which had not been far from her mind all day, as she knew it had not been from Rayne's, either. He had complimented her on her appearance, and she knew it had been meant, for his eyes had hardly left her. Others had done the same, people she knew at the Misses Berry's soirée who had not seen her for months, making her feel welcome and special, and somehow distinguished by being in Rayne's company. Nothing had been remarked, of course, about her new position, but everyone seemed to understand the nature of it. Nor had the two of them stuck together all evening, for that would not have been quite the thing, but their arrival, supper and departure together had been quite enough. As for the silver spectacles, she could hardly count the times she'd been begged to reveal which glasses-maker had supplied them.

Now, she removed them and placed them in their case, recalling the pleasure she had felt at being able to see at last the shelves of merchandise at the Exeter Exchange and the brilliant bolts of fabric at Wilding and Kent's. Faces she was able to recognise from across the street had smiled and called greetings. Men's heads had turned and the occasional whistle had been ignored, but inwardly relished. She also recalled the times when she had told herself how little these things mattered to her, how unnecessary to one's well-being. But she had been mistaken, for never had she felt so proud to be handed in and out of Lord Rayne's curricle, or to fly past with a wave and a smile. This unusual sense of elation had remained with her throughout the evening like a girl at her first ball, even though she was on familiar ground. Rayne had said very little to her on the short journey home, but had held her hand very firmly all the way, escorted her to the door of her room and asked her if she would keep it unlocked for him. What a question, she had thought, nodding her assent. What a shameless thing to do for Perdita's sake. Or was it?

Orla was dismissed, her evening clothes put away, her jewels, her papers, her hair plaited and hanging down her back. What were mistresses supposed to do at such times? Pretend to be reading? Asleep? Standing? Waiting demurely? In a pretty muslin house-gown she stood by the four-poster bed, thinking that no lovelier setting could have been devised for a seduction, nowhere more sumptuously comfortable, velvet and brocade curtained, white and gold painted, shaded with blue like summer cornflowers. There was a blue-and-white patterned *chaise longue* on which she would perch in the morning, and an ingenious washstand with a container to catch the water, brass taps, scented soap, white towels.

She was halfway across the room before the sound of the knock had died. Then she took a deep breath, waited three seconds, and opened it. 'Why, Lord Rayne!' she whispered. 'What a pleasant surprise. Will you come in?'

He caught the ruse immediately. 'Miss Boyce?' he said. 'Miss Letitia Boyce, author of *The Infidel* and others too numerous to mention?'

'The same,' she said, closing the door behind him.

'This is an honour, ma'am. I know it's rather late, but I wonder if you'd write a short dedication in the first eight I've brought with me, and the other twenty-four in the morning. I have them stacked up outside the door.'

'That might take some time, sir. Besides, when I'm told that my characters are not quite credible, or some such, I tend not to write dedications for them until they—'

'I did not say they were not credible, Miss Boyce, I said

that what they did *together* lacked authenticity. That's not the same thing.'

She felt the laughter welling up inside her as his hand took hers and led her gently over to the *chaise longue*, which she had not thought to use until tomorrow. He wore a long dark-green gown with a small leaf-pattern on it that caught the sheen of the candlelight as he moved. On his feet he wore leather mules that made no sound on the carpet, and she suspected that, by the exposed V of bare neck, he wore very little else except the faint aroma of sandalwood.

'Well,' she pouted, 'I have a moment. You could explain exactly what you mean, I suppose, though I can't promise to write…how many dedications?'

'Thirty-two.'

'Do you profess to be an authority on what people do together, sir?'

Wedging himself into the soft bolstered end of the *chaise longue*, he caught her by the waist and pulled her backwards against him, enclosing her with his legs and arms, nestling her against his chest as she had never been before. 'I have made something of a study of it, Miss Boyce,' he said in a voice that imitated exactly one of Miss Berry's guests who had brought along a working model of a beam-engine for discussion. 'I think I may say, with all due modesty, that I am a leading exponent of water pumps, pistons and steam-power, and just about everything else.'

'Is this what you were thinking of, sir, when you appeared to be listening so raptly?'

He sighed, dropping his voice to a chastened whisper. 'I admit, Miss Boyce, that I was not thinking of pounds per square inch in quite the same way that he was. There, now you have the truth of it. I went there only to gaze upon you, as I saw everyone else doing.'

'Now you *are* talking nonsense, sir. They were not gazing at me.'

'Yes, they were. All except Mr Beam-Engine. They all envied me, too, knowing that I'd have you like this before the night was out. In my arms.'

'Doing what people do together?'

'Which was something missing from your stories, Miss Boyce. Your characters don't talk to each other enough. It all happens far too quickly. Could you slow them down a bit and get them to enjoy it? It isn't about what *he* does to *her*, you know, it's about what lovers do *together.*'

Without a shred of awkwardness, he had gentled her into his close embrace where both her mind and body waited to be taught, for now his fingertips played over the inside of her wrists and along her arms and, because it was his touch and no one else's, part of her body was melting with desire. Turning her head against his chest, she whispered, 'Didn't you say once that you wouldn't be doing much talking, sir?'

'Later,' he said, 'neither will you.' He took the candlestick and moved it away to one side so that it no longer shone into her eyes. 'But most lessons begin with a resumé of what's already known, don't they? Take the kiss, for instance.'

Whatever ideas she'd had about learning the mysteries of lovemaking, the timing of it, the range, the depth of the heroine's involvement and the consummation, these were in danger from the very beginning of becoming changed by emotions she had not expected to feel. Her analytical mind had rarely let her down before, but this time it stood no chance against Rayne's skilful teaching for, whether he was using her stories as an excuse or not, it took only one kiss to confuse her organised list of questions.

She thought she knew about kisses, though now she found that those others had been chaste compared to the travelling variety that moved from her lips to cover her face, her neck and throat, then down towards her shoulders. His warm knowing hands preceded them, smoothing the way, slipping her loose gown off her shoulders until the neckline rested on the swell of her breasts, tantalising them both.

But by now the playfulness had changed to something more intent, for he would not make a game of this, her first time. She was a woman, not a child, and this was not a patronising lesson she needed, but a sensitive celebration of new womanhood to be remembered for all time. What was more, the love scenes in her stories, while lacking in reality, were beautifully imaginative, and Rayne knew that she would expect to find out from him, without disgust, what she could hardly visualise for herself. He did not suppose her mother would have been much help to her in this.

She lay quietly in the crook of his arm, all facetiousness gone, her eyes wide, dark with longing and apprehension, looking into his face to find the next move. Her neck had come alive with his kisses, waiting for more. 'You have a most beautiful mouth,' she whispered, touching the corner of it with one finger. 'Beautiful teeth, too.' Her eyes said more. Then, as if she had already learnt something, she reached up to draw his head down to hers, to feel his skin with her lips over his cheeks and eyelids, chin and ears, tasting the male scent of him. She felt waves of heat ripple through her as he breathed out in a rush, half-laugh, half-gasp, his closeness and the gentle male pressure of him alone making her weak with want. Her fingers trembled.

Rayne responded. Gathering her up in his arms and swinging them both off the *chaise longue*, he strode across to the bed where he held her, poised above the linen sheets with her robe slipped down to expose one breast, pushed by his arm to form an exquisite peak. Already aroused by his roving kisses, the nipple stood firm like a bead of dark coral upon a mound of cream velvet.

She saw his lips part and his chest heave under the deep breath. 'My lord?' she whispered, suddenly fearful. 'You are having second thoughts?'

Slowly, he shook his head. 'No, my beauty. I'm wondering how I've managed to keep my hands off you for so long. I'm also wondering how I'm going to show you what you hope for, taking time, making it last as I said it should. You are sensational, Lettie Boyce, yet you are still virgin and I dare not rush through this.'

'I think I understand. But surely we could compromise? You have no experience of virgins?'

'Only once, when I was fifteen. I don't think she enjoyed it much. I've learned a lot since then.'

'Nor do I expect to learn everything in one experience. A little at a time will do quite well, I think. I would not offer myself to anyone but you.'

He swayed her in his arms, smiling at a thought. 'I think we both knew, didn't we? Even then, when I was at my most boorish and you fuming with anger.'

Covering her exposed breast with one hand, she scolded him gently. 'I shall not tell you what I knew then, my lord. It would go to your head.'

Huskily, he laughed, lowering her to the bed. 'Then I shall return the compliment, sweetheart, and take your gift of vir-

ginity with as much care as I can, given that you are enough
to send a man crazy with desire.' Shrugging off his robe, he
was careful, she noticed, not to let her see all of him, but to
rest beside her on one elbow, looking down into her eyes,
though now it was a world of deep shadows and specks of
light upon the gilded bed-posts and the canopy above them.

His hand sought her plait and began to undo it, combing
through the long tresses to free the silver cascade and to
arrange veils of it over her breasts, not knowing how every
slight touch of his fingertips upon her skin sent shockwaves
into her thighs. Pushing the rest of her robe away and
sweeping her hair, he touched her nipples and, when she responded with a cry, he stopped it with a deep kiss while his
hand continued its torment, raking and fondling, kindling and
stoking the deepest fires within her as nothing in her imagination had ever done.

She felt herself being swept along a path completely
unknown to her like a leaf in a whirlwind, giving him control
of every move. Rayne was strong and beautifully made,
bulging with muscle and sinew under her hands, surprising
her with the hardness of him, the touch of smooth skin, the
width of shoulder and deep curve of spine, the soft fuzz along
his arms and chest and the feel of it next to her body, exciting
her still more. Pushing her fingers deep into his hair, she felt
its silkiness like water before his head moved away, bending
to her breast, taking her hands with it.

Her cry became a low moan that did nothing to check him
or the sensation wrought by his mouth. His hand captured her
breast as if to hold all her desire in that one place while he
took his fill, though long before he had finished his mouth had
explored the surrounding areas, too, keeping her on the edge

of an excitement that promised even more delights before returning to the piercing sweetness of his suckling.

Visiting her mouth again, he played tenderly with her lips while his hand smoothed over her stomach and hips as if purposely to take her mind in two directions, giving her the chance to protest. She did, half-heartedly catching at his hand as it slid downwards to the soft mound between her legs. His kiss deepened and, at last, her grip on his wrist slackened, letting it move on to explore the tender folds, which would be the last to yield to his courteous intrusion.

His stroking plunging fingers were, at first, a source of indescribable delight, for this was a sensation so unique that no one ever spoke of it, let alone wrote about it. But then came a sharp and distant pain that was more surprising for its unexpectedness than for its severity, making Letitia yelp even as his kiss came to comfort her, and she clung to his wrist again, nipping at his chin with her teeth in retaliation.

She heard his huff of laughter as he slipped an arm beneath her back, placing himself over her so that for a few delicious seconds she felt his weight, his nudging legs against hers, and it was all so quickly done that she had no time to argue about it. She sensed the change in him as his body hardened above her like a great buttress, his hold on her urgent and sure, guiding himself into her, pulling her close with his arm so smoothly that she was hardly aware of his possession except by the amazing sensation of completeness now replacing the one before it. He waited, pushing the loose hair away from her face, kissing her eyelids.

'Did I hurt you, my beauty? I'm sorry. I tried not to.'

'I don't…think…so. It's all right. Go on. It's wonderful.'

Slowly he began to move, deeper and deeper, filling her

entirely until she was rocked by each tender thrust, his magnificent body sending waves of warmth over her and a presence of domination that had less to do with submission than with a kind of intimate partnership, a binding contract between herself and him that, no matter what happened, would remain for ever. She was his woman. He was telling her so. She felt the primitive message through every part of her body.

It was not what she had intended to happen to her mind, however, for she had not believed it would be engaged on this scale, or that she would feel for him anything more than she had before, though that had grown of late. But how could she remain the same, having taken him into herself, to share the same delight? She was discovering what she had wanted to know, and far more than that, but now she was also discovering things about herself that were not on her list, like a heart that was not as impregnable as she'd thought, for instance. Like a burning bright desire that might not be quenched at her command.

She found no answers, for Rayne knew how to close a woman's mind to everything except the incredible plunging rhythm that brought with it a wondrous comfort and then, with his bold, earthy whispers, a growing excitement. She clung to him, moaning, tossing her silver hair upon the pillow. The fires intensified, and she was lost inside them. She heard herself cry out in a long sighing wail of ecstasy as he moved fast into her, and the whirlwind took her breath for its own, holding it beyond reach as the fire raged and consumed, making her call out again, softly, into his ear.

As if from a distance came the muffled sound of Rayne's deep groan, then the final thrust as he convulsed and relaxed, covering her with his warmth. She knew then with a compelling certainty that what had happened between them just now was not the usual way of things, otherwise the married women of her acquaintance would have spoken of it with more joy than long sufferance. They had provided no details, naturally, but all the implications were that the once-a-month respite was the best part of a husband's attentions. What she had just experienced was beyond anything in her fantasies, something to be accepted whenever it was offered. Perhaps oftener.

Rolling aside, he pulled her into his arms, spilling her hair out across his shoulder, kissing the top of her head and murmuring endearments she had never heard before about how she was now his woman, for all time.

Caressing his face, she pushed the damp locks out of his eyes and let her fingers wander over his mouth. 'You're smiling, my lord. I think you're pleased with yourself, are you not?'

His voice was a deep chuckling rumble that vibrated beneath her hand. 'I certainly am, my beautiful amazing woman, and I'm even more pleased with you. That was something I never thought would happen for years. Some women never experience that at all, you know.'

She knew what he referred to. He should take the credit for it. 'I have little to compare it to, but if I gave you pleasure, it was because you showed me how. My concern now is that once is not going to be enough. My memory—'

With a laugh, he reared up above her. 'Who said anything about *once*? Did you think to be my mistress for a day? A week? I'm keeping you, woman, and even when you think your characters know all they need to know, you'll still be mine. Don't think I don't know what this is all about.' His kiss drew her mind back to the experience they had shared, to its fierce beauty and the violence of their passion, to sensations of which she had known nothing until now.

'No,' she whispered, when his kiss finished, 'that's not what this is all about. I admit that was my original thought, but I am not so cynical that I can pretend to be unaffected by what's just happened, and before. Perhaps we should keep my characters out of the bedroom. They have no place here. Let them fend for themselves, my lord. They're undeserving.'

'They've had their uses,' he said, easing her back into his embrace, 'but it pleases me more than I can say that you want more, sweetheart. Was I too rough with you?'

'Wonderfully so, thank you, my lord.'

His arm tightened as they laughed together. Resting her leg over the top of his, she smoothed the sole of her foot along his skin, thinking that this must be the nearest thing to paradise she would ever come.

Chapter Thirteen

Although the new writing-desk had travelled to London with them, there was hardly any time for writing except for a few notes on their whereabouts, the emotions and sensations remaining in Letitia's mind as being rather too fragile to commit to words until she had time to understand them better.

Rayne had remained with her all night, jubilant that she wanted more of his loving. She was, he thought, a truly remarkable woman, an opinion that was apparently endorsed by his parents and those they had met in town, reminding him of the way people took second glances at Amelie, his brother's wife. Now it was happening to him, too, and, to show her off even more, he borrowed horses from his father's fine stable for a morning ride in Hyde Park, which he had seldom done with other women. Miss Boyce was superb on horseback in her pale grey and silver habit and, with her by his side, Rayne felt more proud and complete than he had ever done.

They returned to Berkeley Square for a light lunch before a walk in St James's Park to see the pagoda and Chinese bridge. When asked if she would not rather go shopping, her reply was that she could do that any time, but now she would rather walk with him and enjoy his company without interference. 'Is that selfish of me?' she asked him, pulling on her cream kid gloves.

'It's the first time in years anyone has preferred a walk in my company to a shopping expedition,' he replied. 'I'm truly flattered.'

'I know very little about you, my lord. I think it's time I did.'

The walk was taken at a sedate pace, neither of them realising how the hours flew as they talked and looked, and by the time they had strolled all round the park and back to Berkeley Square, Letitia had made another discovery that, far from being arrogant, affected, odious, or any of the other epithets she had once used on him, he was in fact very unassuming, knowledgeable and interesting to listen to. Which, if she had not been so prejudiced, she might have been able to see before.

That evening, the Marchioness of Sheen held a dinner party for eighteen guests, never a favourite entertainment with Letitia, who preferred intimate meals. This time, she discovered that the conversation round the great table was quite unlike the shallow isolating chatter at her mother's parties, for the Sheens and their guests were interesting and pleasantly easy-going people.

'My parents,' Rayne told her, 'are enchanted by you, Miss Boyce. In fact, they all were. My father tells me to be quick and snap you up before someone else does.'

She laid her palms upon his chest, trying to appear demure. 'But I thought you *had* snapped me up, my lord. Haven't you?'

'What he means, sweetheart, is that eldest daughters are

quite often snapped up by eldest sons. And I am not an eldest son. I shall have a modest inheritance, but nothing like the property that Nick will have. A little pile in Hampshire is all.'

'Are you telling me that, as a mistress, I don't get a Marble Hill House like Mrs Fitzherbert, or a fleet of carriages like the Duke of Cumberland's mistress did?'

''Fraid not.'

'Oh, dear. No flunkeys, servants, cottage in the country?'

'Nope.'

'Tch! Huh! Well, what am I doing here then?'

With a laugh and a swoop too fast for her to avoid, he swept her up into his arms and carried her across to the bed, holding her on to it before she could roll off. 'This,' he said, 'is what you're doing here, woman. It's what I've waited all day for. Now, shall you submit to me?'

The laughter stopped and he looked down at her in the candlelight with eyes darkly serious, watching the tiny pinpoints of light filter through her long lashes. Her full lips parted for him, and he bent his head to hers, tasting them gently before releasing the longings of the day.

Staying so close to home had reminded Letitia yet again that her mother's threat to publicise Sapphire Melborough's lapse from grace was still a very real one. The damage to her own career was also never far from her mind, though she found it hard to imagine that Mama would go to the lengths of discrediting her own daughter. Uncle Aspinall had been of the same mind.

Upon her return to Number 24 Paradise Road, it appeared that at least one set of parents were showing their disapproval by withdrawing their daughter from the seminary. The formally worded letter from the Reverend Miles Nolan and

Mrs Nolan begged to inform her of their reluctant decision to find a ladies' seminary holding stricter Christian principles than hers for Miss Verity Nolan whose character, at sixteen, was particularly impressionable.

'Well, I'm glad they think so,' Letitia said to Mr Waverley, later that day. 'Personally, I never believed Verity's character was anything like as impressionable as it ought to be, at her age. She meanders through life as if it were a dream, so I doubt very much if she'd even notice what I was doing with mine.'

Mr Waverley's grin was by now more comfortable. Sitting up against the pillows, his multi-coloured face made an interesting contrast with the white cotton, and Letitia was pleased to see that his nose and teeth were undamaged. He tapped the pile of letters she had brought. 'Never mind the vicar,' he said. 'It was to be expected. Look at these, though. Four more applicants. All you need now is more rooms.'

Smiling, she had to agree on all counts. 'That would be ideal, Bart. I have a mind to make old Mrs Sawbridge an offer for Number 20, but I've no idea how much she's expecting.'

'Go round and find out.'

'That would not be improper, would it?'

'Not at all. She may even prefer to sell it to her neighbour rather than to a stranger. Now, tell me how you fared with Mr Lake. Was Rayne businesslike?'

The news that she had a new contract seemed to cheer him and, as she left, she heard the sound of laughter through the open window as two more friends joined him. Dear Bart was on the mend.

But while Letitia had been visiting Mr Waverley, she had missed her own visitor. Miss Gaddestone was eager to give her the rather garbled message that Lady Elyot would call again soon but, meanwhile, Letitia might like to know that her niece, the one who was now Lady Boston living in the other northern Richmond, was to come to take up residence at Number 18 for a period of several weeks.

'When?' said Letitia, taking off her bonnet.

'Next Tuesday, I think. Well, Lady Elyot thinks. With all her family.'

'That's wonderful.'

Miss Gaddestone looked sideways at her cousin, aware of some reserve. 'Are you not pleased? Lady Elyot says you'll like her.'

'Yes, I'm sure I shall. I believe she has a fine voice.'

'Well, that's the other thing. Lady Elyot wants to hold a concert for them at Sheen House like the one at the Melboroughs.' Miss Gaddestone trotted in front of Letitia, spilling out snippets of information like the hare in a paper-chase.

'What?'

There was almost a collision. 'Er…a concert. With the Bostons. They're all musical. And our girls, too, like before. And she wants Lady Boyce to stay with them at Sheen Court, and Uncle Aspinall and Aunt Minnie, too.'

'*Stay* with them? She won't do that. Not Mama.'

'She will, Lettie. I've never known Aunt Euphemia pass up an invitation to hob-nob with the aristocrats, have you? All the families, Lady Elyot said. And that means theirs, as well as ours and the girls' families.'

'Well, we can't. We shall be in London by then.'

'No, we won't, Lettie. Not in ten days' time.'

'Ten…ten *days*? Gaddy, you didn't say we would, did you?'

'Yes, love. I told her… Oh, dear.'

'What did you tell her?'

'That we'd be delighted to meet Lady Boston and her family. Caterina, she called her. Such a pretty name. And that we'd be honoured to help with the concert. Well, we will, won't we, Lettie?'

'Yes, Gaddy dear. Honoured, thrilled, delighted. Is that tea still hot?'

That same evening, Letitia dressed with exceptional care for a private dinner with Rayne before going on to the Richmond Theatre to see a production of *The Duchess of Malfi*, which she afterwards wished she had not, so tragic was it. Later, in her own bed, she made love to him with an intensity that only an experienced lover would identify with fear and a growing jealousy, which he knew how to alleviate with a passion of his own and with assurances that she was all he wanted. Understanding the reason for it, he would hardly have been human not to feel a secret pleasure at the strength of her feelings.

Early on Sunday morning, he took his leave of her, promising to return by nightfall if it was at all possible. Otherwise, it would be Monday.

She had tried all day, to no avail, to place those feelings behind her. They were unfair, prejudiced and unworthy, too. What right did she have to claim all of his heart when it had never been offered to her, when she had not offered hers in return? Of course he had had affairs, many of them. That was no secret to Perdita. But this one involved a member of the family, one who would never quietly disappear like the others,

*and how could she expect to attain the same position in his
heart as one who had been there for years already?*

*Had she not become his lover, she supposed her heart might
have remained intact and proof against such anguish as this,
but she had lain in his arms and become one with him, and
his loving was like a drug. He excited and moved her as she
had never been moved before. She had felt whole, replete and
womanly, and there was little she could do for him that others
had not done before. Perhaps better.*

*Perdita lowered her head into her hands, refusing the tears
that threatened, determined not to give him up before she had
even seen them together. Then she would know. Then she
would decide...what...to turn off this thing called love? Impossible. It was a pain she would have to learn to live with.*

Letitia laid the quill upon the writing-desk and stared at the
page, starting a little at the faint sound below that would
surely be him, come to share the night with her as they'd
hoped. He had been at Hampton Court Palace all day with his
brother, for the Prince Regent's favourite filly was foaling for
the first time, an unpredictable business. The page was left
upon the slope as she folded the lid on top of it, trapped safely
between the wood.

Almost silently, the door opened to let the tall shadowy
figure through with barely enough time to close it before one
arm came across her shoulders, pulling her close, taking the
greeting from her lips, hungrily.

'I'm late, sweetheart.'

'I thought you were not coming.'

'I said I would.'

'Your hair is wet.'

'It's raining.'

'You rode, in the rain? Was there no carriage for you?'

'Riding's quicker. I'm steamy and smelly. Will you still have me?'

'You need never ask that, my lord. Sit over here and let me pull your boots off.'

'This is not quite what you bargained for when you took me on.'

'I think,' she said, looking at her muddy hands, 'we are both getting rather more than we bargained for. Lift the other one.'

'Is this what they call indecent haste?' He grinned.

'Yes, I believe so. Come, give me your coat.'

A week ago, she would have been shamed at her urgent participation, to be undressing a man in her own room for such a purpose. Yet now she felt no modesty or unease, only the same desire as he to give and take the longed-for comforts of body and mind, to wrap him in her arms, to be protected against the world. She had never felt so safe.

Her cry of surrender came sooner than he'd expected, telling him how she'd missed him and needed him by her side. Now, she whispered fierce words in his ear, 'Go on, Seton, go on...do it now...I need you...I want you...quickly!'

'That's my beauty,' he replied. 'You've come to my hand at last.'

'You're gloating.'

'Yes, sweetheart, I'm gloating and you're mine. Mine.' With the last forceful word, he took possession of her, flying like eagles in a storm, softly buffeted, calling to each other, lifted high above the world until, spent and breathless, they came to rest, exhilarated and safe.

The new bond they had forged together was too precious and fragile for Letitia to tell him of her concerns about her perceived rival, nor was Rayne foolish enough to broach the subject before she did. Nevertheless, he sensed as before her need for reassurance, which, he told himself, she was much in want of, despite her seeming confidence in so many other matters. She was, he thought, a delightful mixture of self-reliance and vulnerability.

She was up before him next morning, for Monday was one of her busiest days. Rayne took a more leisurely approach to dressing, his breakfast brought up on a tray by Mr Beck, the new butler. Without the help of his valet, he would have the dubious pleasure of tying his own neckcloth.

Standing before the mirror, his eye was caught by the writing-desk that had given Letitia so much pleasure. Its lid and base were not sitting flush with each other, as if something was caught between them. Lifting the lid by just an inch to see where the problem lay, he was unable to prevent the quick release of a paper to the floor. He let go of his cravat and stooped to pick the page up, but before he could slide it back inside, the elegant writing made him pause, arresting his attention with its beautiful pattern. He turned it and read her last entry.

A sound escaped him, made deep in his chest. 'Oh, sweet lass,' he whispered, staring at the words. 'Is that how it is? Such pain?'

Then he read it again, finally slipping it back into the desk and finishing his cravat with an unusual lack of concentration.

Sure that they'd seen the last of Lieutenant Gaddestone for a while after the last uncomfortable fiasco, Letitia was surprised to see him ride towards her across The Green as she left Mr Waverley's house.

'Cousin Lettie!' he called. 'Good afternoon. I was coming to see you.'

'Cousin Fin? Coming to see me, or your sister?'

'You, of course.' Dismounting, he threw the reins over the horse's head and led it beside her. Steam rose from its flanks and flecks of foam fell from the bit, the nostrils distended and trembling. 'Something I need to discuss with you.'

Guessing what that might be, Letitia steeled herself against anger. 'If it's a question of helping you out again,' she began, 'I don't think—'

'No, it's about the house next-door-but-one to yours. It's up for sale, you know, and I'm interested in it. Just what I've been looking for.'

'How on earth did you hear of it? I've only just heard myself.'

He ignored her question. 'Thought I'd get my bid in first, but I need you to come with me, Lettie. It'll look better if I'm with you, won't it?'

'So the money problem is resolved, is it? That's a relief, Fin.'

'Yes, it's an ideal place. I could give my sister her own suite of rooms, and both of us nearby to help whenever you need us. Just the ticket. We could call now, if you like. On the way home.'

There was something strange about this, Letitia thought, which she could not define. He had ridden hard to get here, but The Green was not *en route* to Paradise Road. She wanted to ask about the prize money, but this was hardly the place to discuss it.

'How *did* you hear about it?' she said.

'Happened to be in the Crickett Players having a drink. There was a young chap there called Ted who does her garden. He told me.'

'Ted?'

'Yes. You know him?'

'Slightly. His father works for me.'

'He seems to know everything that's going on around here. Just seen him again, as a matter of fact, in the Cricketters.'

So that's why Fin was on The Green. Brewer's Lane, with the Crickett Players public house, was just to one side. His drink must have been taken in haste, for his horse had barely recovered. Caution warned her to go back to Number 24, to speak to him in private. 'I have these books,' she said, indicating the two volumes she had just brought from Bart's beside. 'I should take them home first.'

'We're nearly there, Lettie. You need not carry them round. Oh, look, something's happening at Number 18 today.'

'That's Sir Chase and Lady Boston's house. They're expected.'

Boxes, trunks and hampers were being carried up the steps to where an elderly servant stood protesting that they should have gone round to the back, and when Lieutenant Gaddestone tied his horse to the railings only a little further on, it was hardly noticeable amongst the clutter.

It seemed a pity not to take the opportunity to look round Mrs Sawbridge's house, having intended to do so as soon as she could. Now she could safely let Fin ask the questions.

But the ear-splitting yapping of four white-and-brown spaniels was louder by far than the clanging bell, and though old Mrs Sawbridge was very hard of hearing, it was the demented behaviour of the dogs that alerted her to visitors. It was as Lieutenant Gaddestone had said, Letitia's presence and interest in the house prompting the owner to let them look round at their own pace. 'My legs,' Mrs Sawbridge shouted, patting her hip, 'don't work too well up all those stairs. My bed is down here now. Too large…can't keep it up. Yes, you take Mr Ganston round, dear. You know where the rooms are.' This to the accompaniment of hysterical yelps.

Letitia did not think it would be possible to discuss the price, in the circumstances, though this was what she most needed to know. So she took her cousin through one room after the other, stepping over small oddments of the old lady's life while noting the similarities and differences. 'Do we need to go upstairs?' she asked, dubiously.

'Just a quick look, to get the size. It'll need decorating.' There was a musty smell of stale air and old clothes after years of disuse. 'There's probably a good-sized attic up here, too. Is yours like this?'

'Almost identical,' she said, following him.

The attic, however, which in Lettie's renovated house was divided into light well-furnished rooms for the servants, was a shabby dingy place with an old bedstead and mattress in one corner, boxes and furniture thick with dust.

Lieutenant Gaddestone went to inspect the windows. 'Stuck,' he said. 'Well and truly stuck. She's not used this place for years.'

'Ugh! I've seen enough. It'll need some money spending on it, Fin. Am I to congratulate you at last? You've received your prize money and pay?' She turned to go, but Fin had closed the door and was leaning against it.

'Er, no. That's what I want to talk to you about, dear cousin.'

'No? So how are you going to make an offer? Have you borrowed from Uncle Aspinall? Is that it?'

'No, I hoped *you* would help me out.' The boyish grin was gone. The affability with it. Here was a young man of powerful build and serious mien who had lured her into this

ghastly, foul-smelling place for the sole purpose of getting her
to do something she had already said she preferred not to. He
was not going to let her go without an argument.

She decided that to scold him would show him her fear, so
she walked to the front window from where, down below, she
could see the tops of carriages pass along Paradise Road.
'No, Fin. It's out of the question,' she said.

'Not only that, Lettie. I hoped you'd agree to marry me.
We've always been close, haven't we? Remember? It's not too
late. Even though Rayne has got to you first, I'm still willing
to have you. He'll not want you much longer, you know. Once
he's had a woman, he—'

'That's enough! *Enough!* What I do in my private life has
nothing to do with you, nor will it *ever.* Now stand away from
that door and let me go home. I have duties to perform.' Forgetting her intention not to scold, she felt the waves of anger
and fear surge upwards, past the irritation, the exasperation
and sheer annoyance at falling into this trap, ignoring the
warnings any fool would have seen.

'Not before you've heard my proposal, Lettie. You cannot
pretend to be surprised by it, you know. All I need is a little
family help.'

'*Have* you asked Uncle Aspinall?'

'Him? Hah! Some hope. He's told me to find my own
place within the next two weeks, but he's not in line for a
loan. Oh, no.'

'No, I don't suppose you could get him into a disused attic
very well, could you, and then bully him?'

'Oh, come, Lettie. We can never talk at your home with my
sister flapping about. And Rayne, too, with his superior airs.
I had to find a way of getting you to listen, and the old girl

will sell it to me if you're with me. All I need is a loan, Lettie. I shall be able to refund you as soon as my—'

'As soon as your pay arrives? Haven't we heard that rather too often now, cousin? It's not *going* to arrive, is it? What you want is for me to finance your purchase so that you can take your sister on as your unpaid housekeeper. Don't think we have not seen through your plan.'

'Wrong, Lettie. You've missed out the bit that concerns you.'

'Forget it, Fin. We may once have been good friends, but that was years ago and we've both changed. I shall not even *think* of being your wife.'

'Why ever not? I wouldn't beat you. I'm as good as Rayne in bed.'

'Is that so? Thank you for showing me so clearly the workings of your mind. I must say I'm hardly surprised that you know so little about women after being at sea for years. You have a lot of catching up to do.'

'Then who better to help me than our family bluestocking? You run the school for wealthy daughters and we'll have this place for our home, with Rosie to run it for us. What a cosy family we'll make. Now come on, it's the best offer *you're* going to get. Mistresses are never permanent, you know. Especially not with Rayne.'

'Your interest in Lord Rayne does you credit, but I can tell you one thing. He would not stoop to do what you're doing now, asking a lady to lend him money. That is simply not done, you know. Nor would he hold a lady against her will, or force a marriage proposal upon her. Did you really think to win me by such methods?'

'Oh, not *win* you, exactly. Call it what you like, but you'll stay up here until you agree to fall in with my plans.' Slipping a hand into his pocket, he pulled out a key. 'Now, let's just see how long it takes, shall we? The old girl is not going to hear a thing. The windows don't open. I should imagine it gets a bit chilly up here at night, but I'll be back in a day or two, and by that time you'll be talking.'

'And have you thought how you're going to explain my disappearance? I do have a tongue in my head, Fin. I can tell everyone what's happened.'

He smiled and waved the key at her, fluttering the label upon it like a flag. 'Ah, here's the next trick up my sleeve, dear cousin. The young man called Ted, who does the old lady's garden.'

Letitia's heart lurched, uncomfortably. 'What about him?'

'He's eager to make your acquaintance again. He seems to think you owe him some kind of favour.' Deliberately, he glanced towards the bed piled with dusty blankets. 'You've spread your favours for Rayne and he thinks you might be persuaded to do the same for him, now. He had this made for me,' he said, still waving the key. 'He's good with his hands.'

A hot surge of nausea made her breathless with fear. 'That makes no sense at all, Fin. You're talking about loans, favours, marriage, abduction and assault all in one breath and you think I shall say nothing about it? You must be *mad* if you think to persuade me by any of those means. And Mrs Sawbridge may be deaf, but she's not blind as well. She can see that two people came in and that only one went out. She knows me well enough.'

'Yes, I shall say that you went out of the back door, the one that Ted uses. And while everybody is searching for you, I'll do my best to look distraught, comfort my sister, poke about in your rooms, find some money, too, I dare say. That's really what it all boils down to, Lettie, isn't it? Money. I lost mine and you kept yours. Well, now I want *your* share in return for husbandly duties.'

From the distance of the dirty attic floor that lay between them, she tried to read from his face something of the old Fin she had once known, but there was little for her to recognise except bravado. He had always had more than his share of that. 'I'm not afraid of you, cousin,' she said. 'I dare say you would like me to be, but I feel only pity and sadness, because I used to like you.'

'Don't,' he snapped.

She had touched a nerve. 'We were good friends once, but you've changed. Is it the navy? The brutality? I've heard of what happens.'

'*You'd* change. Anybody would, if they'd seen what I've seen. Beatings, lashings, deprivation, starvation. You cannot imagine. No one can. Don't talk to me of *sadness*. They've taken my best years and left me with nothing, so now it's up to me to seek out the weakest and take what I can get. And that means you, Cousin Lettie. Come on, it won't be so very bad. Give me what I want, and we can settle this between us now without…' Pocketing the key again, he moved slowly towards her, shrugging his coat off his shoulders, slipping his arms out of the sleeves while watching to see how she would evade him.

'Without what, Fin? Without hard feelings? Is that what you were going to say?' Fear caught at her throat, drying it, pounding a tight beat into her chest, making her look round in desperation for something to throw, as she had done with Ted in the garden shed. There was nothing to hand but, behind him, the door upon which he had leaned had begun to open, inch by inch, silently, and Letitia knew that she must keep her eyes locked with his, not to mirror what she could almost see, not to reveal her hope even by the widening of an eyelid.

'Hah!' Fin laughed, tossing his coat across to the bed. 'Hard feelings? No, I was going to say without any broken bones.'

'Then, my friend,' said a deep voice from the doorway, 'you had better stop there, unless you want a broken neck.'

Fin wheeled round to face the intruder, his face aghast, his whole body tensed to launch himself upon the man whose voice he recognised. But the intended attack was halted by the sight of not one man but three, one of whom was, apparently, even less welcome than the other two.

'You…you *bastard*!' he snarled at Ted. 'You filthy lying scoundrel. Whose side are *you* on when it comes to the share-out? How much did they pay you?'

'Not on your side, matey,' said Ted. 'Not the way *you* do things.'

'Put your coat back on,' snapped Rayne, 'and lay one finger on Miss Boyce and I'll kill you. You're not fit even to *look* at her. Do as I say.'

For a moment, while Fin went to collect his coat, it looked as if he'd given in. But none of the three believed it, and no sooner had he picked it up than his hand delved deep into the pocket, lifting it to aim the concealed weapon through the fabric at the three men. The most terrifying explosion Letitia had ever heard filled every corner of the room, a flash, a billow of smoke, and a crash as Fin staggered backwards and fell hard against the wall. His yelp as he clutched at his groin was like that of a wounded animal.

'Nice little thing, this,' said the man with the pistol, examining its polished handle and brass mountings. 'Where d'ye get it, Rayne?'

'Bath, last year. A boxed pair of Mantons. Cost me an arm and a leg.' Lord Rayne walked over to Letitia by stepping over the victim's legs. 'Come on, sweet lass. It's all over. Come.' Gently, he removed her hands from her ears and pulled her into his arms, supporting her, smoothing her back.

'Is he dead?' she said into his cravat. She felt his head turn to look.

'Nah! Squawks like a rabbit, so he ain't dead. If it'd been me, I'd have aimed two inches to the left, Chase, but I'm not grumbling. If I carry Miss Boyce, can you two manhandle him downstairs?'

'Carry me? What rubbish…what…oh, heavens…I'm not the swooning kind, my lord, as I told you before but…may I…just…sit?'

'D'ye want me to carry her?' said the man called Chase, grinning. 'I've not carried a blonde for quite a while.'

'You go and carry your own wife,' Rayne said. 'This one's mine. Ted!' he called to the gardener's son. 'I'll catch up with you downstairs, if you can take this great lummock with you. I have a bit of unfinished business to attend to up here first.'

'Aye, m'lord. But I don't want no payment, mind. I just didn't want to see any harm come to Miss Boyce. Scum like him should be… Begging your pardon, ma'am. You all right?'

'Yes, thank you, Ted. I don't know what you did, but I'm more grateful than I can say.'

'It were nothing, ma'am. Nasty character, this,' he said without pausing for breath as he heaved Lieutenant Gaddestone over his shoulder like a bag of garden rubbish. 'A bit o' fun's one thing, but not this kind o' skulduggery. No thanks, Sir Chase. I can manage him. If you'll follow me down, sir?'

'Sir Chase?' whispered Letitia. 'Is that…your friend next

door? Already in, are they?' The sound of footsteps faded with the voices.

'That's him. Sir Chase Boston.'

'You're still friends, then?'

'One of my closest. Why should we not be?'

'Oh…well, I thought…oh, never mind. You're looking as if I'm about to get a scolding.'

'Very bad English but yes, in a nutshell, I *did* wonder how an otherwise intelligent woman could get herself into an attic with a bad penny like Gaddestone who you *must* know by now to be as nicked in the knob as anyone on two legs.'

'I *didn't* know,' she said, 'or I would not have—'

'Then you should have done!' Picking her up before she could struggle out of his arms, he carried her over to the old bed, which was the only place to sit. 'This is going to ruin my coat, and probably my breeches, too, but when a wife has to be chastised it's best to do it promptly, or they forget, like horses do.'

'Like a horse? Like a wife? What are you talking about?'

'Well, it's quite obvious what I'm talking about, little ninnyhammer. How many more times am I going to have to get you out of these scrapes? Eh? Are you going to spend your life being cornered in libraries, garden sheds and attics by all the bedazzled males in Richmond?'

'Not to mention the back-rooms of Hampton Court Pal—'

The furious retort was cut short by his mouth hard upon hers, and no matter that she was not feeling quite herself, his kiss made no concessions to her fragility. When she was able, she mumbled, 'That's hardly fair, my lord.'

'Listen to me, Lettie Boyce. I know this was not part of your plan, and I know it's probably not what you want, but it's what you *need*. And you're going to have to agree, or I shall lock you up in this attic with only bread and water until you *do* agree. If your dastardly cousin can do it, so can I.'

'Do what?' she said, nudging his cheek with her nose.

'Damn it, Lettie. Marry me. For pity's sake marry me and put me out of my misery. I cannot have you as my mistress. I thought I could, but I can't. I want you for more than that. I want you for life, waking and sleeping. You see what happens when I let you out of my sight? This. It won't do, I tell you. You'll have to accept me because I can't live without you. So there.'

'Well, if the alternative is to be locked in here with only bread and water, which I've never liked…'

'Marry me, dammit! How many proposals take place in filthy attics? D'ye want me to go down on my knees?'

'Dearest lord…dearest, most wonderful lord.'

'Lettie, you're crying. Nay, don't cry, lass. Just say yes.'

'Yes. Yes. Yes…oh, sweetest man. Yes.'

Other convincing words were lost as Rayne celebrated the sweet harmony of two minds and hearts that laughed and wept, kissing her damp lips and eyelids, in accord at last upon every vexed question, even who should be first to say the momentous word. Love.

'Learn to give way to your husband, my lady, if you please,' he whispered, rocking her in his arms. 'I shall tell you first, because it was I who *knew* it first when you rode onto my parade ground. And you didn't. I've loved you every moment since then, dearest heart. I've never known a feeling like this for *any* woman, the way I do for you. I never want to let you out of my sight. Heaven only knows what'll happen to you, if I do.'

'Then I shall try to stay where we can see each other, beloved. Thank you, my hero, for coming to my rescue yet again. I never felt so afraid in my life, nor so relieved to see the man I love. Have I told you how I adore you? How much I'm in love with you?'

'No,' he said with a smile, kissing the tip of her nose. 'Never.'

'Well, I am. I have been for…well…' she put on her spectacles again and looked at him over the top rim '…for quite a long time. I found that it hurts badly at first, but now…'

'Now?'

'Now it's like paradise, my love. Safe and exciting at the same time. Will you take me home now? I've had enough of this place.'

'Yes, I will, but we shall certainly have to spend some money making it as habitable as your seminary. A month or two of work, at least.'

'Pardon? What are you saying? You haven't *bought* it?'

'A week ago, my love. And she may be as deaf as a post, but she knows how to drive a hard bargain. It cost almost as much as yours, in the end.'

'Oh, Seton…darling man!' Throwing her arms around his neck with astonishing energy for one so shaken, she showered kisses over his face. 'You've *bought* it! It's yours, after all. So why did she let *us* in?'

'Because I asked her to say nothing. I knew *he'd* come nosing round in time.'

'And young Ted? He doesn't bear you a grudge, as Fin said?'

'Not in the slightest, sweetheart. Men don't, usually. He accepts that he overstepped the mark and got a facer for it. No grudges. He came to find me as soon as he realised what Gaddestone was up to, and fortunately I was at your house waiting for you to return. I met Chase outside and he offered to come and help, so I collected my pistol from the curricle and Ted led the way. Yes, he'd talked in the pub once or twice to Gaddestone, and he'd had a key made. He left it on the hall table this morning, but it was for Mrs Sawbridge, not for your cousin.'

'Oh, dearest one, how could Fin do such a thing? He never used to be like that. Never deceitful. I feel so sorry.'

'Service in the navy and army changes people, my love. I could feel it changing me, too, but I was fortunate to be offered a job afterwards. But now we can put all that behind us, expand your seminary, have a room for your writing, a nursery, a suite for Gaddy, too.'

'You mean, you won't mind if I carry on working?'

'On the contrary, sweetheart, I shall expect you to. I cannot have a wife who floats about in a state of undress all day as mistresses are supposed to do.'

She sighed, rather gustily. 'Ah, no, indeed. But I've hardly had chance to do any of that.'

'Tch! Oh, all right,' he said, lifting her into his arms and striding across to the door. 'A week or two of floating, a month of showing off in London, a splendid wedding after that, then a honeymoon abroad. And *then* I shall expect you to buckle down and plan your next novel and redesign this shabby place. And then, if there's any time left over, we'll make some little Honourable Raynes, shall we?'

Letitia hid her face in his lapel. 'Yes, my lord, if you wish. But how am I to meet Perdita's deadline, I wonder?'

'Isn't she married yet?'

'Not yet.'

'Well, then, lock her in an attic until she agrees,' he said, callously, manoeuvring her round the banisters.

Mrs Sawbridge was in the hall with a messy pile of chewed book covers and pages in her hands, looking rather worried. 'Are these yours, Miss Boyce?' she shouted. 'I should have warned you, the dogs like nothing more than a good book.'

Chapter Fourteen

Having heard from her husband something of the drama enacted that afternoon at Number 20, Lady Boston would not be satisfied until they had both called on Miss Boyce to see if she had recovered from the ordeal.

Lowering his newspaper to treat his wife to a look of mock-reprimand, Sir Chase said, 'You can hardly wait to get a look at Seton's woman, can you? It will be rather obvious, don't you think?'

Caterina did not think anything of the kind. 'Would it be *too* difficult for you to see it as a neighbourly act of concern, Chase Boston, instead of nosey-parkering? It doesn't matter to me whose woman she is, I can still enquire about her poor nerves, can't I?'

The newspaper was dropped into a heap as Sir Chase unfurled his tall powerful frame to stand before her. 'I can see I shall get no peace, Lady Boston, until you've met her. I suppose it serves me right for telling you she's a stunner. Rayne always knew how to pick 'em.'

'Must you be so coarse?' Caterina retorted, pulling the bell-cord.

Even so, she put up no resistance when he pulled her to him with one arm and held her close to his side. 'Only with you, sweetheart,' he said, kissing her.

The meeting both women had anticipated for some time with varying degrees of curiosity took place, after all, in an atmosphere so informal and spontaneous that it was as if they'd known each other for years instead of minutes. From the start, Letitia could hold no doubts that Sir Chase and Lady Boston's infatuation with each other was total and exclusive, their love still shining, new and untarnished by anything resembling jealousy. They had an infant named Charles, and by vague references to their time in Richmond, it sounded as if their wooing had been every bit as turbulent as that of Rayne and Letitia.

As for Rayne, any thoughts Letitia harboured about the exact nature of his relationship with the beautiful, dark-haired and talented Caterina were quickly untangled by seeing them now, sharing the kind of bickering disrespect of siblings, teasing and laughing. At the same time, Rayne made no secret of the fact that Letitia was the only woman in whom he was interested, or could ever be. So it was entirely by coincidence that Sir Chase and Lady Boston were the first to congratulate them on their engagement, and to stay until the early hours of the morning talking like old friends over supper, and discussing next week's family concert.

Miss Gaddestone had spent most of the evening at the surgeon's house where her brother was being tended. But when Lieutenant Gaddestone's failure to return to London caused his uncle some alarm, the Aspinall carriage brought the elderly gentleman to the steps of Number 24 Paradise Road before breakfast was cleared off the table and Wednesday's lessons begun.

Rayne had intended to return to Sheen Court early, to inform his brother of the news. But now seemed like the ideal time to air the problems that had affected Gaddestone and, by association, the rest of them, too, for Rayne had not yet shared with Letitia what he and Sir Penfold had learned while in Portsmouth. That kind of news, he thought, was best coming from family.

'At the place you called the Navy House?' Letitia said. 'Where you talked with the captain who knew Fin?'

'That's it, love,' said Uncle Aspinall. 'What he told us was a bit shocking, but by then I'd begun to have my doubts about my nephew and his many commendations. They turned out to be fictitious, like the prize money.'

'Then what really happened, Uncle?'

'Debt and drunkenness is what happened. He managed to gamble away all his money, couldn't pay his debts, and the punishment for that is to be discharged. He was taken on by another ship via the good offices of a friend, but unfortunately it started again, drunkenness and disobedience, throwing his weight about. He was ordered to apply for discharge, again. That was last month. The rest you know. His pay and prize money all went to pay his debts. It's no wonder he was desperate. Does anybody want that last muffin, Lettie?'

'It's yours, love,' she said, passing him the plate. 'But I wonder why you didn't think to tell me all this. It might have spared me some embarrassment.'

'Yes,' Rayne said, 'in hindsight, it might have done. We both thought your cousin would find a way of making a living, somehow.'

'But he preferred to use mine instead.'

'And there were two other contenders getting in his way.'

'Two? You mean he saw Bart as a threat as well as you?'

'I'm afraid he did, sweetheart.'

'Oh!' Letitia's hand flew to her mouth. 'That dreadful attack…?'

'Was Fin's doing. He paid three men to put him out of the picture.'

'Then he must have heard Bart telling me he'd be going to London early the next Monday, just as he was leaving. Oh, I'll never forgive him for that. Never!' She stood up, leaving the table abruptly and going over to the window. 'What he threatened to do to me was bad enough, but to drag my personal friends into it is *despicable*!'

'Well,' said Uncle Aspinall, munching, 'he'll be out of action for quite some time now. I'm going to send him to a gardener I know down in Cornwall. He'll keep him busy. Now, Lettie, love, come over here and hear this. The news from your mama and sisters is that they've accepted Lady Elyot's invitation to the concert next Thursday. Your Aunt Minnie and me, too. She took some persuading, mind, but she'll get used to it eventually.'

'Then if you were to tell them that Lord Rayne has asked me to be his wife, Uncle, Mama might feel happier about it, do you think?'

The last mouthful of muffin was helped down with a hasty gulp of coffee, the cup crashed to the saucer, and Uncle Aspinall's arms opened like wings to embrace her, his jolly face reddening with pleasure. 'I guessed it would not be long,' he laughed. 'Mistress, indeed! What a *fudge*!'

He did not, of course, see the lift of Rayne's eyebrow and the lazy glance that caught his beloved's blush.

* * *

The concert was, in the end, exactly the kind of glittering family occasion that Lady Elyot had planned, and more, for now there were several other events to celebrate, apart from the visit of the Bostons to their home on Paradise Road. One of them was the betrothal of Lady Adorna Elwick to Captain Ben Rankin who had been kept dangling quite long enough, they all said, the other being the appearance of Lady Boyce, though no one was impertinent enough to question her tactics out loud as they had done with Dorna.

She had arrived at Sheen Court with Garnet and Persephone only minutes ahead of her brother and his wife, still vacillating between pique at having her predictions overturned, satisfaction at having a daughter so well connected, and annoyance at having to moderate her strong opinions in an entire company of Letitia's most ardent admirers. Not least of her qualms was the certainty that she would be obliged to meet Sir Francis Melborough and his family, who had no reason whatever to remember her with any fondness.

Her well-honed acting skills, though usually standing her in good stead, were this time quite overpowered by the warmth of the greetings she received from her hosts, their family and from Letitia also, who shed a tear of relief and joy, and appreciation, too, at the effort her mother had made to be there. She, more than any other, knew what it had cost her to swallow her pride, even if the taste of it was sweetened by her reception. Resplendent in feathery plumes from her hair, Lady Boyce put on her warmest smile to embrace Letitia and, for the first time, to congratulate her on her happiness, turning to Rayne with a lie as great as any she had ever told with a conviction that would have rivalled the actress Mrs Siddons.

'And my *dear* Lord Rayne…yes, I always *knew* you'd be the one.'

Dutifully, he received her kiss to both cheeks. 'Really, my lady?'

'Oh, silly boy,' she said, tapping his arm. 'Of *course* I did. A mother always knows these things. Is that not so, Lady Sheen?'

The marchioness smiled and agreed, drawing her towards all those friends she could have met months ago if she'd not been so intransigent. But if Lady Boyce had hoped to delay her meeting with the Melboroughs, Sapphire had a way of demonstrating her complete lack of resentment and, in a gown of embroidered muslin, white and virginal, she ushered her parents forward. 'Do come and meet her,' she was saying to them. 'This is Miss Boyce's mama. Lady Boyce, do allow me to introduce my parents. They *long* to meet the mother of our most famous author. They're both great admirers of hers, you know. Mama has just finished reading *Waynethorpe Manor*, have you not, dearest? And now Papa has got it. *So* wicked!' She laughed merrily, blinking at Lady Boyce's perplexity. 'Surely you're one of Miss Boyce's dedicated readers, too, are you not?'

Standing nearby, Letitia felt the disbelieving stare of her sisters, the quick shifting blink of her mother and the uncomprehending frown of Aunt Minnie all at the same time, but it was Sir Francis who stepped into the breach as if he sensed what was happening. 'Well, of course she is, dear child, but you can hardly expect Lady Boyce to admit keeping up with the racy exploits of her daughter's characters. What mothers *do*, and what they *admit* to doing, are two quite different things. Don't you agree, Lady Boyce?' He held out his hand to her, smiling. 'Francis Melborough at your service, m'lady. And my good wife. You are fortunate indeed to have such a multitalented daughter. Sapphire has the greatest admiration for her, you know. Cannot wait to tell all her friends that she is taught by the author of *The Infidel*. You should see their faces.'

Lady Boyce's recovery was a marvel of improvisation. Caressing Letitia's face with a smile of motherly pride, she accepted Sir Francis's outstretched hand and allowed it to be taken to his lips. 'Yes,' she cooed with all due modesty, 'we tried to keep it to ourselves for a while, but these things have a way of rising to the top, don't they? I have to admit to borrowing my twins' copies, and they don't always get them back.' She sent another smile over to the twins with a silent demand for them to change their shocked expressions forthwith. Aunt Minnie was less responsive. 'And,' she told her audience, 'she's had *such* a success with the seminary. Always been a talented gel, you know, and so brave to strike out on her own without her mama's protection. Yes, I always knew she'd do well. And, Lady Melborough, you have a lovely daughter who is going to sing for us, I hope?' Linking arms, Lady Boyce strolled away, trailing a pile of black Chantilly lace behind her over the chequered marble floor of the hall, her black ostrich feathers nodding in agreement.

'Shall we play chess with her, sweetheart?' Rayne whispered in Letitia's ear. 'Black Queen in trouble, d'ye think?'

'Did you *ever* hear such dissembling in your life?' she said.

'It was a tricky situation. She got herself out of it rather well, didn't she? Keep your nerve, here are your sisters.'

There was no such pretence for Garnet and Persephone, only praise and compliments and a lot of questions that begged for answers, excitement, incredulity and a mountain of wonderment, which she scarce knew what to do with. They went off to tell Uncle Aspinall and to deal with Aunt Minnie's confusion.

'Where is Sapphire?' Letitia said, looking round. 'I have to find out how she knew, before we begin. Did she do this on purpose?'

'She's here. Ask her. But I doubt it. She's not malicious.'

Sapphire had noticed nothing amiss. Her explanation was simple. 'Oh, I didn't think it was a secret, Miss Boyce. You left your writing on your table, you see, and I had absolutely nothing else to do but read it until Lady Boyce had gone. I could easily tell the writing was the same as the other two because we've done about styles in our writing class. You have that lovely way of telling how your heroines are suffering. I can hardly *wait* till it's published.'

'Just one moment, Sapphire dear. Are you actually saying that you read my manuscript that day…?'

'Yes, ma'am. That dreadful day. You told me to stay in your room, and it helped to take my mind off things. It was the best four hours I'd spent for ages, except for the riding, of course.' Her blue eyes peeped up mischievously at Lord Rayne, quite unaware of the stir she had caused by her disclosure.

'Then I suppose all the girls know, do they?' said Letitia, wearily.

Sapphire's eyes sparkled again. 'Oh, yes, and they're all so proud of you, Miss Boyce. We're all going to give the performance of our lives tonight, to show everyone what a *brilliant* seminary we attend. But I must go and speak to poor Mr Waverley. He's not looking at all well, is he?'

In fact, Mr Waverley was looking better that evening than he had for a week, though he was still confined to a chair and his face was mottled with every colour of the rainbow. He was also receiving an inordinate amount of attention from the pupils, who had missed him greatly.

But the attention that evening was divided evenly between the performers, all of whom excelled themselves, and their headmistress who had brought them to such a high standard, who was now Lord Rayne's intended wife, and who was also the author of the novels few in the audience had not read, either from cover to cover or in a more probing manner. It seemed to Letitia, as she sat beside the man she adored, that her world had moved on into an entirely new phase, for now she had one more bonus to make her evening perfect. The approbation of her mother. Why it should matter so much to her when she had everything else she could have wished for, was not something she tried to analyse, for it went deeper than she cared to delve.

Lady Boyce sought her daughter out in the supper room during the interval, when the crowd around Letitia parted, knowing that this was to be a private moment. She took Letitia's hands and held them tightly, slightly trembling, her eyes awash with tears even before a word was spoken, her smile struggling against the things she felt but could not begin to say.

'Mama,' Letitia whispered.

'Lettie.' The hands shook, then loosened, sliding up her arms to hold her close, and Letitia knew that it was not for show, for her mother would never have wept in public for any reason other than genuine emotion. 'You've done well, dearest,' Lady Boyce croaked. 'I'm so proud. I didn't…'

'Shh! Hush, love. Say no more. We've missed a few months, that's all. We can soon make it up. No harm done.'

'Yes, we'll make up for it. Perhaps you could come and do this at Chesterfield House? You'll all be in London next month, won't you?'

Letitia's embrace was garnished with a laugh. 'Of course we will, Mama. We'll do it all over again for your friends.'

'I shall start planning for it straight away. And before we go home tomorrow, I want you to show me round your Paradise Road house, will you? I have one or two friends with daughters…' Lady Boyce wiped beneath her eye with the tip of one gloved finger '…who really ought to see *your* gels.'

'Of course, Mama. Come, I believe Lady Boston is about to give us another song. She *is* lovely, isn't she?'

Until that evening, Lady Boyce would hardly have heard any other meaning behind her daughter's observation, yet now it was as if she'd tuned herself to a higher frequency. They had been about to move off, but she lay a hand over Letitia's arm, sensing her concern. 'Lettie,' she said, 'I believe Lord Rayne has found in you something he's been looking for, for many years. I know what a fuss I made about it at first, because I was afraid for you, on your own. But I see that I need not have been. I've been watching the way he looks at you, even when you're not standing together, and there's no doubt at all in my mind that you are the only woman he sees. Don't allow doubts to cloud your relationship. They can, you know.'

If Letitia had not known of her mama's liaison before her marriage, she might have accepted the advice as no more than kindly platitudes. But she did, and the significance was unmistakable. Later, as she sat beside her betrothed, she looked across the vast room to see her mama sitting beside Sir Francis in close conversation, like two good friends.

'What's the smile for, sweetheart?' Rayne said. 'Your mama?'

'For the deepest happiness I've ever known,' she said, sharing the smile with him, 'and for the most wonderful man this side of paradise. That's where I first saw you, you know. On Paradise Road. Looking superior.'

'Then I shall take you back there tonight, some time before dawn, and show you how excessively superior I can be, my beauty.'

'Will you, my lord? And shall we not delay the making of the Honourable Little Raynes until we're quite settled? Please?'

'Oh, I think we may put some practice in, certainly. Where better than a ladies' seminary, after all?'

The sound of sweet music-making filled the hall, heads swayed, fingers tapped, and the applause reached the goddesses sailing on clouds across the ceiling.

It was a night to be remembered, especially later in the comparative peace of Letitia's bed where the two lovers pressed themselves along every warm surface with the music still echoing in their heads.

'Perdita is being sadly neglected,' said Letitia, drowsily.

Rayne's hand moved silkily over her buttock. 'Mmm…? So what else does she need to know?'

'What it feels like to make love when she's half-asleep.'

'And is that part of the story?'

'It could be. If the author knew something about it.'

'Well, then, perhaps she'd better find out. I take it her pains have been dealt with by now?'

'Oh, quite. Utterly. How did *you* know of her pains?'

'Don't all heroines go through anguish and torment?' His hand moved to the tender inside of her thigh, resting in the valley of her groin.

'Mine seem to, yes.' She yawned, noisily. 'Usually unnecessarily. Silly, really.'

Lifting himself on to one elbow, he lay above her, smiling at the double-talk. 'Then let's celebrate Perdita's discoveries, shall we, sweetheart?'

Her arms wrapped softly around his neck. 'And Letitia's,' she said.

Epilogue

In the circumstances, Letitia found it difficult to complete the manuscript on time, but complete it she did, even in the middle of the celebrations meant to mark the end of hostilities with France. It was the busiest time of Letitia's life, and the most successful and enjoyable, for she became all the rage at a time when it seemed that uniqueness must have run its course. Even without the wonderful entourage of scholarly pupils and tutors, even without the charming spectacles and superb costumes, the revelation that she was the *author*, eldest daughter of Lady Boyce and soon to be Lady Rayne, was enough to set a new standard that few of her contemporaries could reach. Not that she was aware of it; she was far too busy with domestic standards to concern herself with the ideals of society.

The seminary at Number 24 expanded in the following year into Number 20, which also became the Richmond home of the Rayne family, all six of them. Letitia's seminary was to develop, many years later, into Richmond's first National School on the site of what is now Eton House, 18–24 Paradise

Road, the address of the publisher of this book, Harlequin Mills & Boon, who still specialise in romantic fiction. As Letitia did.

* * * * *

Author's Note

For those who would like to know more about Lady Elyot, her story is told in *A Scandalous Mistress*. Her niece Caterina's story—i.e., Lady Boston—is told in *Dishonour and Desire*. The story of Lady Dorna's ancestor, the Adorna Pickering of the Elizabethan era, is told in *One Night in Paradise*.

MILLS & BOON
Historical

On sale 5th September 2008

Regency

THE SHOCKING LORD STANDON
by Louise Allen

Rumours fly that Gareth Morant, Lord Standon, is to be wed.
He cannot honourably deny them, but he won't be forced into
marriage. Encountering a respectable governess in scandalising
circumstances, Gareth demands her help to make him entirely
ineligible. But he hasn't bargained on the buttoned-up Miss
Jessica Gifford being such an ardent pupil…

Regency

HIS CAVALRY LADY
by Joanna Maitland

Alex instantly fell for Dominic Aikenhead, Duke of Calder,
even knowing he would never notice her. To him, she was
Captain Alexei Alexandrov, a young man and a brave hussar!
Alex longed to be with her English Duke as the passionate
woman she truly was. But there was danger in such thoughts.
What if Dominic ever found out the truth…?

MILLS & BOON

Historical

Undone!

A seductive new mini-series where scandal is the talk of the ton!

Starting in October 2008

NOTORIOUS RAKE, INNOCENT LADY
by Bronwyn Scott

Wilful debutante Julia Prentiss seeks out the *ton's* legendary Black Rake, Paine Ramsden, for one night of passion that will free her from an unsavoury marriage…

To be followed by more sizzling tales of
COMING UNDONE
only from Mills & Boon® Historical

Available at WHSmith, Tesco, ASDA, and all good bookshops
www.millsandboon.co.uk

Celebrate 100 years of pure reading pleasure with Mills & Boon®

To mark our centenary, each month we're publishing a special 100th Birthday Edition. These celebratory editions are packed with extra features and include a FREE bonus story.

Plus, you have the chance to enter a fabulous monthly prize draw. See 100th Birthday Edition books for details.

Now that's worth celebrating!

July 2008

**The Man Who Had Everything
by Christine Rimmer**
Includes FREE bonus story *Marrying Molly*

August 2008

Their Miracle Baby by Caroline Anderson
Includes FREE bonus story *Making Memories*

September 2008

Crazy About Her Spanish Boss by Rebecca Winters
Includes FREE bonus story
Rafael's Convenient Proposal

Look for Mills & Boon® 100th Birthday Editions at your favourite bookseller or visit
www.millsandboon.co.uk

FREE

2 BOOKS AND A SURPRISE GIFT!

We would like to take this opportunity to thank you for reading this Mills & Boon® book by offering you the chance to take TWO more specially selected titles from the Historical series absolutely FREE! We're also making this offer to introduce you to the benefits of the Mills & Boon® Book Club™—

- ★ **FREE home delivery**
- ★ **FREE gifts and competitions**
- ★ **FREE monthly Newsletter**
- ★ **Books available before they're in the shops**
- ★ **Exclusive Mills & Boon Book Club offers**

Accepting these FREE books and gift places you under no obligation to buy; you may cancel at any time, even after receiving your free shipment. Simply complete your details below and return the entire page to the address below. You don't even need a stamp!

YES! Please send me 2 free Historical books and a surprise gift. I understand that unless you hear from me, I will receive 4 superb new titles every month for just £3.69 each, postage and packing free. I am under no obligation to purchase any books and may cancel my subscription at any time. The free books and gift will be mine to keep in any case.

H8ZEE

Ms/Mrs/Miss/Mr...Initials ....

BLOCK CAPITALS PLEASE

Surname ....

Address ....

....

....Postcode ....

Send this whole page to:
The Mills & Boon Book Club, FREEPOST CN81, Croydon, CR9 3WZ